politically
I·N·C·O·R·R·E·C·T

JEANNE McDONALD

Politically Incorrect
by
Jeanne McDonald

PUBLICATIONS
http://www.enchantedpublications.com
enchantedpublications@gmail.com

Visit the author's website at www.jeannemcdonald.com

Edited by: Amy Gamache of Rose David Editing
Cover Design by: Jada D'Lee Designs
Interior Formatting by: Lindsey Gray Formatting Services
Cover images by: rh2010 via Adobe Stock

First Edition: August 2016
ISBN-13: 978-1535457613
IBSN-10: 1535457619

Dedication

For Sarah Canady
Without you this story never would've
been written. Thank you for
seeing potential in my drabble.
Love ya!

"Love is blind; friendship closes its eyes." ~*Friedrich Nietzsche*

One

Dark garnet liquid reverberated in the wineglass as I circled my finger around the rim. With every swirl, the motion of the wine increased. The effect was almost hypnotic.

"Elizabeth?"

The flicker of fingers snapping in my face drew me from my entranced state.

"Elizabeth, are you even listening to me?"

Truthfully, I'd tuned out the conversation a while back, but I wasn't about to tell him that. There was only so much a girl could listen to when it came to what it took to make ugly people beautiful.

For the most part, this date had been a complete and total failure. At least he had good taste in restaurants, however, with the location being inside one of the most elegant hotels in Dallas, I was sure he had more than dinner on his mind. He could think again.

"Of course I am," I schmoozed, gracing him with my most polished smile.

Dr. Jack Gamble had met all my criteria on his dating profile. First and foremost, I needed a professional man. Having been out of the dating game for far too many years, gainful employment was pretty much my main criteria. I didn't have time to babysit a man who didn't have a job and I certainly wasn't going to become someone's sugar mama. Work took up a lot of my time and I would never apologize for loving my job. If a man couldn't understand that then he wasn't the one for me.

My second criteria – he had to be good looking, and Jack fit the bill there. He was handsome with his ocean green eyes, wavy black hair, and perfect smile. While the black suit and red button-down shirt hid his body, it was easy to see he spent many hours at the gym ensuring he stayed fit.

And my third criteria, which was probably the most important of all, was he had to be a Democrat. There was no way in hell I'd be caught out on a date with a Republican. I'd never hear the end of it. I worked too long and too hard to make a name for myself as *the* political strategist of the Democratic Party. I might've enjoyed the occasional tryst with a Republican, but dating one, nope. Not gonna do it.

"Oh, really?" He leaned forward and rested his elbows on the table. The luxurious white linen table cloth bunched beneath the Italian silk of his well-tailored jacket. His dark brow lifted and his lip curled into a half grin.

"Yeah, really." I batted my eyelashes and widened my grin. Another tactic I'd learned while working with politicians. Lie all you want, but do it with a smile on your face.

Taking my wineglass by the bowl, I swirled the alcohol twice and took a sip, savoring the rustic flavor on my tongue. Up to this point there had been food sitting in front of me, which allowed me to keep busy. Now, the only place to direct my focus was on Jack and my wine.

This wasn't the first date I'd been on since my daughter, Jordyn, persuaded me to get out there again, but this might very well be my last for a while. Men my age were full of themselves. They wanted a little thing, more like my daughter's age, that they could dangle on their arm as a trophy, not a successful woman who spent her life raising a child and making a career for herself.

Yep. It's certain. Perpetual bachelorette life for me.

And why couldn't I remain alone? What was wrong with it? I was happy. I had a full life. Just because I didn't have a man didn't mean I was incomplete. No. Dr. Jack Gamble had officially made me realize that finding Mr. Right wasn't in the cards for me. Mr. Good for Right Now was all I needed. At least with him, I could toss him back when I was done. No harm, no foul.

Jack stroked the stem of his wineglass between his thumb and index finger. It took all the self-control I had not to roll my eyes at his unconscious sexual suggestion. He leaned back in his seat, continuing to tease the stem of the glass. As if to challenge me, he lifted an eyebrow and rolled his tongue along his bottom lip. "Okay. What did I just say then?"

Dammit! He *had* to ask that.

I had no clue what he'd said. For most of the date I'd

been off in La-La land. He talked so much that I really didn't need to worry about doing anything more than nod and ask the occasional appropriate question. This man was dull and entirely full of himself. He even had the audacity to mention his last girlfriend was only thirty. Who gives a fuck? I sure didn't. It was right about then when I completely tuned him out.

I positioned myself so that my cleavage would draw in his attention. Just because the guy wasn't getting any, didn't mean I couldn't use the gifts the good Lord gave me. I might be forty-five, but I still had a great rack. Pursing my lips, I peered over the rim of my wineglass as I took a sip. "You were talking about a patient," I guessed.

He didn't waver. His eyes flickered down to my breasts, but only for a moment. Those blue-green eyes remained locked on mine as a smirk curled the corners of his mouth. "Which one?"

I gulped down the last of my wine without so much as enjoying it. My gaze dropped to the black screen of my cell phone. If only it could give me the correct answer. "The one who had a facelift." It was a viable answer, and I had a fifty/fifty chance of being right.

"Wrong," he snapped. "I was talking about the penial extension I performed last week. You haven't heard a word I've said all night, have you?"

Every inch of my skin crawled at him admitting to discussing such a terrible topic. In my line of work, it was customary for me to go to places no one else wanted to go. Dark, dirty, sweaty, smelly, seedy, or forbidden. I'd seen it all and did it all in the name of a win, but for him to discuss this, well, that was too much for even me.

My fingers drummed against the screen of my cell phone. The one night I wished it would ring, it was silent.

"Okay. You caught me." I released a sigh. "I'm sorry. I just have a lot on my mind."

Jack leaned forward and took my hand in his. "I can tell by the way you stare at that phone; you're anticipating it to ring. Trust me. I know the feeling. My life is a constant on call fiasco."

On call? Who was this guy kidding? He's a plastic surgeon not a heart surgeon. Good grief!

His thumb rubbed along the outer shell of my index finger. "I turned mine off to be with you. So, how about you put it away for the night?" His thumb continued to rub along my fingers. "We can get a room and I can help you relax a little."

I slipped my hand from his, resting it in my lap, creating distance. "It's a sweet offer, Jack, but we've only just met."

"But I feel as if I've known you all my life."

Face meet palm. Of all the pick-up lines he could choose from, he went with *that* one?

I scratched the back of my neck looking for the waiter. It was time for me to make my exit and fast. "That's sweet, but I think we need to get to know one another a little better first. Besides, I told you when I agreed to this date that I'm leaving town in the morning. I have to get back to DC for work."

Jack ran his fingers through his perfectly coiffed hair. "I know what you said, which is why I want to spend the night with you," he stated in a slight huff. "And quite honestly, you're making me feel like a sleaze here. I only want to help you relax. You seem so tense."

Nope. Just bored.

"Thanks, but really, I'm fine."

"Okay. Fine. I understand and I'd never take advantage of a lady."

I nodded, my eyes searching the room for the waiter.

Jack reached into the pocket of his jacket, retrieving his wallet. He pulled out a little black card and handed it to me. "How about you stop by my office tomorrow before you leave for some Botox."

My smile dropped and my brow furrowed. "I beg your pardon?"

"Many of my patients tell me it's very relaxing, and it'll take about ten years off your face. It's only an hour of your time and you'll feel like a million bucks afterward."

This asshole was serious!

My perfected persona dropped. It was a rare person who could cause me to break my polished demeanor, but somehow, Jack Gamble had managed it.

"Listen here, buddy, I don't know who you think you are…"

Just as I was about to tell this prick what I really thought of his offer, my cell phone started playing the Star-Spangled Banner and flashing the name Guy Harper across the screen.

Saved by the bell, dickwad!

"Hold that thought." I paused and took in a deep breath. "I need to take this."

Without giving Jack a chance to respond, I grabbed the phone from the table, slid my finger across the screen, and answered, "McNeal."

"My, my. So professional," came Harper's jovial tone.
"How can I help you?"

"Oh, right. I forgot. Tonight's date night! I take it's not going very well." Harper's chuckle only added to my bad mood. He was taking too much pleasure in my torture.

"You might say that."

"Wow! This guy must really be a doozy." Harper chuckled low.

I glanced up at my date. A look of frustration brightened his tanned skin. Served him right after insulting me like he did.

"You don't know the half of it…"

"Well, then, ditch him, Bet, and get over here. We have business to discuss."

Harper and I had known each other since high school. He was my ex-husband's best man and Jordyn's godfather. It was safe to say, he was pretty much family. I trusted Harper with just about everything, which was saying a lot. Trust was a high commodity in politics, and was never given freely. While I worked my way through college, Harper coasted through life on his family's dime. He came from a long line of old money, but no one would suspect it if they'd seen him on the street. When I entered the realm of politics, he joined me by donating to campaigns for many of my most promising candidates. He always said his donations weren't wagers on the candidates, but on me, because I was the safe bet. Hence, the nickname. Over the years, he'd developed a good eye for finding the right person for the job, so when he said we needed to talk business, I knew exactly what he meant.

I didn't have to look up this time to know I was being

stared down by the man across the table. Frankly, I didn't care. Harper had given me the out I needed. "I'll be there in forty minutes or so."

"Perfect. See ya then."

I ended the call and slipped my phone into my clutch.

"So that's it? I try to help you by offering my services and you're going to give me the brush off?" Jack sneered.

My eyes jolted up to meet his death stare. I stood up and leaned over the table, coming nose to nose with him. "My dear, Jack, your services are *not* necessary."

"I beg to differ. Not only do you need some work on those crow's feet, but I can help you get rid of those extra ten pounds you can't seem to run off in the gym." His mouth bowed and his thick brows lifted as if he'd actually one-upped me.

He didn't.

I took in a deep, cleansing breath and plastered a smile on my face. "I'll have you know I look *damn* good for my age. Now, if you're interested in spending your time with a twenty-year-old blonde bimbo, go find one, but don't you *dare* try to Dr. Frankenstein a woman to meet your stereotypical idea of perfection."

"At least a twenty-year-old woman would know how to be engaging on a date. She'd listen to me."

"Jack, if you'd had anything interesting to say, I might've listened to you." I let out a half-hearted laugh. "But from what I did hear, I can tell you this. You and I are on the same side of the coin. We both tell people how to look, but the difference between us is I tell them how to act. So, the next time you try to tell a woman how she should look or what standard she should try to achieve, think of me and what I do. Because no matter how pretty you make her, she'll never be what I turn my clients into. You see, Jack, I create power." I moved in a little closer to him. "I create legends..." I paused for dramatic effect, "I create gods!"

I reached into my purse, pulled out a one-hundred-dollar bill from my wallet and dropped it on the table. "Don't say I never paid for your services." I dusted my hand over his shoulder, pretending to remove lint from his jacket. "It was nice meeting you, Jack."

With a flick of my blonde locks, I grabbed my belongings and started to walk away. "Oh, and Jack," I called out without so much as a glance back to see the baffled expression on his smug face, "the next time you want to implant something, how about you implant some brains in that head of yours, because you're thinking with the wrong one, buddy."

Throes of laughter reverberated behind me as I slipped into my frock coat and exited the building with my pride intact.

Two

Long highway stretched out before me, lit only by streetlights and the headlights from oncoming traffic. The night sky was devoid of life. No moon. No stars. Just a blanket of darkness hung overhead.

Heat blasted from the car vents warming my cheeks. I wished I'd shed my coat before getting behind the wheel, but it was too late now. I moved to turn the heater down a smidge and ended up increasing the stereo volume in the process. My hands returned to the steering wheel where I tapped to the beat of the music while singing as loud as I could with Dolores O'Riordan. Nineties rock music always put me in a good mood, and The Cranberries was my ultimate indulgence.

As I reached the climax of the song, the music disappeared as my Bluetooth connection announced an incoming call. I almost growled in aggravation. I loved that part of the song.

There were only three people who might be calling me

at this hour. It couldn't be Harper. We'd already spoken. I doubted it was my ex-husband, Russell, because we rarely spoke, so that left only my daughter, Jordyn, who was probably calling to tell me she made it back to DC safe and sound.

Per our usual holiday tradition, we'd spent the last two weeks in Dallas. Jordyn visited with her dad, and I, well, I spent time reading some Nietzsche and catching up on a years' worth of lost sleep.

I pressed the button on my steering wheel. "McNeal."

"Hey, Mom." Yep, number three's the winner.

"Hi there, sweetheart. How was your flight?"

Girls giggled in the background and Jordyn called out hi to someone. "It was fine. It snowed here last night."

I veered into the right hand lane, preparing to make my exit. "I bet you're excited about the fresh powder. I'm sure you and the girls will be heading to Snowshoe before classes start."

One of the things I both loved and feared when it came to my daughter was her obsession with extreme sports. Jordyn had never been afraid of anything and would try everything at least once. She loved to snowboard, surf, and skydive. Name anything dangerous and she was into it, as well as being damn good at it. When she was twelve, she broke her collarbone snowboarding. It scared the crap out of me, but it didn't stop her. If anything it pushed her to try harder. I lost count at the number of broken bones she'd suffered, but I never got tired of watching her push herself to be the best. One might say, the apple didn't fall far from the tree. At least in my sport, death wasn't a possibility.

"We talked about it, but nothing's set in stone yet," she

paused, "So…"

My eyes cut to my side mirror checking the lane beside me. "So, what?"

"How'd it go with sexy doctor-dude?"

I dropped my head slightly, shaking it. "Terrible. All looks and nothing else."

Jordyn groaned. "No, really? His profile seemed perfect for you."

"It just goes to show that no matter how great people seem on paper it doesn't mean they're in fact a well-rounded person."

I spent a few minutes giving Jordyn an overview of my night, sparing her no detail. When I was done, Jordyn remained silent for a moment. A loud gust of air expounded from her lungs through the phone. "You. Can't. Be. Serious."

A light laugh echoed in my chest. "I wish it were a joke, but he actually said that to me."

"What a peckerhead! Is he fucking blind?"

"Language, Jordyn!" I didn't mind my language, but my daughter was better than me and shouldn't be using such vulgarity.

She blew off my comment as any teenage girl would. "The guy's a douche if he couldn't see the gorgeous, sophisticated woman sitting in front of him. Frankly, he didn't deserve your company."

Another laugh burst through my lips. "Sweetheart, do you think I'm offended by what he said?"

"Aren't you? I would've been crushed."

The gravel beneath my tires crunched as I turned down a long, winding road. There were very few streetlights, making it difficult to see, so I flipped on my brights. I was truly in the country now. Well, as country as the city of Dallas could get.

"Pissed, sure, but he didn't hurt me. He's a small-minded person who doesn't deserve another thought from me."

"How do you do it?" Jordyn inquired.

"Do what?"

"Let stuff roll off you so easily."

This wasn't the first time we'd had a conversation like this, and I'd bet almost anything it wouldn't be the last. Though, I never minded having a repeat occurrence with my daughter. All women needed to understand that independence wasn't a dirty word. It was a key to womanhood and security.

I curled my lips upward, contemplating my words carefully. "Hmm. It's simple really. You have to like yourself, and you have to know who you are."

"That's all?" Her voice rose an octave in disbelief.

A tiny chuckle escaped me at her skepticism. She definitely was her mother's daughter. Never take anything at face value. Look deeper. Understand everything. Then make your conclusion.

"Think about it. When you like yourself what others say doesn't matter because you already know the truth. I know who and what I am. The good doctor doesn't. He attacked what he considers to be my shortcomings, because those are exactly the things he hates about himself. Age scares him. Being undesirable scares him. Simple-minded people attack what they fear. So, yeah, that's it."

"I hope one day I'll be as strong as you are," Jordyn

boasted.

I scratched the top of my head and pulled up to the entrance gate of Lone Star Ranch, one of many estates belonging to the Harper clan. This was a place I knew all too well, having spent a great deal of time here with Harper during our business adventures. I rolled down my car window, only to be met with a burst of cold air mingling with the heat trapped inside my car. A deep shiver skittered down my back as I pressed the buzzer on the callbox.

"You're already stronger than I'll ever be." Which was the absolute truth. I couldn't begin to imagine growing up in the electronic age where anything and everything you did could and would be caught on camera. That was something I incessantly preached to my candidates. A good rule of thumb to follow was if you wouldn't do it in front of your grandmother, don't do it in public. Plain and simple. People will catch you and they will always use it against you.

A crackling sound came from the box and I heard a voice resonate over the speaker. I stuck my head out of the car and waved up to the camera to announce myself.

"Where are you?" she asked.

"I just arrived at Harper's. He called while I was on my date with Dr. Douche wanting me to come by to see a new potential."

"So, Uncle Harper rescued you from your date?" she teased.

"For business."

"Right," she drawled. "You know, Mom, I always thought you and Uncle Harper should get together."

"What?" I squelched through a snort.

"Yeah. It'd be the perfect matchup. You know each other well. Besides, Uncle Harper's hot for his age."

For his age. Good grief. Harper wasn't too much older than me. Oh, to be eighteen again and think forty plus was old.

The gates opened and I slowly pressed on the gas. My car moved past the entrance and the metal enclosures slid shut behind me.

"Sweetheart, we've talked about this before. There's got to be a certain chemistry between two people for even an inkling of a relationship to work."

"I know, and you and Uncle Harper have chemistry."

"No, what we have is a warped form of sibling rivalry." I laughed. "He's like a brother." Granted, Jordyn wasn't lying. Harper was a pretty sharp looking guy for a man pushing fifty, but we'd known each other for far too long. The thought of anything happening between Harper and me was out of the question.

"You're probably right."

At the end of the long, winding driveway, stood a house that looked as if it belonged on one of the plantations in *Gone with the Wind*. Bright lights lit up the front, with its large pillars and dual winding staircases leading to the balcony and glittery windows. Though dormant due to the winter, the vines of ivy which grew up toward the roof added a shade of elegance to the abode. From what I knew, Lone Star Ranch had been in existence since 1902 when the Harper family struck oil. Money and crude flowed freely through Harper's veins and this house was evidence of it.

"I know I am." I drove to the front of the house. "But anyway, I'm here. Can I call you back in a little bit?"

"Just call me tomorrow. I'm about to crash for the night."

"I'm on a morning flight to DC, tomorrow. How about you just stop by for dinner?"

"Okay. I'll see you then. I love you."

"Love you, too. Goodnight."

I cut the engine just as Jordyn disconnected the call. Reaching into the backseat of my car, I grabbed my leather briefcase and pulled my makeup bag from the hidden pocket. With the overhead light turned on, I quickly applied a fresh coat of lipstick and mascara. Not that I was the kind of woman who could be considered narcissistic, I had no time for that sort of self-love, but I was the kind of woman who knew appearance meant everything and the lack of lipstick could suggest scandal. So I never left home without it.

I quickly combed my fingers through my golden tresses, giving my flattened hair a little bit of its former body back. A fingernail over my eyebrows ensured they were perfectly sculpted around my hazel brown eyes. My lips rounded in a satisfied grin with my appearance. I returned my makeup bag back to its hidey-hole in my briefcase, before tossing it into the backseat. Grabbing my purse, I slid out of the car, closing the door behind me. I buttoned the front of my frock coat and slipped my clutch under my arm. The sound of gravel crunched under my heels as I made my way to the front door of the Lone Star Ranch. My finger perched on the doorbell, I rang it and waited.

God, this was turning into one long night.

Three

The door opened and I was welcomed by the elegant black and white tiles of the foyer. A large chandelier dangled from the raised ceiling above my head. I stepped inside the house, clutching my purse beneath my arm. Light sparkled around me in subdued hues, producing an elegance that only these old homes could. Engulfed by the warmth of the house, I released my grip on my coat and adjusted my black A-line skirt. With the tip of my fingernail, I brushed my bangs away from my face.

A tall, slender man bowed his head in my presence. "Ms. McNeal," resonated the butler's New Yorker accent.

"Good evening, Ivory," my thickened southern drawl resounded. I'd spent so much time in Washington, DC that my Texas accent was pretty much non-existent anymore, but it never failed, when I returned home it reappeared in full force.

Ivory adjusted the bowtie at his slender neck and closed the door. One last shiver skittered down my spine from the burst of icy wind that managed to slip past the door before it shut.

"May I take your coat?" Ivory addressed me with polished social grace.

My gut instinct was to wrap my coat tighter around my chest, but decorum wouldn't allow it. I slipped my frock coat off my shoulders, juggling my clutch between my hands in the process. Ivory held his arm out for me to drape the jacket. With my clutch secured under my arm, I deposited my coat along his forearm.

"Mr. Harper is expecting you in the den." His white gloved hand extended toward the hall.

"Thank you. I know where to find him. Bourbon in hand, I'm sure."

Ivory slipped a little chuckle, but snapped his mouth shut as soon as he realized I'd noticed. After all, it was unwise to comment, even if only a simple laugh, on his employer's bad habits. I waved him off with a wink, letting him know his secret was safe with me. Ivory bowed his head and departed the area.

Each step I took echoed as I walked down the long hallway toward the den. Even from the hall I could smell the pungent scent of cigar smoke. Harper was already in celebratory mode, which meant he knew he had a winner.

To the side of the room, Harper stood in front of a blazing fireplace. Deep in thought, his arm rested on the mantle, a crystal glass, half filled with bourbon, dangled from his fingertips. In an ashtray, mounted on the mantle, a cigar burned but remained otherwise untouched.

My fingers brushed against the dark, smooth wood of the den door. It opened with a creak. Harper lifted his head at the sound, and a sincere smile appeared on his lips. "Elizabeth." The way he spoke my name seemed to linger in the room. His pale blue eyes sparkled in the firelight and his handsome, yet rugged features were merely accented by the warmth the fire provided. Dark brown hair, peppered with gray, and a chiseled jaw dusted with silver stubble. Harper had aged well over the years.

He placed his glass on the mantle and extended his hands out toward me as he made his approach to where I stood. Dressed in his usual fitted jeans, cowboy boots, and starched brushpopper, he fit the perfect stereotype of a Texan. Over the years I teased him about his style, but he held true to his heritage. Just one of his many endearing qualities.

"Harper," I replied, taking his outstretched hands.

"So glad you could stop by."

"As if I could ever turn down an invitation from the great Guy Harper," I jested.

Harper pulled me into a hug, holding me tight against his hard chest. For a man who was nearly fifty, he had the body of a thirty-year-old. A body that, as Jordyn would say, could melt the panties off any woman. Not that I ever understood that phrase. Never had I known a man who could melt my panties off. Nope, they typically stayed intact until I willed them to be removed.

I closed my eyes, wrapping my arms around him, breathing in the musky scent of his cologne mixed with the spicy aroma of the alcohol he'd ingested. The combination reminded me of home.

"You're not going to regret dumping your date for this. I promise."

I stepped out of his embrace and marched over to the mantle, snatching up his abandoned glass. In one gulp I downed the crisp liquid. "That remains to be seen. What ya got for me?"

Harper chuckled at my abrasiveness, but didn't hesitate. He stepped behind the bar and poured himself another drink. "So I take it you haven't heard the news?"

I placed my purse on the leather chair near the fireplace and walked over to him, presenting my commandeered glass for a refill.

"What news?"

Harper clapped. "Oh, you've got to be kidding me? I can't believe you don't know. This is a first."

Instead of pouring bourbon for me, as he had for himself, he grabbed the decanter filled with scotch and doled out two fingers full. "I must bask in this moment. I can't believe the Queen of Politics doesn't know..."

I gritted my teeth. Harper knew how much I hated that nickname. I wasn't the queen of anything. I just happened to be the best at my job. "Stop gloating and tell me what I'm missing." I grabbed my glass, taking a swig of its treasures.

Harper's lips quirked in a ghost of a smile. "Thomas Bailey's stepping down," came his hushed voice.

My glass nearly hit the floor from my shock. Somehow I managed to catch it without spilling a drop.

"Nice catch."

"Are you kidding me?"

He laughed, shaking his head. "Nope. Christmas is a little late this year, or maybe it's a little early, but either way, I'll take it."

My hand shook with each word for emphasis. "Senator Tom Bailey is stepping down?" I asked in disbelief. "That man's been in office since the dawn of time."

"Seems that way. But it's true. He announced it about an hour ago, but I got the inside scoop yesterday. His wife's Parkinson's has worsened, and a little birdy told me she's dealing with dementia, too. They're not giving her much time and he says they want to be home for her final days."

For a moment I actually felt sad. "I'm sorry to hear that. Doris is a sweet lady."

"She is and I feel for them, but do you know what this means?"

I gulped down the rest of my drink, grinning on the inside while maintaining my solemn demeanor. "It means there's a senate chair open for the taking."

"It does."

The glass in my hand clanked against the wood of the bar as I rested it for another refill. "And I bet this next drink you already have a candidate in mind."

He poured me a double.

My laughter filled the room at winning my little wager. "Who is...he?" It was never good to assume that the suggested candidate would be male, but it was still the norm, even with the first female president currently residing in the White House.

"*He*," Harper confirmed, "is the perfect candidate."

I crossed my arms over my chest. "I'll be the judge of that. Besides, you realize you're asking an impossible task of me here. It's not going to be easy to sell a Democrat to fill a Republican's seat. I'm in for a heavy year if I take this on, which means," I examined my fingernails, fighting back the grin trying to expose me, "this won't be cheap."

Harper hummed in acknowledgement. "Is that so?"

I lifted my shoulder in a nonchalant shrug. "It is. So, I'm curious. Will your candidate be able to cover my fee or will he have someone bankrolling this venture for him?"

Harper dropped his head back in laughter. "Money's not an option with this one. I've got him covered."

"Interesting. So you really like this guy."

"He's different. I think he'll overcome the stigma. We need fresh blood, Bet, and fresh ideas. This guy's got them. I've been following him for some time. He's the real deal. The breath of fresh air that Texas and the democratic party needs."

Skeptical, I rolled my eyes. "Promises, promises. Tell me about him."

A smirk twisted Harper's mouth. He pulled his glass to his lips and took a drink. "I'd prefer you to meet him," he mumbled over the rim of the glass.

I dropped down on the sofa, crossing my ankles and tucking my long legs back. "He's here?"

"Yup. I invited him here because I knew if I simply told you about him, you'd probably laugh in my face and turn me down. But just like Ross Cooperman, I know as soon as you meet him, you're going to fall in love with him."

"Cooperman's on board? You're telling me that the DNC is giving him their full support?" A hint of shock and sarcasm peppered my tone. The Democratic National Committee in Texas was usually as skeptical as I was, so for Cooperman to actually be on board before I was even introduced to the candidate really had me suspicious.

Smug as ever, Harper scratched his jaw and shrugged. "Full backing."

"Who the hell's this guy that he already has the full backing of the DNC?"

Harper placed his tumbler on the counter and strode over to the sofa where I sat. He reached across me to the phone on the end table. His lips twitched as he spoke into the mouthpiece, "Send him in," and hung up. Crossing his leg over his knee, Harper leaned back and rested his arm behind me along the top of the sofa.

Almost as soon as Harper got comfortable, a dark figure emerged at the den entrance. Every inch of skin on my body electrified at the sight of the shadowed frame. My breath caught in my throat and I uncrossed my legs, pushing myself to the edge of my seat. Clenched fingers curled into the fabric of the cushions. I lifted my chin and squinted my eyes to see this man as he entered the room. Focused on his face, my heart raced in my chest. Perspiration formed on the back of my neck. My stomach fluttered in excitement. If I didn't know better, I would've thought I was high. This feeling was unlike anything I'd ever felt before and it frightened me.

I stood up, only to realize how tall this man was. In heels, I met most men eye-to-eye. This man, however, towered over me still. I took one step toward the door and halted; for he moved into the light and the world stopped on its axis. My heart thundered in my chest and air rushed in my ears.

With a light shake of my head, I straightened up, forcing back the wiggly feeling in the pit of my stomach.

That wasn't me. I wasn't some silly school girl or hormone crazed teenager. I inhaled deep, adjusted my skirt, and put on my best smile.

"Elizabeth McNeal," Harper extended a hand out toward the god standing before me, "I'd like to introduce you to Congressman William Baxter."

Four

"My friends call me Liam," the tall drink of water noted, extending his large hand to me.

Out of habit, I accepted his offering. We both froze, locked in that simple action of shaking hands. His skin was warm against mine and the smell of his cologne was tantalizing. He moved forward, closing what little gap remained between us. His hooded eyes were glued to mine. Long, smooth fingers engulfed my small hand. For a moment everything around me faded into the background. Gone was the smell of expensive alcohol and the crackling of the fire. I couldn't even hear myself breathe. Only this man stood in the haze of my thoughts.

Deep chocolate eyes, so dark they appeared almost liquid, stared down at me under long, chestnut lashes. Lips, full and pink, spread into an award winning smile — one I was certain he'd perfected over the years, and like any good politician, he'd used it to get his way a time or two. He was dressed in a tailored slate gray three-piece suit with a silk orange tie that was virtually bright as the sun. Aside from the monstrosity of his tie, I had to admit this man was almost perfect. But me being me, I had to find imperfections, no matter how small they might be.

I blinked several times and licked my lips, my gaze running up and down his tight, hard body. Broad shoulders dropped to a trim waistline. He was an athlete; of that I was sure. His body was too firm not to be. The mere way he stood, with near perfect posture, suggested former military, which would also explain why his golden brown hair was cut far too short. A buzz cut might be standard for military personnel, but for a senator people expected a man with hair — unless he was naturally going bald. Don't ask me why, I'd never been able to explain the American public perception, but naturally balding men equates distinguished and wise while a buzz cut elicits fear.

Then there was a little scar above his left eyebrow. No one would notice it if they weren't scrutinizing him, as I was, but it made me wonder what the story was behind such a tiny imperfection. While his smile was charming, his two bottom incisors were crooked. There was a small bump on his otherwise perfectly straight and narrow nose.

A sports injury, perhaps?

Up and down, my eyes raked over him, and trust me, that was no easy feat. The man had to be six-four, maybe six-five. His height alone was intimidating.

Out of all his physical imperfections, which really weren't imperfections at all, they actually added to his handsome demeanor, the one thing I noticed — the most important thing I noticed— was his youth. Since Harper was suggesting him for the senate seat, I knew he had to be over thirty, but not by much. This man was barely a man. He was still a child when it came to working on the Hill.

I released his hand and took a step back. My heart thundered in my ears, but I managed to ignore it. Instead, I allowed my professional nature to take over. I swiveled around by my hip to catch Harper's eye. "Please tell me this is a joke." I thrust my thumb upward toward Liam, who seemed incapable of taking the hint that I needed space to breathe as he'd, once again, invaded my personal space. The hairs on the back of my neck tickled with excitement. I rolled my shoulders to push back the completely inappropriate and unwanted attraction I had toward this guy.

"I beg your pardon," Liam scoffed.

Harper's lips curved into a cocky smirk. He shrugged a shoulder and gave me a wink.

"No wonder you said money wasn't an option!" I huffed in frustration. I raked a fingernail over my eyebrow. "Do we even have a clue who the Republican candidate or *candidates* might be?"

Harper's smile dropped. He clasped his hands together over his knee. "Not exactly. But I'm pretty sure we both know who it'll be."

My hand smacked over my forehead. "Governor Keating," I groaned. "Now, I know this has to be a joke. There's no way you'd send this guy, a nobody, up against Keating."

As shrewd as politicians came, Bonnie Keating fit the bill. Her wily antics and cunning charisma could lull a person into a false sense of security. She had the ability to make a person believe she could change the world so it would no longer revolve around the sun but rather around you before cutting you down to size in a matter of a few words. Bonnie would do just about anything to get elected, which she'd proven time and time again. Her crooked tactics were what landed her in the Governor's office. If she was the person we'd be up against, we needed a hard hitter not the rookie kid who was still wet behind the ears.

"Where do you get off..."

I whipped back around to Liam, raising my chin to meet his dark gaze. "Look, I'm sure you're a nice guy, and maybe even a great Congressman, but this is the big leagues, *kid*, and I'm afraid you'll be eaten alive."

His once adorable smile turned downward and bright red burned through his cheeks. "I don't know what makes you think you have the right..."

Cutting him off again, I snapped, "Years of experience."

I turned back to Harper, my temper flaring. "You called me here for this?" I flung my hand backward, uncaring that I'd just smacked the Congressman in the chest. "He's barely reached puberty."

"She can't be serious?" Liam barked.

Harper crossed his arms over his chest, his mouth screwed tight in an attempt to fight off laughter.

"I know you said she's the Queen of Politics, but I'm not taking this ageist crap from anyone. I don't care if it's the Pope himself. I appreciate your support, Mr. Harper, but I'm out if it means I have to work with someone who's as prejudice as she is."

If my blood wasn't already boiling before, it was now. I jerked back around to him, my teeth gritted. "Ageist?

Prejudice? I'll have you know I'm neither of those things, but what I am is a person with a great deal of experience. I was running high-profile campaigns while you were discovering hair in awkward places. How old are you anyway? Thirty? Thirty-one?"

"Thirty-four," he reluctantly replied.

"And that right there is my point. The odds are already stacked against you being a Democrat in Texas. Not to mention the fact you'll most likely be running against a well-known politician, where no one even knows your name. Those two issues alone put us in the weeds, but you add being under forty to the mix and we might as well kiss that seat goodbye."

He puffed out his chest and dropped his chin, locking his eyes on mine. I knew his stance was meant to intimidate me, and the truth was, it did, but I'd never let him know that.

"Lady, you don't know me." The tension in his voice was so tight it sounded like he could snap at any moment. Yet somehow he managed to hold it together. "So don't pretend to. I might be young but I have a lot of experience under my belt, and I won't allow some know-it-all consultant to tell me I don't have what it takes to serve the American people because I'm not old enough."

I tried to interject but he lifted a finger to my face, almost touching my lips. My whole body was enraged by his display of authority. No one ever spoke to me like that. Ever. They knew to trust me and to accept my advice. This little punk was challenging me, which felt both exhilarating and infuriating.

"Age is but a number," he continued. "It doesn't equal

knowledge or experience. An eighteen-year-old can have more experience in their short life than a sixty-year-old. And, frankly, I am not some sort of statistic. We live in a world where a woman is the president of the United States. A black man has held that coveted seat in the oval office. There are no limits on what a person can or can't do. Age, race, sexuality, and religious creed no longer define us. My age is a benefit. Bonnie Keating is old news. The Texas population is young and they want someone their age to help lead them into this new era. They thirst for new ideas and leadership. And, Ms. McNeal, I'm the person for the job."

My mouth gaped open. Somehow, in the interim of his speech, we'd moved so close together that if he leaned forward just a little and I perched up on my toes, our mouths would surely meet. While that thought was tempting, there was something about his speech that thrilled me even more. His words were unrehearsed. They were natural. They came from deep inside him and with honest conviction. It was unusual to see so much raw passion exude from someone in politics. His impromptu speech breathed life into my chest. It excited me.

I glanced over my shoulder to Harper who was on the edge of his seat. Wide-eyed, his expression mirrored how I felt. Engaged, intrigued, and sold. Harper gave me a simple nod, as if to tell me Liam had just proven him right. I returned the nod, agreeing with him. It was yet another perk to being friends with someone for so long. Words weren't needed between us. We knew what the other was thinking, and we were both thinking we had ourselves a candidate.

I stepped back, steepling my fingers together. "Okay."

I floated down onto the couch next to Harper. With a pat on the knee, I side-eyed him. "The kid has moxy," I admitted.

"Moxy?" Liam echoed.

Harper and I ignored him. I shifted sideways, turning toward Harper. "Full DNC support?" I reiterated.

"Not only does he have full DNC support, but he also has complete backing of Harper Industries. Funding won't be an issue."

I nodded, drumming my fingers against each other as I calculated how best to play out this campaign. "I have provisos."

"I expect nothing less." Harper scooted back in his seat. He glanced up to Liam and held out his hand for the young Congressman to take a seat in the armchair adjacent from the sofa. Liam seemed hesitant at first but unbuttoned his jacket and dropped into the chair.

Note to self: Dark colors are good for his tanned skin. But the neon ties have to go!

"Let's start off with cosmetics." I glanced over at Liam, a look of confusion on his face.

"Okay," Harper chuckled.

I stood up and circled around Liam, resting my hands on the back of the armchair. "He has nice form. Commands a room well, but the hair. It needs to be grown out."

"What?" Liam glanced up and over his shoulder at me. God, those eyes. Empires would fall over those eyes.

"Your hair, Congressman. If you want people to take you seriously, you need to grow it out a few inches. This," I circled my finger around the top of his head, "might work well in the military, you were in the military, right?"

He nodded. "Yes, ma'am."

"I thought so." I dared to touch his short hair. It was soft, baby-fine and I wished it was already grown out so I could run my fingers through it. I jerked my hand back at such a thought. He was my client now. No fraternizing with a candidate was rule number one. But it was more than that. He was far too young for me. Almost eleven years too young. "But politics is sort of like Hollywood. People have certain expectations on how candidates should look."

"No one had an issue with my hair before. Why now?"

I balled my hands at my side, putting my campaign face on. "Because as a US Congressperson for the state of Texas you're one of thirty-six faces. It's easy to overlook some things. However, as a US Senator you're one of two. People are finicky and a man who purposely chooses to have no hair is either military or part of some cult. No one wants a KKK member as their senator. Ya get my drift?"

Liam's eyes grew so large they were almost cartoonish.

"Okay, so we grow out his hair. What else?" Harper asked.

I stepped around to the side of the chair, catching his profile. Liam cocked his head to look at me, his brows raised in anticipation of what I might suggest next. "The tie."

He lifted the bright orange excrescence and glanced down at it. "What's wrong with my tie? I happen to love this tie."

"It looks like something Big Bird would wear. We need you regal and that makes you look comical."

Liam dropped his tie and crossed his arms over his chest. "What else?" he challenged.

"Are you in a relationship, Liam?" My heart stopped in my chest as I waited for the answer.

Liam leaned back in his chair, crossing his leg over his knee. His long fingers wrapped around his ankle and a cocky smile perked his lips. "Are you interested?"

I rolled my eyes, slumping my shoulders forward. "For professional reasons only, I assure you."

If he only knew.

He lifted his shoulder in a half shrug. "No girlfriend."

"Wife?" I shot back. My eyes locked on his.

"Nope."

"Boyfriend?"

Neither of us flinched, nor did we blink.

"Not gay."

I sat down on the arm of his chair, crossing my legs. He didn't even bother to scoot for me to have room. His elbow rested right against my backside. Again, another challenge from him. He wouldn't back down. That was fine.

Challenge accepted.

"If you must know about my sex life, I haven't had a steady girlfriend in about three years, and even then it wasn't serious. I've been too busy doing what I was elected to do."

"Casual sex then?"

"Absolutely not. Sex is too intimate for it to be casual."

I looked over to Harper who'd gotten up to pour himself another bourbon. "Is this kid for real?"

Liam's fingers squeezed around his ankle. "I'd appreciate if you'd stop calling me a *kid*. I'm a grown man and *your* Congressman. I'm to be respected and addressed as such."

I lifted my knuckles to my lips, stunned. Clearing my throat, I acknowledged, "You're right. Please accept my apologies, Congressman."

"Apology accepted, and yes, I'm for real. No matter what, I will never lie about who or what I am. You have my word on that."

Chills formed over my arms. For the first time, in all my years in politics, I found myself actually believing a politician. It was an unsettling feeling.

"Okay." I paused, meeting his deep stare. "Then I must ask, do you have a friend —of the female persuasion— who might be willing to accompany you to special events? We need to make you look stable and having the same young lady by your side will give that impression."

A gleam twinkled in his eyes. "Yes. Kristin Page."

I bounced off the arm of the chair, grabbing my clutch. I pulled out my cellphone and opened up a new memo to start taking notes. "Who is she?"

"Childhood best friend."

"Is she in a relationship?"

"Not at this time," he answered as quickly as I asked.

"Good." I jotted her name down to run a background check on her later. One could never be too careful about who was involved in the inner workings of a campaign.

Harper moved back to where I'd initially found him when I entered the room. He placed his full glass on the mantle and began poking at the dying fire, bringing it back to life. Heat moved about the room and I relished the feeling. I hated the cold. Give me summer heat any day.

I drifted back to the sofa. "Since you claim to be honest…"

"I am honest."

Harper glanced back to us, but said nothing.

"Yes," I noted, attempting to appear unfazed by Liam's interruption. "As I was saying, are there any skeletons in your closet I need to know about? Any at all? I don't care how insignificant they might be to you, if it can be used against you, I need to know about it now."

"No, ma'am." He enunciated each word with precise deliberation. A practiced military response, but there was an attorney's authority that I picked up on as well. For one so young, he might actually have some experience.

Again, our eyes locked. Those dark chocolate orbs were mesmerizing. His full lips pursed, almost begging me to challenge him. But I didn't have the facts, which bugged me. With over four-hundred Representatives in the US House, sometimes one would slip off my radar. William Baxter happened to be that one. And since I didn't know enough about him, I wouldn't challenge something I wasn't entirely certain to be true.

I dropped my gaze and made a quick note on my phone. It never failed, when I vetted a politician, I'd find some sort of skeleton. No matter how much they declared I wouldn't. My guess was William Baxter would be no different.

"So, Liam, when you campaign, do you go by William or Liam?"

"William."

"Good. If you'd said Liam, I would've suggested a different strategy."

He nodded.

I brushed my hair from my eyes and relaxed back into the sofa. "Well then, there's only one other demand I have."

Harper turned around, holding his hands behind him close to the fire. "And this is the biggie, isn't it?"

I laughed. "You know me well, my old friend."

"I do. So what's the deal breaker?"

"Congressman," I addressed Liam, "who's your current press secretary?"

Liam looked a little confused by the question. "Victor Knolls. Why?"

Ah, good ol' Victor. Nice guy. Been in the business for years, but he was soft, which made what I was about to demand even easier to request. "Because you need to let him go."

Liam jumped forward in his seat. His huge feet hit the ground and his hands clasped together as he rested his weight on his knees. "What? Victor's been with me from the start. No. I won't do that. He's been nothing but loyal."

"Loyalty is great and appreciated..."

"I won't do it. I won't fire someone on my staff because you said to. Absolutely not. You have no right to tell me who to hire."

"You're right, and I'm not telling you who to bring on as your chief of staff, which by the way, who is your chief?"

"My brother, Aaron," he growled.

"Aaron Baxter. Got it." There went another note into my phone. "Now, as I was saying, when it comes to the press we need someone who knows how to handle national campaigns with, shall we say, flare. Victor won't be able to handle what I need him to do."

"Who do you have in mind?" Harper asked, plopping down beside me. The warmth from the fire resonated from his skin. I placed my phone on the table and scooted in a little closer to enjoy the heat.

Liam cocked a single eyebrow. I furrowed mine, hating he could do the whole one eyebrow thing. I'd always envied people who could do that and roll their tongues.

I wonder if he can roll his tongue? I bet he has a talented tongue.

Dammit! I had to stop thinking things like that.

"Scout Whitaker," I replied.

"Scout," Liam balked. "Is that some sort of press nickname?"

I cocked my head and smirked. "No. That's actually her name and she's the best in the business. She's a heavy hitter and that's what we're going to need if we're to play hardball with the Republicans."

"I can't do that to Victor," Liam stood firm.

I shrugged. "Well, then I can't run your campaign. It's really that simple."

The room grew into a heavy silence. I stood up and made my way to the bar, pouring myself a club soda. I had to drive back to the city soon and needed to be sober, plus I didn't want to be slobbering drunk in front of my client. I was a practice what you preach kind of gal, and appearances always came first.

I took a sip of my soda and watched as the man, who was the most honest person I was sure to ever meet, wrestled with what to do next.

"Listen, Liam, I know it's a sacrifice, but if things don't work out with Scout, you could always hire Victor back," Harper encouraged. "And, I'll even chip in a hefty donation so you can give him a great severance package."

I downed the rest of my drink in a single gulp. It was probably wrong of me to make the poor man encounter such a moral crisis from the beginning, but if he couldn't handle firing one little employee as a means to win then he wasn't worth the office he was running for.

"Okay," Liam finally agreed. "But I have some *provisos* of my own."

The corners of my lips turned upward. This man really did have some balls. I leaned forward, resting my elbows on the bar, my empty cup secured between my hands.

Liam stood up in a graceful, fluid motion. He marched over to the bar and leaned toward me. "You will not ask me to do anything that is immoral ever again."

Immoral. Hmm. I could think of a good many immoral things I could do to this man.

"By immoral, do you mean...?" I wiggled my eyebrows.

With the best poker face I'd ever seen, he whispered, "You know exactly what I mean, Ms. McNeal."

I swallowed hard, my skin burned as he pulled the glass from my hands. He walked around the bar and poured me another soda before pouring himself one as well. I had to respect his alcohol restraint. For me, it was a good sign that I wouldn't have to worry about him making an ass of himself in public.

"I refuse to terminate another employee without just cause. I wouldn't do it now, but Mr. Harper's offer is one I don't think I can refuse. You understand?"

The serious look in his eyes meant there was no room for debate. This wasn't a challenge. It was a demand.

All I could do was nod.

"I will not allow you to take advantage of people. All business dealings are to be handled legitimately. Nothing under the table," he added.

Liam slipped my glass back into my hand. His touch was like an inferno that consumed me, warming me more than the crackling fire that heated the room. He wiped the corners of his mouth with his fingertips and smiled. "Do we understand the word *immoral* a little more clearly now?"

I nodded again, fixated on his intense eyes and the way his lips moved as he spoke.

"Good." He inclined his head a little closer so only I could hear. My chest rose and fell with rapid breaths at his invasion of my personal space. "Oh, and one other thing," he murmured, his voice decadently smooth. "I keep my ties."

Inapposite laughter rattled in my throat. The fighter in me wanted to scream out no, but the winner in me debated otherwise. I could give him something as insignificant as a tie. Besides, if they turned out worse than the one he was wearing, I could lay down the law and force him to wear one of my choosing. "Fine," I agreed.

"Then I propose a toast."

Harper jumped up from the sofa and met us at the bar. I lifted my shoulders, wiping away the white noise that had become my brain.

Liam lifted his glass. "To making changes."

Harper and I lifted our glasses. "To making changes,"

we chimed in. Three glasses clinked together before we all took a drink.

"So," —I winced, swallowing down my fizzy soda— "does this mean we have a deal?"

"I believe it does. Welcome to Team Baxter." Liam once again extended his hand in an offer to shake. I raked my teeth over my bottom lip and rested my glass back on the bar to accept his hand. Stronger than before came the rush of magnetism toward this man. My mind fought against the pull I felt. I told myself it had to be the unspoken challenges he blasted at me from the moment we met. It couldn't be this polished, young man who captivated me. No. There had to be more.

I waited for the answer to strike me down where I stood, yet as his fingertips brushed along the inside of my wrist, feather light, but so enticing, I found no such answers. Liam slipped his hand from mine, lightly spreading his fingers into my palm as he released me. He had to know what he was doing to me, but he played coy.

Well played, ki...Congressman. Well played.

"Fantastic!" Harper exclaimed. "Bet, you won't regret this."

Out of the fog, I squeezed my eyes shut. "I hope not."

"You won't, *Bet*," Liam teased.

My eyes flew open to find him grinning back at me. "Elizabeth," I grumbled.

Liam laughed and finished off his drink. "Well, I for one, am calling it a night. Thank you again for your hospitality, Mr. Harper."

"I told you before, call me Harper. Everyone does."

Liam granted him a slight nod. With a bow of his head

and a swaggering wink, Liam turned to me. "And, *Elizabeth*, I'll be seeing you soon."

Damn him and his charm. He had the charisma down pat. And while the woman in me wanted to succumb to his allure, the professional in me refused to give him the satisfaction. I stood taller and rounded my shoulders. "Count on it."

Liam placed his glass on the bar and strolled out of the room, not even taking a glance back, though I couldn't take my eyes off him. That suit contoured his body well, an enticing little wrapper for a woman to rip off him.

As soon as Liam was gone, I felt like I could breathe again. I took in the deepest breath imaginable and released it almost as a sigh. "Well, I guess I need to be heading out of here. I have an hour drive back into the city." I set my glass down beside Liam's vacated tumbler.

Harper grabbed my hand. "There's no need for you to drive back. Stay here tonight."

I squeezed Harper's hand before releasing it. "I wish I could." In short strides, I moved to the table and grabbed my purse and phone. "But I leave out for DC tomorrow and I still need to pack. Besides, you already have a house guest this evening."

"As if I don't have the room," Harper argued.

"Okay, but I don't have a change of clothes or any of my necessities with me."

Harper moved toward me, taking my belongings from my hands. "We both know that's not true. You always carry your makeup bag in your briefcase and I'd bet my fortune you have a suit in the car."

Longtime friends should never know that much about

each other. Such as the knowledge I had of a certain porn stash he hid in his office.

"That's true, but it doesn't change my flight plans nor the fact that I have nothing to sleep in."

"Jordyn left some pajamas here while visiting last week. You can wear those." Harper slipped his arm around my shoulders, walking us out of the den. "I need you to change those plans anyway. Tomorrow I'm hosting a little dinner to announce William's intent to run. You need to be here for it."

I stopped mid stride. "You had that much confidence that I'd say yes?"

"Yes," he stated without hesitation. A gleam of deviltry played across his face.

"Oh, you are wicked," I jested. "Fine. I guess I'm staying. My usual room?"

"You know where it is."

"I need to go get my stuff from my car." I pushed up on the tips of my toes and planted a friendly kiss to Harper's cheek. "Thank you for saving me tonight."

Harper tweaked my cheek. "And thank you for accepting Liam. I really think we have a shot with him."

Movement in my peripheral vision grabbed my attention. I scanned down the hall, but saw nothing. I shrugged it off as my imagination. It had been a long night.

Sleep. That's what I needed. And maybe a good kick in the head for the project I'd just agreed to take on.

"You know what?" I rubbed along my jaw to my chin. "Add another million to my fee. I'm gonna need it with the amount of work I have cut out for me with this one."

Five

Sleep was my enemy. No matter how hard I tried, I simply couldn't find rest.

I was haunted by molten chocolate eyes, smooth lips, and an unwitting smile. Strength, not only in that masculine body of his but in his personality, burned through my thoughts. I wanted so badly to either smack him across the face or kiss him as hard as I could. Either sounded inviting but neither were possible. What bugged me the most was I couldn't place him. Washington DC, was my domain. Anyone of importance I knew and knew well. I could tell you who they were, who their families were, and even who their mistresses were. This guy was never even a blip on my radar.

As if it mattered now.

Still, not knowing anything about him haunted me.

Frustrated, I smacked my fists down onto the soft, pillow top mattress. Cotton linens with God only knew what kind of outrageous thread count bunched beneath my balled hands. I was wasting time trying to sleep. My mind wouldn't let me rest until I knew all there was to know about Congressman William Baxter.

Kicking off the covers, I threw my legs over the side of the mattress onto the plush rug beneath my feet. I wiggled my toes into the soft fibers and pushed myself out of the bed. The heat was on, I could hear it running, but there was no eliminating the constant draft that invaded the bedrooms of the old house.

Harper had given me a pair of Jordyn's pajamas to sleep in. It wasn't uncommon for Jordyn to spend time with Harper. After all, he was her godfather. He loved spoiling her. One year, Russell and I nearly killed him for buying her a mare of her own for Christmas without discussing it with us first. But that was Harper. Always giving. He loved Jordyn and I couldn't begrudge him any opportunity to spend time with my daughter.

I stood up and tugged at the pant legs because they were far too short for my long limbs. They fit more like capris than pants.

A hiss escaped my lips as I meandered across the hardwood floors to the chair where my briefcase sat. Chill bumps multiplied over my skin with each step I took. The floors might as well have been covered with ice considering how cold it felt against my bare feet. I slipped my laptop out of my bag and rushed back to the bed where I could get warm again.

Back under the covers, I fired up my computer. The bright screen lit the room with an eerie white glow. A few keystrokes was all it took to appease my weary mind. Images of William Baxter covered my screen. A full background check would take a few days to complete, but the internet was a great place to get started.

Fox News, CNN, MSNBC, C-Span, AP all covered stories on William Reid Baxter, the charming Democrat from North Texas. There was even a Wikipedia entry on him. Then again, I had a Wikipedia page, so that wasn't saying much.

It didn't take me long to compile a skeleton history of the man I'd be supporting in the upcoming Senate election.

William Baxter, born in Lewisville, Texas, but grew up in Grand Prairie. He played on his high school basketball team all four years. That didn't surprise me considering his height. I had to give myself a pat on the back for recognizing him as an athlete. Then again, that rock hard body of his was a dead giveaway. Anyone with two ounces of brains would've figured it out.

After high school, Liam attended the University of Texas at Austin and graduated with a bachelor's degree in Philosophy, which led him to Yale Law School. Straight out of law school he clerked for the Fifth Circuit Court of Appeals for a year. He had such a promising career in law. It shocked me to see he went into the military after one year as a clerk, yet there it was in black and white. Not only did he go JAG Corp, but he was also deployed for six months to Baghdad. Honorably discharged from the Army upon completion of his four years of service, Liam returned home where he set up a private practice until he ran for Congress a year and a half ago and won.

I sat there staring at my computer screen like I was reading the greatest literary work ever written. Every word jumped off the screen at me and explained so much about the man who stood up to me earlier in the evening. For one so young, he'd lived so much already.

While his career history intrigued me, the one thing I noticed was nowhere did it mention any kind of scandal involving him. Not even an inclination of any wrong doings. There was no smear campaign during his run for Congress, which seemed really odd since he was young and single.

Several pictures popped up with him and the same young lady – Kristin Page. That explained why he was so quick on the draw when I asked if he had someone. His last campaign manager used the same tactic. So, I dug in a little deeper on Ms. Page. Much to my surprise, there wasn't much available on her. Every mention of her included Liam. That didn't concern me much. I'd get full intel on her once I pulled a complete background check.

When national news didn't provide desired results, I resorted to the lowest level possible. I scanned some of my favorite rag-mags, expecting to find loads of filth on the young Congressman.

No time for casual sex, my ass.

In all my years I'd never met a man who said sex was too intimate to be casual. That was a woman's line and it was used to keep from screwing whatever ugly bastard she'd found herself shackled to at the time. No woman, at least not in this day and age, would ever turn down a hot man who wanted to screw her brains out. And since no woman would, I found it difficult to believe a man would.

However, the deeper I looked the less I found. Kristin's name popped up countless times. Speculations about the true nature of their relationship, but even that fizzled to nothing. There was an obscure entry on a nameless ex-girlfriend, but the article was so vague it could've easily been Kristin they referenced.

"What the hell is wrong with the media? Have they forgotten how to do their jobs?" I complained to the laptop.

I scratched my head and stared at the handsome face with the broody, dark eyes staring back at me.

And what the hell was wrong with the American woman…and men…if they weren't throwing themselves at this guy? Geez!

"Fine," I snarled at the picture. "Let's see what kind of hobbies they say you have, Mr. Too-Good-To-Be-True."

I clicked a few links and found a site that showed pictures of Liam playing basketball with some inner city kids.

"Photo op," I sneered and closed the site.

Worthless.

But I was relentless. I wouldn't give up until I found what I sought.

And my stubbornness paid off.

A few more clicks and I hit the jackpot. There was Liam bundled up in a thick winter coat on a fresh-powdered mountain with a snowboard perched beside him. Another man, a couple of inches taller than him, which shocked the hell out of me because Liam was a giant, stood at his other side, also holding a board. That had to be his brother, Aaron.

Part of me felt sorry for their mother, because she had to give birth to those two. Then it got me to wondering how tall their parents were. More photo ops proved their mother to be around my height, which meant she was tall for a woman. Their dad, a rather handsome silver fox, stood as tall as Liam.

Height runs in the family.

My curiosity about his family was satisfied for the moment, I flipped back to the snowboarding picture. It had to be one of my favorite photos of him. Liam's face, bright red from the cold, beamed from ear-to-ear. Snowboarding took courage, agility, and a lot of skill. I knew all too well how treacherous it was through all of Jordyn's blunders over the years.

"Well, I'm sure you'll have Jordyn's vote after she sees this," I chortled.

Between the cold air and the drinks from earlier, my bladder started to holler at me. Reluctantly, I closed my laptop, but not before bookmarking the page, and slithered out from under my covers.

For a house that big, I couldn't believe there were only three bathrooms and one of them was downstairs.

Damn historic builders.

My feet hit the floor and I winced at the cold. I stood up and once again tugged at my sleepwear. Certain it was both dark enough and late enough that I wouldn't be caught wearing Jordyn's silky —too small for me— pajamas, I tiptoed to the door and turned the knob. The hinges creaked as I slowly pulled open the door, but not so loud I felt it would wake anyone. Opened just enough to slip my lanky body through, I left my room and slinked down the hall to the bathroom.

When I reached the door, I looked to my left and then my right. For the most part the hall was still dark. Only fragmented light from under the bathroom door gleamed into the pitch black. Assuming the light was from a nightlight left on for guests, I turned the knob and pushed the door open.

One step inside and I stop dead in my tracks. There was Liam climbing out of the shower. Beads of water glistened down his rock hard chest. He rubbed his hands over his head, spraying water around him. I stared in awe of the naked man reaching for a towel. Taut, tanned skin pulled over sinewy muscles taunted me. Tempting me. Gone was the well-tailored suit and hideous tie. In its place was sex incarnate.

My fingers itched to touch him. I could almost taste the water dripping down his body on my tongue. Inside my chest, my heart lurched, wanting to feel him all around me. Instead, my eyes feasted on the gorgeous man that was Congressman Baxter. Frozen where I stood, my gaze drifted down his well-defined torso to the main attraction between his legs. My eyes widened at the sight.

Fuck me! He'd definitely get the female and gay vote over that package.

His towel was midway around his waist when he noticed me. He stopped and something about his movement triggered me to look up, allowing my mind to escape the cloud of sexy flesh in which it was enveloped.

His dark stare met my hazel one. He cocked his head to the side and raised an eyebrow. I smacked my hand over my face, covering my eyes, trying to back out of the bathroom as fast as I could. "I'm sorry. I didn't see...I didn't know..." I shrieked, turning around, nearly hitting the corner of the door in the process.

Behind me, I could hear Liam rushing to wrap the

towel around his hips. "Elizabeth," he called out after me. "Wait!"

"I'm sorry," I cried back.

"Elizabeth! Stop!"

But I didn't stop.

Once I cleared the bathroom door, without breaking my nose, I dropped my hand and dashed down the hall toward my room. The memory of Liam's naked form would forever be scorched into my memory.

Safe and secure in my room, I slammed the door shut and locked it. I pressed my ear to the cold wood to hear if anyone was coming. My heart raced in my chest and my breathing was erratic. I felt like a teenager who'd just been caught by her mother with a boy in her bedroom. I was absolutely humiliated. This wasn't like me. I *never* lost my cool. Ever. Yet I ran like a fool.

"This is silly! I'm a grown woman," I reminded myself. "I've seen naked men before. Gah!"

But none like him.

What the hell is wrong with me?

What an idiot I was over a little bare flesh. Not only did I interrupt a man's privacy, but I gawked at him like a dog in heat.

Minutes passed and there was nothing. No one called my name. No one came to my door demanding an explanation for my childish behavior or why I'd invaded a Congressman's privacy. Nothing happened.

I pressed my back to the door and slid down it, uncaring of the freezing cold floor beneath me. What I should've done was got my ass up and went to apologize to the man, yet my body couldn't move.

Stupid!

I hugged my knees close to my body to keep warm. I dropped my forehead to my knees and closed my eyes. Gone was the urge to pee. It wouldn't have surprised me if I'd wet myself during my run back to my room, but I was too cold and angry at myself to tell.

The whole scene replayed in my mind. His body, hard, long, and wet. His fingers clutching the terrycloth towel, about to wrap it around his hips. Water dripping from the top of his head. Those chocolate orbs boring back into mine. The look in his eyes upon catching me staring at him. What was that look?

Shock?

No, that wasn't it. Well, it was, but not exactly.

Anger?

Again, it didn't fit.

Arousal?

I lifted my head and shook it slightly.

Pissed off. That's what it was.

Arousal. Blah! My imagination's wishful delusion.

As time passed, I started thinking like myself again. My actions had been unprofessional and I needed to own up to the situation. It was an accident. No harm was done, and no one but Liam and myself needed to know it had occurred.

I pulled myself up and dared to slip open the door. I half expected to find Liam waiting in the hall for me to finally grow a pair and confront him, but he wasn't there. The hall was dark. There wasn't a single sound. Not even the glimmer of light from under the bathroom door shone anymore.

Liam was gone.

Okay. I could deal with this. In the morning, I'd do what I was best at, averting scandal. Calm and rational, I plotted out in my head how to fix the situation. Yet, no matter how hard I contemplated my next move, the image of Liam's naked body resurfaced in my head.

I'm screwed. So very, very screwed.

Six

No amount of makeup could cover up the dark circles under my eyes.

For someone who was used to running on little sleep, I was suffering. And for what?

Guilt?

In my line of work guilt was a liability, but I felt guilty for not going straight to Liam's room to clear the air about what happened. The whole thing was an accident. My teenage girl seeing cock for the first time routine be damned.

When the sun finally came up, I didn't hesitate. I donned my spare black sheath dress, perfected my usual makeup, and sucked up my shame.

Much to my dismay, however, he was already gone when I knocked on his bedroom door.

Frustrated and a little hungry, I hightailed it downstairs to the kitchen for a cup of tea and maybe a waffle. I knew from years of experience that Harper wouldn't be up before noon, and since there was no telling where the young Congressman had scampered off to, I'd be eating alone. Well, as alone as one could be in a house filled with staff who were already bustling about for the evening festivities. I dodged in and out of traffic on my way to the kitchen, doing my best to stay out of the way.

Now, I'd never been a wiz in the kitchen. My mother tried to teach me how to cook when I was younger but I had no desire to learn. I was more interested in reading and boys. Some years later I regretted that decision. As a young, single mother, I struggled to make my growing daughter a well prepared meal. After many nights of burnt soups, and yes, one can burn soup, I finally figured out a few minor cooking techniques. Not that I ever became a good cook, but I did learn how to boil water for tea and make some mean waffles.

Once in the kitchen, it didn't take long for me to find a tea kettle, but with all the people rushing about, there was no way I'd be able to make waffles.

Tea would have to do.

Damn my luck!

I filled the kettle with water and placed it to boil on the only stove burner available.

The faint smell of barbeque floated through the air making my mouth water. Food was a must, so I slipped in between two women, both wearing chef's uniforms, to get into the double-wide refrigerator that was bound to have something I could eat.

Much like the rest of the house, Harper had renovated the kitchen once he took over the estate. Polished hardwood flooring, painted white wood cabinets, gorgeous white and black tile backsplashes, and amazing black granite countertops created a look of elegance for the enormous space.

A giant kitchen and three bathrooms.

Three fucking bathrooms and I had to walk into the one where Liam was taking a shower. Why the hell was he taking a shower at such a crazy hour? Better yet, why wasn't there any steam from said shower? That might have at least tipped me off.

Right. As if anything would've but his enormous...would've caught my attention in that moment.

Naked Liam resurfaced in my mind. Damn, he did look good.

Stop that! He's too young!

Too young was right. Ten and a half years too young. Not only that but he was a politician. No self-respecting campaign manager would be caught dead with a politician. We knew too many dirty little secrets about the underbellies of politicians that the American people would die if they knew.

I shuddered at the thought.

No, I could admire him from a professional distance. There was nothing wrong with that.

I placed my hands on the door handles, ready to pull open the fridge when I caught sight of Liam through the kitchen window.

Of course he appears right now.

I almost had enough restraint not to take a closer look. Almost.

I released the handles and side stepped to the window. Resting the palms of my hands on the countertop, I leaned forward. The morning fog still rested on the ground, but there was Liam doing pushups in the grass. Up and down he went, his arm and leg muscles flexing with each repetition. I watched as his lips moved each time he came up.

He's counting. I chuckled to myself.

The tight, black compression shirt looked soaked through and his black and red basketball shorts dragged the ground as he pushed himself up. How he wasn't freezing in a sleeveless shirt and shorts astounded me. My ass would've been a popsicle.

His face scrunched with the intensity of his workout, and I became mesmerized by how consistent his movements were. They were fluid in motion, not jerky. His body knew what it was doing without even being told. It was trained, poised, and ready.

The longer I observed him, the bigger that pit in my stomach grew. Once again I was guilt-ridden that I had somehow managed to stumble on yet another private moment in the life of William Baxter.

I backed away from the window, leaving him to his workout.

I hated this sudden moral conscience I was experiencing. I'd worked so hard over the years to squash it.

With a roll of my shoulders, I pushed back the feelings. Once Liam came inside, I'd sit down and discuss what happened with him in a rational, professional manner. I was a closer and I would close this. Sure, I might have to eat a little crow. This whole damn situation was my fault and I was woman enough to own up to my mistakes.

All my plans to apologize reformulated in my head. I'd explain that I was caught up in work and I didn't notice the bathroom light on. It wasn't a lie. I was certain Liam would understand and even agree to let this whole thing go for the sake of the campaign. There was no reason for anything to be awkward. We were both adults.

Okay, so I was the adult. He just surpassed the brink of manhood. Tit for tat.

Secure in my decision, I moved back to the fridge. Cold air blasted against my face as I opened both doors. My eyes scanned the shelves, searching for anything that might fill my stomach. So much food and nothing appeared appetizing. I opened and closed the drawers, barely paying attention to what was really in them.

About to slam the doors shut, I was stopped by the warmth of his breath fanning over my hair. His chest pressed against my back and the smell of the outdoors flooded my senses. My body burned with kinetic energy. I tried to calm my erratic breathing, but there was no controlling it. His mere closeness caused me to tremble. Even if I wanted to move, I couldn't. He had me pinned between him and the cool refrigerator.

A strong, defined arm reached over my shoulder and a huge hand appeared in front of my face. I glanced up to see Liam standing over me, sweat peppering his brow. His mouth pulled into a crooked grin as our eyes met.

Inside I was screaming in aggravation. This man was exasperating. Here he was, rubbing his nasty, sweaty, smelly...hot, gorgeous, amped up, body against me when I was clean and dressed for the day.

"Do you mind?" I snarled.

"No, I don't," he buzzed, grabbing a bottle of water from the fridge.

I tried to shove him back, but it was no use. He was hard as stone and acted like he didn't even notice my attempt for escape.

Liam pulled his arm back slowly, letting the bare skin of his wrist brush against my neck.

Ugh! What the hell?

I raked my nails through my silky locks, fighting the irritation crawling under my skin. No matter what, I had to get myself under control, apologize, and put this crap behind me so I could get to work on important stuff – like making sure Liam won the race.

I turned my eyes heavenward and sighed in resignation. With my chin lifted, I closed the fridge doors and swung around to face Liam.

He backed away keeping his eyes locked on me. A bemused smile played across those sexy as fuck lips.

"Sleep well?" he queried, hoisting himself up onto the large island behind the refrigerator. He dragged the bottle of cold water across his brow to cool his face. "Because you look quite exhausted."

Thrown off task by his comment, not to mention that seductive little move of his, I gritted my teeth into a polished grin. "I slept fine. Thank you."

He shrugged. "Could've fooled me." Taken back by his candor, I examined his expression. His eyes darkened with mischief. "You really should sleep more if you intend on helping me win the election. From what I hear it's going to be time consuming, me being the dark horse and all."

Liam twisted the lid off the bottle and brought it to his

mouth. His throat bobbed as he gulped down the water. Lost in his actions, I smacked my lips, drawing my tongue out over them. Liam twisted the lid back on the bottle and dropped it to his lap. His gaze traveled down my body, heating every inch of me. I dared to meet those smoldering eyes of his, only to get lost in my memory of him. Tanned skin. Firm muscles. Defined torso. An exceptional....

Oh shit! I just looked at his crotch!

I jerked my eyes away from him, feeling something warm rise in my cheeks. No way in hell could I be blushing.

No! No! No!

But there it was. My blood surged through my veins. The thrum of my heartbeat pounded in my ears. Tension mounted inside me and at any moment it could explode.

And it nearly did at the sound of the kettle chirping, which caused me to jump clean out of my skin. "Jesus!" I screeched.

"I've been called many things, but that's a new one for me."

The seriousness of his tone caused me to laugh. "How about asshole? Have you heard that one before?"

As I whipped around to turn off the stove and collect my screaming kettle, he tapped his chin and laughed.

"You seem rather jittery this morning," he evaluated. "Maybe you should take a *shower*. I hear it can be quite cathartic."

It was a good thing I'd set the kettle down on a potholder or I might've dropped the damn thing. I jerked around to him, my mind whirling with what to say next. It was time for me to own up and make amends. I rounded my shoulders and straightened my back, bringing myself to my full height. "I guess we need…"

"There's nothing like hot water spraying down your *naked* body to help you unwind from a hard day. Wouldn't you agree?" he interrupted me.

It took only a second for me to realize that this little snot was needling me. Well, two could play that game. I collected my wits about me and returned to my task of making a cup of tea. Mug in hand, I inserted the tea infuser and poured in hot water. "Absolutely. And locking the door to the bathroom is a good way to keep from being disturbed."

Wrapping the chain between my fingers, I bobbed the infuser to help my brew along, careful not to look at Liam. It was bad enough I could feel him staring a hole into my back.

"Doors are only meant to be locked if someone has something to hide."

"Again, I won't argue there, but something so *small* should really be concealed behind a locked door."

Boom! There ya go. Dig the knife in a little deeper.

I turned around to find his brow lifted and lips pursed.

"Small?"

I brought the cup to my lips, feeling the steam rise against my nose. "More like tiny."

Liam shoved off the island and moved toward me. People tried to push past him but he was solid as a wall blocking their way. Instead they simply moved around him. "Not tiny at all."

Through it all, I stood my ground. For the first time since last night I held the upper hand and it felt good to be back on top again. "I beg to differ."

Much like he had in our previous encounters, he closed the gap between us in a single stride. He took my teacup from my hands and placed it on the counter beside us. "I'd hate to argue with you, since you're the expert and all, but on this fact, I must."

Without a flinch, I met his gaze, which wasn't easy, and produced my best smile. "You're right. I am the expert and you should trust me on this."

He bowed his head, his lips ghosting my ear. "Maybe the expert on politics, but this, you need a little instruction on."

Heat rolled through my veins. An uncontrollable shiver scampered up my spine so hard we both felt it. "That's what I thought," he whispered so soft it tickled my skin. Liam took a step back, giving me a chance to breathe. "Now, I need to go take a *shower*. My run was quite invigorating this morning."

In a militaristic manner, he turned on his heel and started to walk away.

What possessed me to call after him, I wasn't sure, but I did. He stopped but didn't look back.

"Elizabeth. Don't."

His single warning burrowed its way deep inside me. In that one word I understood. This incident was between us and would stay that way. First impressions remained unscathed. Authority would be a tug-of-war between us. A game of sorts and this was only the first round. There was no winner or loser here. We had a draw. A draw in which we both agreed on. But next time there would be a clear winner and clear loser and the game would play out until

Election Day.

My mouth snapped shut, as he lumbered off.

A worthy opponent.

I reached for my cup and sucked down the bitter brew, my focus remaining on the exit where Liam had disappeared. The world returned around me, all the hustle and bustle of preparation. My stomach growled reminding me that I still hadn't eaten. I chuckled deep in my throat and snagged a mini quiche from a passing service tray.

It was official. William Baxter was going to be the death of me and if I wasn't careful, he'd also be my downfall.

Seven

"There you are. I've been searching all over for you. I thought you might've left."

Harper plopped down in the armchair across from me. On the table, piled in neat stacks, were plans I'd started jotting down for Liam's campaign. Mailer ideas. Polls to set up. Things steamrolled out of my head faster than I could write. I'd already called my office in DC to have the intent paperwork submitted, and contacted Scout about coming on board to Team Baxter. All of the pieces were falling into place far too easily, which worried me. Nothing smooth ever worked in my favor. I always anticipated a snag in the road, because no matter what, there always was one.

"I've got too much to do. Besides, my client is here, remember?" I teased.

Legs crossed out in front of him, Harper slunk down in his chair, locking his fingers behind his neck. "I figured you'd want to run home for a dress tonight."

"Yeah, about tonight," —I leaned forward and flipped through a pile of papers until I found the one I wanted and handed it over to Harper— "I don't believe we should announce Liam's intent to run this evening. I've been giving this some thought, and I think he needs to do a public announcement. We want his name out there, for people to see him. A private event won't give us the coverage we need."

Harper shoved forward, taking the paper. His eyes scanned over the document. "You want him to announce here?"

I smirked, snapping back the sheet. "Scout agrees with me."

Harper smacked his lips, a wide grin growing across his face. "The Old Red Courthouse is a ballsy move."

I shrugged, stacking my pile back on the table. "He's young, Harper. He's going to need a lot of gutsy moves if he's to be recognized as a real contender."

"This is like Obama epic. You realize that, right?"

I wiggled my brows, full of arrogance. "Why do you think I'm suggesting it?"

Harper laughed, tapping his fingertip to his lips. "Okay. So, how do you plan on procuring it?"

A few clicks on my laptop and a very important email appeared. I turned my computer for Harper to see. "Already done. I called in a favor or two. It's set for tomorrow afternoon."

"And Liam?"

I was about to make some offhanded comment about how he hired me to do a job and he better let me do it, when I heard, "What about Liam?"

My eyes shot up and Harper glanced over his shoulder at the lanky man strolling into the room. Dressed in black slacks and a crisp button down shirt, sans a God-awful tie or jacket, his collar unbuttoned and his sleeves rolled up to his elbows, Liam looked like any other businessman ready for a day at the office. His hands stuffed in his pockets, with a manly black watch peeking over the fabric, he strolled through the study toward us, a carefree smile lighting his face.

Damn him for wearing a watch. No one wears watches anymore. If men only realized how sexy that was.

I swallowed hard and straightened up, turning my laptop back toward me. "Good afternoon, Congressman."

"Good afternoon, Elizabeth. Harper." He nodded to Harper and strolled toward the sofa, taking a seat beside me. He leaned forward resting his elbows on his legs, and peered at my computer screen.

"Sleep well?" Harper questioned, stretching his own arms over his head.

His dark eyes shifted to me and a smile tweaked his lips. "My accommodations were comfortable," he dodged. Gooseflesh formed over my skin as he scooted closer to me. "The Old Red Courthouse, huh? What are we doing there?"

I blinked several times, cutting through my memories of this man. He raised a brow, his head tilted in a way he could look between Harper and me rather easily. I tapped the computer screen with my fingernail and began to explain my plan for his candidacy announcement. Once I started talking, all thoughts of Liam naked dissipated, leaving me with nothing more than my work. Plans set in motion, as I gave him a step by step of my ideas.

"Scout's already getting several major networks on the horn to televise it." I took in a deep breath and beamed.

Yep. They can say it. I'm a genius.

"Okay." Liam nodded, grazing over a few of my notes I'd thrust into his hands.

"Okay?" I replied back in shock. "Just okay?"

Liam leaned back into the sofa, crossing his leg over his knee. "I hired you for your expertise, Elizabeth. Everyone claims you're the best and from what I've seen so far, they're not far from the truth. If you believe this is the best way for me to announce my candidacy, then I'm on board."

I'd expected a fight. Some sort of argument. Not a simple *okay*. "Well, alrighty then." I reached for my pile of paperwork and sifted through it. "Next we need to go over policies and strategies. I need to know where you stand on certain issues. If Keating is running, which I have my feelers out to verify, then she's going to come out pitching, and we need to be ready to bat."

Liam crossed his arms over his chest. "You really love your baseball metaphors. Are you a fan?"

I chuckled, shaking my head. "Nope. Never seen a game in my life. Would you prefer I start using basketball metaphors?" I jibbed.

Liam let out a good, hardy laugh. "The ball's in your court."

"Damn! That's the only one I know," I whined.

"There's always — slam dunk, home court advantage, no harm, no foul, and my personal favorite, full-court press," Harper jumped in.

Liam and I turned to look at Harper, both a little stunned that he'd pulled those out of thin air so fast, but also a little surprised he was still in the room. I scratched my jaw and chuckled. "Well, I guess I'll add those to my list and use them when necessary."

Liam shifted his eyes back to mine, his smile cool and inviting. "You better now that you have them in your arsenal."

I rolled my eyes and fought back a laugh, tapping my well-manicured nails on the papers sitting in my lap. "Okay, smarty pants, let's get to work here. Policies, first."

"Ugh. This stuff bores me," Harper groaned. "I'll be in the stables if you two need me for anything." He stood up, stretching his arms over his head, his joints cracking with the movement. "And please, no bloodshed, you two. They just cleaned the carpets this morning."

"If I must spill any of his blood, I promise to keep it off the carpets." My eyes cut to Liam whose lips were pursed in a mocking grin.

"I'm not one to lie, so there's no way I'll make that promise."

I shook my head. "You might want to grab us a tarp then, Harper. Looks like the gloves are coming off."

"Seriously, woman? A boxing idiom?" Liam squawked.

"Make that two tarps!" I hollered at Harper who was already halfway out the door.

After Harper left and Liam was able to calm his snarky laughter, we spent the next two hours discussing strategies and policies. Debates became heated. Creative ideas flowed between us, almost as if we were one mind. I was astonished by how many good ideas he had. Good, but I made them better. By the time we were done, I was exhausted but excited. It'd been ages since I had a campaign thrill me this much.

Usually my clients simply took my word for things, always giving me and my staff carte blanche on all aspects of a campaign. Not Liam. He wanted to be hands on with everything. Compromises were made, plans slated. I felt like a kid in a candy store, or better yet, a woman who'd been thoroughly fucked.

By the end of it all, Liam and I were sitting so close our knees touched. I became immersed in the musky hints of his cologne and the heat emanating from his skin. Light touches and soft, innocent brushes of our skin left me aching for more. There were two things, however, that kept me grounded — his age, but more importantly, his candidacy.

"Well, I guess that covers the prelims." I tossed the pen I'd been chewing on to the table.

Liam slumped back into the cushions of the sofa, his size fourteens brushing against the back of my ankle. "You know, after all that, I'm a little exhausted."

I grabbed my bag from the floor, sliding my laptop into it. "Me, too, but this was a great start, Congressman." I tilted my head sideways and graced him with a sincere smile. "After all this," —I pointed toward my ever growing mound of notes— "I have a feeling the voters are going to adore you."

"So I'm not going to be eaten alive?"

I bit the inside of my cheek as my harsh words were thrown back at me. It wasn't often that I had to eat crow, but with this guy I felt like that was all I ever did. "I was out of line when I said that. I was having a bad night and I took it out on you."

His brow furrowed into deep lines. "What happened?"

I chuckled, slipping all my paperwork into my satchel. "Nothing you should worry about."

Liam reached out, wrapping his long fingers around my wrist. "Tell me?"

My eyes dropped to where his fingers perimetered my skin. He rubbed his thumb along my pulse line, unabashed by the personal nature of his actions. A deep sigh expelled from my lungs, feeling a little embarrassed that I'd opened myself to him. I never talked about my personal life with clients. It was unprofessional, yet with Liam it felt natural. "When Harper called me last night I was on a date."

Liam's hand tightened, but not to the point it was uncomfortable. "A date?"

I shrugged. "Yeah. It wasn't a good date, as you can imagine since I rushed right over after receiving his call."

"I'm sorry."

A derisive laugh fell from my lips. "No need to apologize. It is what it is. I really don't expect much, if you know what I mean."

Liam released my arm and straightened up. His face contorted into a strange, almost hard, expression. "I'm afraid I don't know what you mean."

With a dismissive wave of my hand, I managed a deadpanned expression. "Men want to settle down with girls like my daughter, not *old* women like me."

"I beg your pardon?" Liam's mouth set in a straight line, his face contorted in surprise. "You're not old." He stopped as if something struck him. "And you have a daughter? Will I get to meet her?"

I chuckled, taking a moment to close my bag and depositing it at my feet. "Yes, I have a daughter, and I'm sure you will. She's a freshman at Georgetown."

A little pang smacked me in the chest at the thought of her. Rare was the time I cancelled on Jordyn. I lived by the creed that my daughter came first and my job second. In times like this, nonetheless, my darling girl understood why I needed to stay. We made arrangements to get together once I returned to DC, and I wouldn't break them again no matter what was thrown my way.

"You must be proud, but there's no way you're old enough to have a daughter in college."

I got up from my seat and stretched my tense muscles. "You're too kind, but that's not what my date said last night."

"Then your date deserved to be left. He's a fool."

I bended at the hip from side to side. "What about you? You say you don't have time, but really, who doesn't have time to date?"

Liam bent forward, touching his fingers to his toes. If I didn't know any better, I'd say it was his way to keep from looking me in the eye. "I just haven't met the right woman, I guess."

"C'mon. I know you fed me that line last night with Harper around, but it's just us now. Tell the truth. Are there any women on the side taking care of the good ol' Congressman's needs?"

He shot back up and squared his shoulders. "I won't say this again, Elizabeth. I don't do casual sex. People today toss sex around like it's a toy or a game. I don't see it that way."

"So are you saying you're a virgin?"

A deep laugh thundered from his chest. "No, I'm not a virgin." He stepped in closer to me, his lips moving near the shell of my ear. "I happen to enjoy *sex* a great deal."

I became a little lightheaded at the throaty, sensual tone of his voice. "Good to know," I choked.

Liam stepped back, his thick brows raised. "But to me, sex isn't a toy. It has meaning and depth. Two bodies sharing a connection. I will only ever engage with a woman I have true feelings for."

I brushed my bangs back from my face and reached for my bag. Now it was my turn to hide my face. "A very rare quality. Most men don't think like that."

"And most men miss out on what it feels like to make love to a woman for the first time. I assure you, there's no greater rush."

I draped my bag over my shoulder, chuckling a little.

Liam stretched his arms over his head. His shirt pulled against his tight stomach. A small gasp perched at the seam of my lips at the thought of that stomach, bare, wet, with just the right amount of light brown hair trailing to…

I diverted my eyes from going any further. I couldn't allow myself to go there again, so I blurted out the first thing that came to my mind. "I guess I kind of know what you mean. Until recently I didn't date much, either. Jordyn's the reason I started dating again. For some reason she thought I was lonely after she moved into the dorms. She said I was working too hard and needed more social interaction that didn't include a political function."

"It's nice to have someone worry about you. Aaron worries about me constantly."

"Yes, about Aaron. Will he be here tonight?"

Liam glanced down at his watch. "Actually, he should be here…"

"Hey, you two," Harper called out, entering the room. "Look who I found."

Aaron followed behind Harper, standing a good head and shoulders above him.

"Speak of the devil," Liam mumbled.

Introductions were made, and I determined rather quickly Aaron belonged in the realms of politics. He was nothing like Liam. Where Liam came off as honest yet frustrating, Aaron had that smile to your face but lie behind your back vibe. He came off as a bit of a trickster, countering Liam's seriousness. It was safe to say, I felt comfortable with Aaron Baxter and had a certain assurance he would be able to get politically dirty if I needed him to.

"Liam told me all about you last night," Aaron stated, glancing over to his brother. A look passed between them making me wonder how much Liam had told him. "If you have a moment, there are a few things I'd like to discuss with you."

"Aaron, can we do this later?" Liam stated. "Elizabeth and I just spent the last two hours talking policies and campaign strategies. I need a break to clear my head." He rubbed his forehead, his long lashes fluttering. "This woman's a tyrant."

"I'd say, if she made you fire Victor," Aaron noted with a grin. "I've been begging you to do that for a year. Besides, we don't need you here if you don't want to be."

"You know I always want to be involved," Liam growled. "And she didn't make me fire anyone. I agreed to it. I even made the call personally this morning. It's done."

Aaron turned his green eyes to me and grinned. "I'm looking forward to seeing what else you can get this knucklehead to do. Lord knows he won't listen to me."

"I said she didn't make me…"

"Yeah, yeah, yeah. You keep telling yourself that." He shrugged Liam off. "So, Ms. McNeal, I'd really like to discuss new staff arrangements, which, by the way, will we be meeting our new press secretary tonight?"

"Aaron." Liam's tone darkened with authority. So much, in fact, it made my girly bits quiver. What woman didn't enjoy a man who exerted his power when necessary?

Down girl.

"What? You started without me. I can't help it if I need to get up to speed."

"Later," Liam declared. "We need to let Elizabeth get ready for tonight."

"Oh, yeah. That reminds me, Bet," Harper interjected, "your dress arrived. I had Ivory take it upstairs to your room."

I'd been so beguiled by the power struggle between Liam and Aaron that I'd barely noticed Harper. I patted my old friend on the back. "Thanks." I adjusted my bag on my arm. "Aaron, to answer your question, Scout will be here tonight, but more than likely she'll be a little late. She's flying in from Nebraska."

Aaron crossed his arms over his broad chest. "Nebraska? She's not a Texas native?"

"No, is that a problem?"

Liam shook his head. "None at all. Right, Aaron?"

Aaron smirked, nodding. "Nope. Not a problem at all."

"With that, I think I'll bid my leave and go get ready for the evening." I nodded to Aaron. "It's nice to meet you and I promise we'll go over everything I have planned for your brother's campaign and then some. Maybe we can talk tonight after the party so you can get a feel for what Scout has in mind as well."

Aaron nodded. "I'd appreciate that."

Liam reached for my arm, his long fingers slinking around my wrist. "Am I allowed to be a part of this little impromptu meeting?"

I had to fight the feeling of excitement at his touch. This had to stop. I had to get myself under control. "Of course, Congressman. Although, you might be bored. I'll only be recapping what you and I have discussed today."

Liam lightly trailed his fingers down the inside of my palm as he released me. "I could never be bored."

"Well," Harper reached for my arm, "I'll make sure everything is arranged in the den where you'll have more room to spread out." He tucked my hand into the crook of his elbow. "I'll escort you upstairs, Liz."

"I think I know where I'm going," I slipped my hand from his arm, "but thanks."

Liam smirked, appearing almost pleased by my interactions with Harper.

How odd.

I shuffled the thought to the back of my mind and nodded to each man. "Gentlemen, if you'll excuse me, I'm going to take a shower and prepare for the evening."

As I started out of the room, Liam called out, "Be

careful. The door on the guest bathroom upstairs has a faulty lock. I'd hate for someone to walk in on you while showering."

I stopped for a moment, feeling heat rise up my neck.

Dammit! He made me blush again.

"Thank you, Congressman," I managed. "I'll keep that in mind."

I rushed out of the room without so much as a glance over the shoulder. He'd won that round, and he knew it.

Liam 1 - Elizabeth zip.

You picked on the wrong girl, buddy. Just wait. I'll own your ass.

I trampled up the stairs, chuckling to myself at the thought. One way or another, I'd get him back. All I had to do was wait for the perfect moment. And I was patient. I could wait.

Eight

Excitement, the thrill of the hunt, purred inside my chest. My hand brushed along the smooth bannister as I sashayed downstairs. In the distance, I could hear soft music playing and the warm chatter of voices mingling. Lone Star Ranch was alive with wealth and intrigue.

Over the years, I'd become the master of working a crowd. In my younger years, I was intimidated by mingling with the rich. My old boss and mentor, John Beckman, use to tell me that private donors were like puppies. They would piddle all over your floor, but as long as you showed them the right amount of love, you could train them to eat from the palm of your hand. He was right, of course, which was why he was the best in the business until the day he retired and passed that torch on to me.

The house was fragrant with the aroma of barbeque and of course, money. Bright lights glistened throughout the room adding elegance to an already exquisite decor.

The women were beautiful in their evening best laced with diamonds, and the men were dashing in their five thousand dollar suits and elegant ties. As for me, I wore a black tea length cocktail dress I'd ordered from my favorite Dallas boutique. To finish my classic look, I pulled my hair back in a loose ponytail at the nape of my neck and finished my ensemble with the pumps I'd worn on my date the night before.

I flattened my hands over my stomach, glancing around the room for my first target. Okay, more like my first victim. Hell, they should've smelled me coming a mile away, and if they didn't it was because they were rookies and I was about to pop their political cherries. Not to mention their oversized pocketbooks.

"You look beautiful." Harper stepped up behind me, resting his hands on my satin covered shoulders.

I turned around and gave him the once over. "You look pretty sharp yourself."

He tugged on the hem of his jacket. He hated suits but understood this world as well as I did and wore them when necessary. That didn't mean he was going to wear a tie, however. Instead he finished his outfit with a gold bolo tie bearing the Lone Star of Texas. Very typical of Harper. "Well, what do you think of our little turn out?"

I shifted back around to view the room. It was packed with the who's who of Democratic Texans and some of DC's finest. "Not too shabby, but I have to know, how on earth did you get Gerald Samford here?"

Gerald Samford was a money man from way back. We're talking, he was around when Plato wrote the Republic, kind of way back. While he might've been the oldest son-of-a-bitch alive, every Democratic candidate would give up their first born child to garner Samford's support. His name spun gold in Washington. To have him in attendance was an honor, more so because his feeble body didn't usually allow for travel. Hell, a good strong Texas wind would topple the poor bastard over. Probably a good thing we weren't in Lubbock. He wouldn't have made it out of the limo.

"He called me," Harper admitted.

I glanced up at my friend. "Really?"

"Yeah. Apparently the word's out that Liam's preparing to announce his candidacy."

I huffed, blowing my bangs from my eyes. "Dammit. I was hoping it'd stay quiet until tomorrow, but oh well." I jerked my shoulder in a jagged shrug. "I should've known once the paperwork was filed there'd be no secrets."

"Meh. You'll still have your epic announcement."

I laughed, patting Harper on the back. "We both know I always get what I want. No one's taking that away from me. So, where's our golden boy anyway? I expected him to be down here by now."

Harper grabbed two glasses of champagne from a passing waiter's tray. He handed one to me. I took a sip of the bubbly liquid, but nothing more. I needed to be clear, sharp, and on point tonight. My job was to get Liam in front of the right people at the right time. These folks were ready with checkbooks in hand. They simply needed me to supply them a pen.

"He said something about a call to his office regarding a bill or something. He and Aaron were going on about it. I kinda zoned out."

I glanced up at Harper, swirling the rim of my glass with my fingertip. "For someone who puts as much money into politics as you do, you really are clueless about the on goings."

Harper shrugged, downing his drink. "That's what I have you for."

"My, oh, my," I chortled, handing him my glass. "We better get out there."

Harper sucked down what remained in my glass in one gulp and grinned. "I'm already out there, my dear. They're in my house. That's all I need to do."

I rolled my eyes. "Suit yourself. I have some fundraising to do." With a wink, I left Harper shaking his head and laughing.

I made my way around the room, hobnobbing with the best of them. At one point, Gerald Samford latched onto my arm. I didn't complain, because the more I could talk up Liam to him, the better chance we had of gaining his support.

Amidst all of the hustling, because let's face it, that was my job, I caught sight of Liam near the staircase with Aaron. My eyes grazed over him, stopping at his neck. Yet another hideous tie dangled there like an electric blue beacon.

Was there an ugly tie store I was unaware of?

I forced my gaze to move downward, assessing the rest of the attire. He'd matched his terrible tie with a slim-fit, double-breasted blue-grey suit. Had it not been for that God-awful tie, he would've been quite dashing.

A deep breath in and a hard exhale out, I plastered a smile to my face and started toward the young

Congressman and his taller, more appropriately dressed, older brother with the good ol' Samford still dangling on my arm.

At the sight of me glaring at his distracting tie, Liam's face exploded in a smile. He slipped his fingers around it, slowly running down the length. Annoyance simmered under my skin. Again he was taunting me. I clenched my fist into a ball, digging my nails deep into my skin to maintain a semblance of control.

"Congressman Baxter." I tried to force my voice to sound pleasant. It wasn't. To make things worse, Liam's dark eyes danced with amusement. Oh how I ached to slap that smirk right off his face.

I extended a hand out to Liam in introduction. "I'd like to introduce you to Mr. Gerald Samford of Samford Innovations." Tilting my head slightly, I gave Samford my most polished grin. "Mr. Samford, this is Congressman William Baxter and his chief of staff, Aaron Baxter."

Liam accepted Samford's outstretched hand for an awkward handshake. Like a true politician, Liam's smile never faltered, but his attention never left me either. The way he looked at me was almost a dare for me to say something, anything that he could taunt me with.

"Mr. Samford, it's a pleasure to meet you," Liam quipped.

The old man released me, latching on to Liam. "Congressman," he gruffed, "the pleasure's all mine." He returned to my arm before I could give him the slip. Such was my luck. "This pretty lady's been telling me all about you."

Liam raised a brow and his teeth grazed over his

bottom lip. "All good I hope."

There he went with that single eyebrow bit. Aggravation pulsed through me from his silent taunts, but no matter what, he would never get the better of me. This was my domain and I would rule supreme.

"Representative Baxter, I'm shocked you'd think otherwise. As I told Mr. Samford–"

"Gerald," the old man interjected.

I gave him my grin and continued, "Ah, yes, Gerald. As I was saying, Texas needs strong, young Democrats, like yourself, in office."

"She's right. And, son, it's impolite to question the integrity of a beautiful woman," Samford scolded.

Liam laughed, good and hard. He patted Samford on the shoulder, his gaze locked on mine. "You're absolutely right. I wouldn't dream of it, sir."

I fluttered my eyelashes. "Why, thank you, Gerald, but I can assure you, Congressman Baxter is the epitome of honesty and serenity," I drawled.

By the look on Liam's face, he had a million rebuttals, but none could be said in the presence of Samford.

Take that, Baxter!

As the three men chatted, I checked out of the conversation and perused the crowd for Harper. I located him, trapped by a group of people to whom I knew he couldn't stand in the least, but like me, he'd mastered the art of the rueful grin. A slight nod and wink told me he was ecstatic to see Samford and Liam talking. If Samford approved of the young Congressman, we had a fighting chance against the Republicans.

Off in the corner, another sight captured my attention.

In the back, where he thought no one could see him, stood Victor Knolls. Standing at least a foot shorter than me, he almost succeeded in his desire to be masked by the crowd. Gray, thinning hair puffed around his head in a sort of halo effect. Even from a distance, dark age marks were visible on his forehead. In his heyday, he was a handsome man, but time had not been kind to him. Drink in hand, he stared at me in the most menacing of ways.

It occurred to me then why Aaron asked about Scout's origins. Victor was a native Texan. It seemed that the Congressman had enjoyed employing Texans in his office.

Nice plug, kid, but diversity is the name of the game.

Samford patted the top of my hand, giving it a shake. I dropped my gaze to the hunched man and smiled. In turn, his wide, toothy grin lifted up to Liam as he said, "I like you. You can count on my support. It's nice to see young men with a sense of chivalry today. So many forget the practices of a true gentleman."

What the hell did I just miss?

I made a note to ask Liam later. For now, I was more interested in why a former employee was shooting daggers at me from across the room. Not that he frightened me. Victor was more of a nuisance than anything. My biggest concern was his presence and how it might cause trouble for Liam's campaign.

Liam rested his hand on Samford's shoulder. "I appreciate your support, Mr. Samford."

Victor downed the rest of his drink. I slipped my hand from Samford's arm, about to take my leave in order to extract the party crasher when Liam excused himself. Samford gushed about Liam after he walked off. I nodded and smiled, pretending to be engaged in the conversation, all the while I watched as Liam approached Victor and disappeared from the room.

It didn't take a rocket scientist to figure out Victor was pissed. When the opportunity presented itself, I excused myself from Samford, leaving him in Aaron's capable hands and slinked off to help Liam defuse the situation. Liam had been smart in taking Victor out of earshot. I had to admit, the Congressman was quick-witted, which would take him far.

As inconspicuous as I could be, I slipped into the dark hallway, prepared to bring security in, if necessary. I stopped at the sound of my name being mentioned.

"This is not how you want to run your campaign, Liam," Victor yelled. "That woman would steal blood from a dying man if it meant getting what she wanted."

"Victor, I know you're upset, and I don't blame you, but Ms. McNeal has nothing to do with my decision. Your irrational behavior right now is a good example as to why I released you. This is not how I want my staff to…"

"No!" Victor hissed. "I'm not being irrational. I'm being protective. I've put a lot of time in creating your persona. I don't want some snake of a woman destroying everything you've worked for."

"And I appreciate your concerns, but I feel…"

"Did you know that she left her husband for that oil guy? What's his name?" I heard the snap of fingers. "Guy Harper. Yeah. She left her husband and kid to run off with him."

Seriously? That was the best he could do? Some made up shit? I rolled my eyes in disgust. It was obvious this guy couldn't find sand in the Sahara. A good press secretary would've built his story and been ready to make it come to life. What an idiot.

There was a long pause and a heavy sigh. "This is beneath you, Victor."

"You're blinded by a pretty face and campaign promises."

Everything inside me wanted to jump in and rip Victor to shreds. Not because he was tearing me apart. I thought nothing of that. People spat on my name daily. Especially if they lost a race to me. What pissed me off was the crass nature of Victor's argument. I'd known Liam all of twenty-four hours, and in that short time, I'd come to understand that he wasn't the type to jump into any situation without careful consideration. Victor's accusations were that of a scorned man.

"That's enough," Liam growled.

Oh, how I wanted to round the corner to see Liam in action. I could imagine the stern expression on his face and his towering figure looming over Victor.

"You know me better than that, and I will not allow you to talk about a woman like that, no matter how much you dislike her policies. I find Elizabeth to be a smart, creative, and empowering woman. Her tactics are exactly what I'm going to need if I want to get that Senate seat, and believe me, I intend to get it. Now, as I told you this morning, if things don't work out with the other press secretary, I'll consider reinstating you, but after tonight, those chances are slim and none."

"Liam…"

"Let me finish," Liam commanded, his voice steady

but stern.

A moment of silence surrounded me. I sucked in my bottom lip waiting to hear what he had to say next.

"I want you back in DC tonight. You will remove your belongings from my office and we will not speak another word of this again. I respect you, Victor, and I appreciate all you've done for me, but I will not tolerate being treated this way."

"Fine," Victor spat. "But you'll regret this. Mark my words."

Great. A threat. That never bode well in my book.

"You don't mean that. We're friends. That's not changed and it won't. But I need to do this. You understand that, right?"

"No! I don't understand. You don't need her and her bullshit."

"Look, my mind is set and you can't change it."

As their conversation came to a close, I slinked into the kitchen. I didn't want to take any chances Liam might see me as he returned to the party. What I'd heard would remain my little secret.

Inside my chest a little ember burned. Liam defended me. Not many people would've done that. They would've simply agreed with Victor, because he did speak the truth. I was unscrupulous when it came to winning, but what he failed to understand was Liam needed my lack of conscience in order to succeed.

Time moved slowly as I waited for Liam to have a chance to return to the party. So, I replayed the conversation over in my mind. Each word, each nuance, I analyzed. If only I'd been able to see his face when he spoke to Victor. The command in his voice and the manner in which he defended me and his campaign left a mark on my soul.

Once I was certain Liam and Victor had moved on, I slipped back into the main room, but not before I dared to glance around the corner where Liam had taken Victor. It was empty as I expected, and maybe it was my imagination, but I swore I could smell the faint scent of Liam's cologne lingering in the air — a composition of spice and lavender, but most of all, Liam — as I walked past.

I laughed at myself for being silly and slinked back into the crowd, doing what I'd been hired to do — sell the idea of William Baxter as the new United States Senator from Texas.

Nine

I stretched my arms over my head. The sound of my joints popping echoed through my body. Every muscle inside me ached from being on my feet all night. My throat burned and my jaws hurt from constant smiles. The event had been a success. Now, what I wanted more than anything was to kick off my shoes and soak in a hot bath. Instead I was stuck in Harper's den listening to two hot heads squabbling over nothing.

"That's not how Victor and Bridget handled things before and it worked great for us," Aaron snapped.

And there he went bringing up Bridget Malone again. Bridget had a reputation for running a "clean" campaign, which was great for a state or local election, but when it came to national, you had to be ruthless. And by my count, she'd lost nearly every national campaign she ever ran. Liam was one of her rare wins.

"I don't care what Victor or Bridget did before," Scout sneered. Piled in a messy bun, her bright red hair matched the color of her temper. She was over caffeinated and running on very little sleep. Her flight had been delayed due to some extreme weather up north, so while the rest of us were dressed to impress, she was still attired in her traveling clothes of jeans and an oversized cashmere sweater that swallowed her slender body whole. "This campaign is going to be different from last time. The Republicans are expecting us to go out there with *guns a blazin'*," she drawled, "as you Texans like to say. They won't expect an inspirational speech from him."

Aaron, perched next to the fireplace, shook his head with vigor. "I get that, but Liam needs to get his message out there from the start. I think it's important he highlights his platform tomorrow. The public needs to know he means business."

Eyes snapped shut, I rubbed my temples. Lack of sleep and the incessant squawking between Scout and Aaron caused me to feel nauseous. Though my body was tired, I couldn't sit still. I'd shifted every which way in my seat and when I couldn't take it any longer, I stood up and meandered to the bar where I poured myself a seltzer to ease my stomach.

"Yes. I agree. His platform's important, but it's too much too soon. If you want, include hints in his speech, but nothing more."

Aaron straightened to his full height, his hands resting on his hips. For most men that stance would look feminine, but due to Aaron's stature, it made him appear formidable. "You act like I haven't been working on Capitol Hill for the last year!" His deep tone rumbled throughout the room. "I know how to handle constituents, lady. I do it every damn day, and I also know my brother better than you do. He's honest. That's why people like him."

Scout met Aaron's stance, which was kind of entertaining since he was three times her size. It was like watching a mouse face off against a pit bull. Only problem was, I couldn't determine which one was the mouse and which one was the pit bull.

Scout flung her arm toward Liam who was sitting on the sofa next to Kristin. "People like him because he's young and hot!"

Liam's face flushed a light shade of pink. Kristin covered her mouth with the ball of her fist, snickering. Although I was a little aggravated, okay, more like pissed, by Kristin arriving to the party so late, I couldn't deny that from the moment I met Kristin Page, I liked her. She was a tall, slender woman, with absolutely no curves. Not that I would tell her, but she reminded me of a twelve-year-old girl just about to reach puberty. Her mousy brown hair was pulled back into a sleek ponytail, exposing her long neck. She'd chosen a pink tulle cocktail dress for the evening, which only accentuated her little girl persona. Soft spoken, she came off as timid and shy. It was almost a treat to see her giggle at the interchange between Aaron and Scout.

"So you're saying people only voted for him because he's *hot*?" Aaron added air quotes.

"No. I'm not saying that's the only reason, but it's a good one. Your brother will capture the female voters' hearts, young and old, and we don't want to turn them off by him jamming his platform down their throats too quickly."

"Yeah, because we all know women don't like having

it rammed down their throats." Aaron wiggled his brows.

"You would know, wouldn't you?" Scout delineated.

Irritation flashed in Aaron's eyes. "What's that supposed to mean?"

"You know exactly what it means. From what I've heard your fly's open more than a Google homepage."

That was my cue to step in. I took a swig from my cup and cleared my throat. "Children, please. Don't make me separate the two of you."

"But..." Scout threw her hands in the air. Her green eyes burning hot with her temper.

I raised a hand, stopping her oncoming tantrum. "No. Here's what you're going to do and I'm not going to hear any complaining from either of you. Understand?"

Scout slunk down into the oversized armchair that Harper usually fancied. Harper'd already escaped the debacle over an hour ago. I envied him, all tucked away in his nice warm bed, while I was stuck managing the bickering children. Aaron folded in next to his brother, punching his knee, almost cocky, as if he'd won.

He hadn't.

I circled the room, ticking off my fingers as I listed the details of what I expected Aaron and Scout to accomplish before the next day. In my trek, I noticed the distance between Kristin and Liam. They were close, but their movements were calculated. They were comfortable in each other's presence, and while I couldn't put my finger on it, something was off between them. He maintained a cordial stance with her, his hand always at the center of her back, directing her around the room. Rarely did he ask her to speak. And even now, they leaned into each other, but it reminded me of how I settled in with Harper. It was clear, they were not a couple.

"So," I finalized, "all we need now is to make sure everyone is where they need to be and doing what they need to do." I pointed to the sofa. "Kristin, you'll be on stage next to Liam tomorrow when he makes his announcement."

A look of terror crossed Kristin's face. Liam bounded out of his seat. "No. Absolutely not."

"Why not?"

Liam maneuvered around the coffee table in a fluid motion, glancing over his shoulder to Kristin. The knot of his tie had been loosened and the top button undone. Gone was the jacket that had contoured his body so well, leaving only the crisp white shirt with the sleeves rolled halfway up his arms. He adjusted the band of his watch against his wrist. "I agreed for her to be at my side during social events, but I won't force her into the public eye more than I have to."

Again I asked, "Why not?" challenging him.

The expression on his face caused alarms to sound off in my head. I'd struck a chord with him. He was protective of her. No man would react that way over something so trivial. He was hiding something for her and I needed to figure out what it was and fast. If she could hurt him, then we needed to find a replacement.

"Because we're not together, and if that's not enough, then let's settle for I said no," he etched out between gritted teeth.

I mimicked Aaron's earlier stance, propping my hands on my hips. "Well, I don't care what you say. She needs to be on that stage with you."

"I refuse to put her in that position," he grinded.

"You refuse?" I spat.

"Did I stutter?"

Oh, this was war. No one treated me like that and got away with it. Kristin tried to intervene, but we paid her no mind.

"Listen here, buddy. You hired me to run your campaign, and that's what I'm doing. When you go up there tomorrow, she" —I thrust my finger in Kristin's general direction— "must be on stage with you. I don't give a damn if you two are fucking or not, but what I do care about is making it seem like you are."

Aaron laughed. Scout chuckled. And it sounded like Kristin gasped. But Liam stood speechless in front of me. His mouth clamped shut, his jaws jutted and rage seared in his eyes. Air poured from his nose like fire, expanding his nostrils with each exhale.

"You have no right..." he began.

"I have every right," I shot back. "This is what I do. It's how I make sure you win."

Unlike when Aaron faced off against Scout, Liam had lowered his face to meet mine. The smell of coffee and peppermint clung to his breath. Sweat prickled my skin. The urge to wipe it away tickled my fingertips, but I refused to be the first to back down. He was wrong. I was right.

Closer and closer we drew together. I wiggled my fingers at my sides. Air rushed in my ears, filling the silence that penetrated the room. Liam was pushing my limits, but I wouldn't lose. Not to him.

"Liam," Kristin's soft voice broke through the silence.

Liam blinked and when he did, I realized how close we were standing to each other. Nearly stomach to stomach, our mouths were a breath away from touching. Somehow, in our standoff, we'd pulled so close together that not even a sliver of paper could've slid between us. If we'd been naked, it was safe to say our bodies would've been connected in an unholy manner.

In a jerking motion, Liam twisted around to meet the voice of his friend. I glanced around to see Aaron's mouth twisted in a smirk, his brows raised almost to his hairline. Scout crossed her arms over her chest, her head tilted in an analytical way.

"I'll do it," Kristin muttered.

"What?" we both replied in unison.

She squirmed under the several pairs of eyes burrowing into her from around the room. "I'll stand with you if it's important."

Liam moved away from me, the scent of his cologne lingering in the air around where I stood. With him out of arm's reach, my dander simmered down, slowing the pounding in my chest. The twitch in my fingertips that had played along my leg in a piano-like manner stopped. This man had gotten me all riled up again. The pull toward him made me nervous. It was a confusing feeling.

A slight thud resonated as Liam knelt to the floor in front of Kristin. He took her hands in his, giving them a slight squeeze. "I won't let you put yourself in that position, Kris. You do enough for me as it is. This would be too much to ask."

She slipped her hand from his, resting it against his

cheek. Her thin lips moved into a meek smile. "Liam, you're always protecting me, and I adore you for it, but you can't guard me from the world. You never ask enough of me, and I want to do this for you. It's not like they're asking me to marry you." She lifted her gaze to meet my stunned expression. "Are you?"

The softness of her question brought laughter to my belly. I bit my lip, preventing the chortle from escaping me. "I'd never ask such a thing," I fibbed, because that was definitely something I'd ask a candidate to do if it meant winning the election. Hell, I'd done it before.

"Sure you wouldn't," Liam berated, sarcasm coloring his cadence.

"I would," Aaron chuckled.

"Me, too," Scout chimed in.

I covered my face with my hand, this time unable to hide the amusement. My laughter broke the ice in the room, sending almost all of us into hysterics. Kristin appeared confused for a moment, but soon joined in. Liam never wavered, maintaining his poker face. The man didn't even crack a smirk.

He lifted himself from the floor and crossed the room to me, tugging his ear. My amusement vanished at the seriousness of his expression. "You won't ever ask her to do that," he growled so only I could hear.

My hackles rose. Under my skin, my blood began to simmer. "I'll do whatever I have to do to get you elected."

He stepped in closer, his mouth moving to my ear. I could feel the warmth of his breath wash over my skin. A slight shiver rushed down my spine. "You didn't hear me then. I said you *won't* ever ask her to do that. Do you understand?"

I tilted my head, defiance rippling through me. He could make demands all he wanted, but in the end, this was my arena and he'd play by my rules. I rolled my shoulders, putting a little distance, but not much, between us. This conversation needed to remain private, or at least as private as I could make it. My finger pressed against his broad chest. "Yes," I spoke with authority, poking his breastbone, "but know this, if you or Kristin are hiding something, I will find out. So it's best to come clean now."

"We're hiding nothing."

Bullshit! But it was too soon to call him on his bluff. I needed my ace to win.

"Okay." I poked his chest once more for good measure. "I'm in this to win. I told you that last night and I'm not in the habit of repeating myself. So, I'll say it one last time, just so it sinks into that thick skull of yours, I'll do whatever it takes to win. Are we clear?"

Liam took a step back. Stern consternation placated his features. "Crystal," he claimed. For a moment he remained still, his focus stationed on me. He was sizing me up. And I must have met his expectations, because his shoulders dropped and his stance became less hostile.

Score!

Liam 1 - Elizabeth 1

A bit of pride swelled inside me as I ticked off the score. He was a fierce competitor. Few had ever taken me on and even fewer had ever given the challenge that Liam presented. The man had some serious balls, and I couldn't wait to see him in the throes of a debate.

On the heel of his polished cap-toes, Liam circled

around to Kristin. I couldn't see his face, but from the way his body relaxed I had the inclination that he smiled at her. "No one would ever ask that of you, Kris, and I'd be honored to have you stand by my side tomorrow. That is, if you really want to."

Kristin lifted up from the sofa, her tulle skirt rustling as she approached Liam. Her long, skinny fingers clasped his bicep. "As long as you have a barf bag nearby, I'll be there with bells on."

A hearty laugh reverberated from Liam. "I'll make sure they have as many as you need on standby. Right, Bet?" He cocked his head to see me from his peripheral.

My mouth dropped at his blatant use of Harper's nickname for me. This was him attempting to regain power. Well, I wouldn't have it.

"Absolutely!" Scout interceded before I had the chance to smart off.

Aaron sprang off the couch and rushed to the couple, pulling them both into his arms. "Of course we'll take care of our little Krissy."

"There," I announced. "That's settled." Feeling drained, I rubbed the back of my neck. "With that resolved, I think I'll head off to bed." I clicked my fingernail against my teeth, trying to pull my thoughts together. With a snap of my fingers, I pointed to Scout, shaking my index finger. "More than likely, I won't be here when you get up in the morning. I have to run home, grab some clothes, and pack for my return to DC. I'll meet you at the courthouse around eleven to start setting things up."

Liam tugged on the end of his tie, his mouth drawn into a straight line, but he said nothing.

"Aaron, please listen to Scout about Liam's speech tomorrow. I beseech you. Put your differences aside and make it a kick ass speech. All right?"

Aaron squeezed Liam and Kristin tighter in his grip. Poor Kristin winced at the additional pressure. He cast his cocky grin to Scout. "We won't let you down. I promise."

Kristin wiggled free of Aaron's hold. Relief expressed in the way she shook her tiny body to release the stress Aaron caused. Liam scratched the side of his neck, still not looking at me. I'd finally gotten under his skin. Was about damn time. I was getting sick of being on the defensive. I preferred being on the offensive. It suited me better.

"We'll be fine," Scout reassured me. "Don't worry. I know Elizabeth McNeal quality and I won't let anything ruin that reputation."

I gave Scout a two-finger salute. "I knew we hired you for a reason."

"It takes the best to know the best," she boasted.

With a wink, I laughed. "That it does. Now, you kids play nice. I'll catch you all at the courthouse tomorrow. And Liam," —his gaze met mine in what could've easily been our next face-off— "please try to wear a sensible tie tomorrow. I swear to God, if you pull out a neon pink tie, I'll have to strangle you with it."

"Is that a threat?" he quipped, that confident smile blooming across his face.

"It's a promise."

Ten

The morning sun trickled in through the heavy curtains. A stream of light rippled in a long, bright line across the floor. I stood at the foot of my bed, my toes touching the tip of the rays, as I rubbed my temples to alleviate the pressure behind my eyes.

I couldn't remember the last time I'd had a headache, but I woke with the worst one imaginable. With only a few hours 'til Liam's announcement speech, I could barely think past the headache to what I needed to get done before I left for the courthouse.

Finish packing. Right. That was the first thing I needed to do.

My open suitcase was spread out across the bed like a political mistress with her legs wide open. Clothes were strewn everywhere. Nothing was folded or even placed in the luggage. For me that was a horrific no-no. Everything in its place was my logic. Clean. Tidy. Wrinkle free! Yet, in my current disarray, it appeared as though Jordyn was packing for me.

I trotted into my bathroom and rummaged through the medicine cabinet for some Tylenol. I needed something to knock that damn headache out.

My recent bout of insomnia was killing me. All night long I tossed and turned thinking about Liam only a few doors away from me. No matter how badly I needed to pee, I wasn't about to go near that bathroom. Not if it meant I was chancing a run in with a naked Liam again. That was one image forever burned into my memory.

Tall. Wet. Pleasingly hard in all the right places.

I clapped my hands over my eyes trying to block the image from my mind.

Perv!

Since I couldn't sleep, thanks to images of Liam dancing through my head, I left Harper's house while it was still dark out. The hour long drive to my place gave me a chance to clear my head. I opened the sunroof of my car, unconcerned by the cold air rushing in, and blasted my stereo with the throaty vocals of Bush. Come to think of it, that probably didn't help my head in the least likely bit, but the sound of the electric guitar vibrating through the speakers took my mind off the young temptation for a moment.

Why the hell did he have to be so damn young? That alone was cruel. Then to make him my client. Talk about the ultimate forbidden fruit.

After two pills and a gulp of water, I went back to work packing for my return home. Once Liam made his announcement, I was scheduled for the first flight back to Washington. There was so much to do and I couldn't do it without the support of my full staff.

That reminded me of my second task. I needed to check in for my flight.

Before I forgot, I grabbed my phone from the charger and navigated through the airline's website. Much to my surprise, my assistant, Brandy Turner, had already completed that task for me. I adored that woman. Her knack for organization and discretion, made her the perfect assistant. Relieved, I returned my phone to its charger and continued with my mediocre packing job.

In the midst of folding my delicates, my phone chirped. I swiped the device from my nightstand and glanced down at the screen to the message indicator. Of all the people in the world, the text had to be from Liam.

I slid my finger across the screen and the message burst forth in a blaze of light. I blinked a few times to focus on the little black letters.

William Baxter: I need your opinion on something.

A little curious, I plopped down on the bed where I typed out a quick response.

Elizabeth McNeal: How can I help?

I tucked my feet beneath me and leaned forward so that my elbows rested on my knees. Within seconds a new message appeared. This time it included attachments. I clicked the attachments and my jaw hit the ground. There were two selfies of Liam from the chin down. One was of him in nothing but a pair of black boxer briefs and a bright yellow tie. The other was in the same underwear with a chartreuse tie. I blinked, shook my head, and pulled the phone away from my face to make sure I wasn't imagining he'd sent me such a thing.

When I determined my headache wasn't screwing with my vision, I quickly replied.

Elizabeth McNeal: ARE YOU NUTS? Why would you send me something like that? You have to be careful with what you send out electronically.

While I scolded him, I couldn't drag my eyes away from the nearly naked man in the photographs. His body was alluring. A feast for the eyes. Hardcore perfection. A body made by the gods for the gods. My phone chirped again, causing me to jump. I returned to the messages to read Liam's reaction.

William Baxter: It's not like you haven't seen it all before. So, tell me, which tie should I wear?

I placed my phone in my lap and rubbed my temples again. If my head wasn't already pounding it would've been after that little stunt. I grabbed my phone and tapped out a response.

Elizabeth McNeal: I thought we were going to let our little incident go?

I hopped up off the bed and closed my suitcase. It was time for me to get dressed. Instead, I was texting with this man.

William Baxter: Did you really think we could ever let go of what happened the other night? I own you for that and don't you forget it.

Oh, those words sent my blood into flames. They were both sexy as fuck and infuriating as hell. To add insult to injury, I could imagine that damn grin of his slapped across his smug face.

Elizabeth McNeal: No one, and I do mean no one, owns me. Least of all you.

There. I told him.

William Baxter: If that's what you'd like to believe. Now, answer my question. Which tie would you prefer I wear?

Infuriated, I stamped my feet and let out a shrill shriek.

Elizabeth McNeal: It's not what I believe. It's what I know. How about a nice blue tie? And I do mean blue. Not that electric blue thing you wore last night.

I grabbed my dress off the bed and started toward the bathroom. Every inch of my body was on high alert. It was almost as if Liam was in the room with me. I didn't like feeling so out of control and every encounter I had with Liam Baxter left me feeling exactly that way.

William Baxter: You only have these two to choose from, or I'm going with the bright pink one you demanded I not wear. ;-)

My fingers flattened to my lips, I stared at that little emoticon like a bull stares at a muleta just before charging. That damn winky thing was worse than nails grating over a chalkboard.

Elizabeth McNeal: I thought you were supposed to be a nice guy. Those pics and threatening me with an ugly-ass tie isn't very nice of you!

I slid my phone across the counter and shimmied out of my sweats. The phone chimed with a new message as I threw off my tee shirt. Determined not to respond immediately, I turned my back on it. If I didn't see it, then I wouldn't be tempted to answer it. I needed to get ready and he was distracting me.

My phone chimed again, reminding me to check it.

Stupid technology. And they wonder why the whole

damn world is addicted to it.

Unable to resist, I picked up my phone and read the message.

William Baxter: You're mistaken then. I never once referred to myself as a nice guy. Although, I wish I was there to see that blush on your cheeks right now.

I glanced at myself in the mirror, a stunned expression stared back at me. My blonde hair hung in waves past my slender shoulders. I'd yet to straighten it for the day. My hazel brown eyes shifted up and down from the mirror to the phone, examining the light pink hue on my cheeks.

"I don't blush!" I screamed at my reflection.

My thumbs rushed across the screen of my phone.

Elizabeth McNeal: I don't blush! And seldom do I make a mistake. You said you don't have casual sex. Remember? That equals nice guy in my book.

With that message sent, I slipped into my dress. At this point I was running late. Playing text tag with Liam was silly, juvenile, and deep down I was having far too much fun with it.

The text indicator chimed and my fingers itched to read his message. Like a drug addict ready for their next hit, I snatched up my phone.

William Baxter: Just because a guy doesn't fuck everything that walks doesn't mean he's a nice guy. It means he has some respect for himself and the women in his life. And, my dear Elizabeth, you do blush. Our little incident is proof of that.

I met my own gaze in the mirror, my heart thumping loudly in my chest. My imagination whispered *fuck* in his voice. It sent a salacious shiver through my nervous system, tantalizing me.

Too young. Too young. I chanted over and over.

It was the truth. Even if he wasn't my client, a scandal waiting to happen, he was still far too young for me.

It was time for me to nip this little texting game in the bud. Scout and Aaron would be at the courthouse soon and I still needed to apply my makeup and fix my hair. I wet my lips and tried to conceptualize a great comeback. Nothing came to mind, so I simply stated the obvious.

Elizabeth McNeal: We both know you're a nice guy, William Baxter. Now, I need to finish getting ready. I have this thing to attend to.

Almost as soon as I hit send, I received a new text.

William Baxter: Just remember, nice doesn't always mean safe. ;-) Now, since you never told me what tie to wear, I'm wearing the pink one. See you in a bit.

Dammit! No! Not a pink tie!

I slid my phone across the counter and pressed my palms along the edges, hanging my head.

Liam 2 - Elizabeth 1

I'd lost that battle. A deep breath in, I reminded myself it was okay as long as I won the war.

And this was war.

Eleven

Lost in thought, a lone ink pen dangled between my teeth. The angsty chords of Radiohead blared from the turntable in my quaint office at Baxter campaign headquarters. From my desk, I had a great view of Capitol Hill – one of my favorite sights in the city.

Upon moving into our new headquarters, I expected a tussle with Liam over this office. It had a huge pane window that opened the room up unlike any other office in the building. But he spared me the argument. That left me a little disoriented at first, especially with our constant battle for control, but after a few weeks I realized it had been a tactical move and I fell right into his trap.

So, I chalked it up as another point on Liam's scorecard.

At my last count, I was up by one.

Liam 10 - Elizabeth 11.

But that number fluctuated frequently, so I stayed on my toes.

With my bare feet propped up on top of my desk, I slinked down into my chair, allowing the haunting melody and melancholy lyrics to wash away the events of my day. This had been the longest of days and it was far from over. I'd spent the better part of my afternoon rallying staffers, buried under paperwork, and conducting countless meetings. The campaign trail was calling and that meant four weeks on a tour bus in Texas.

A trip of this magnitude required a great deal of planning. Since only a few of the staff members would be on the road with us, I needed to ensure everyone was on task while I was away. So far, we were leading in the polls, and I refused to lose that lead because some staffer lost focus without me being on top of their every move.

In my lap rested a copy of the late edition of the *Statesman*. On the front page was a picture of Bonnie Keating with her mouth wide open and hands raised in the air, as if she were preaching the gospel. As we'd expected, Keating became the Republican front runner and her camp wasted no time going after Liam once he announced his candidacy. If only they were more creative about the shit they liked to sling. Anyone could attack his bachelorhood or his platform. Those were no brainers. Even a rookie could come up with a good speech to bash the obvious.

Keating's latest interview took place on The Rachel Maddow Show. Throughout the entire interview, I died of laughter. Keating spent most of her time looking like a damn fool stumbling over how someone Liam's age wasn't prepared to help make the big decisions for our state and country.

Idiot!

It was people his age watching that interview. My favorite moment occurred when Maddow mentioned Liam's military service. That shut Keating right up. Though politicians loved throwing mud at the wall to see what might stick, when it came to military service, they had to be careful. The attack must be clever and provide a semblance of proof to back up the claim. John Kerry's 2004 scandal was indicative enough of that. And Keating had nothing.

I folded the paper and tossed it on my desk at my feet. As the coda of the song peaked, I closed my eyes and dropped my head back against the headrest, immersed in the music. My head bobbed from side-to-side with the beat, the ink pen bounced between my teeth. Something about this song always relaxed me, no matter how depressing it might be. Of their own accord, my hands lifted and my fingers started to flick with the thrum of the electric guitar. I screwed my eyes tighter, my face scrunched. Lord only knew what I looked like, but since the door was closed I didn't care. Wasn't as if anyone could see me.

Or so I thought.

"Radiohead. Nice," Liam's voice, husky and low, interrupted my moment of clarity.

My eyes popped open. The pen dropped from my mouth and rolled down my chest to the floor. Disoriented, I grunted, "Huh?" I hadn't even heard the door open.

Liam leaned into the doorframe, a charming grin on his lips. His blue Oxford shirt with a white collar and cuffs was perfectly tucked into his crisp khakis.

Oh be still my heart.

Scout and I had been dead on when it came to Liam and ladies. The women flocked him. Not that I blamed them. Every time he walked into a room my chest would tighten along with other lower extremities. He could charm anyone, except me. We constantly butted heads, but that was part of his appeal. He hadn't been joking when he said nice didn't necessarily mean safe. For me, Liam Baxter was most definitely not safe. He was dangerous and mysterious, a toy to play with.

Yes, a toy. That's all he was. Nothing more. Not someone who tantalized my senses every time he came near me. No. He wasn't a temptation. An uncontrollable desire.

Just a toy.

Yeah. Who was I trying to convince?

Liam tilted his head, scrutinizing me. I realized then that my skirt had hiked its way up my thighs during my little head banging session. I dropped my feet to the floor and slipped them back into my black patent leather stilettos. Covered by the mask of my desk, I straightened my houndstooth pencil skirt back down to my knees.

"Radiohead," he thumbed toward the record player on the shelf. The song had come to an end and the tick of the needle bouncing clicked through the speakers.

"Yeah? What's wrong with Radiohead?" I inquired, shuffling papers around my desk.

Liam pushed off the door and stepped into my office. He picked up the needle, placing the stylus in its stationary position. "Nothing's wrong with Radiohead," he stated, plucking the album jacket off the shelf. "Personally, I love them." He shrugged a shoulder, flipping the cover in his hand, perusing the back. "I just took you as more an eighties girl, that's all."

Outrage surged through me. That was the insult of all insults in my opinion. It ranked right up there with being called a Republican. I rose from my seat. The sound of my heels clacked against the linoleum flooring as I approached him. I ripped the cover from his hand. "Watch your mouth before I smack it."

He crossed his arms over his chest, his eyes dancing. "Threats of bodily harm. Hmm. This is serious." He did that whole eyebrow raising thing, which made me want to smack him even more.

"The eighties hair bands are nothing compared to the nineties grunge bands. The eighties guys were all show. There's no emotion in their work. They were the Lady Gaga's of their generation."

The smell of his cologne permeated my senses. Liam stepped toward me, as always, invading my personal space. He looked into my eyes, a hint of a smile played with his mouth. "Amazing. We really can agree on something."

"You call this agreeing?" I motioned between us.

"There's always a first time for everything."

I slipped the album jacket back onto the shelf where Liam had found it. "I guess you think I'm old fashion for listening to my music on vinyl." I felt shy in admitting that. Kids never listened to records anymore. It was practically impossible to find vinyl, and while digital had an amazing sound, there was something lost in the perfection.

With his fingertip, Liam traced the length of the bookshelf housing my favorite albums. A contradiction of cool confidence and boyish shyness oozed from him. "Not at all. There's something about vinyl that makes the music feel real. The pop and crackle of the needle against the album adds an additional layer to the artist's work."

I stared at him in disbelief.

He'd basically verbalized my thoughts.

Get out of my head!

While I was a little weirded out by his ability to see into my soul, I was also intrigued. It was rare to find someone so young who understood the art behind the music and how digital eliminated the unique sound of human imperfection from a track.

"What's bothering you?" he queried, drumming his fingers along the bookshelf.

The intense look on his face burrowed itself deep inside me. Unlike anyone I'd ever met, Liam had a way to challenge a person to be truthful, and I don't know why, but I longed to spill my deepest, darkest secrets to him. That scared me.

I told myself it was because Liam understood my world. He lived in it with me. Not even Russell or Harper understood the details of my life. It was for that reason my marriage fell apart.

I'd never even been fully open with my ex-husband. Russell didn't mind being a stay-at-home dad. He was proud of having a successful wife, but he wanted me to share the details of my job with him. At the end of the day I was so tired I didn't want to give him a play-by-play of what I'd done. He respected that for a while, but when the midnight calls from clients who found themselves in the center of some scandal that could break them started to interfere with our family time, he wasn't so understanding. Our marriage crumbled. It was my fault. I took the blame then and still did. Hence the reason I didn't date until recently.

Casual trysts were easier, cleaner, in a manner of speaking. No one's feelings were involved. Both parties were in it for the physical gratification. All the touchy feely shit was left at the door.

"I was thinking how amazing it is to find someone so..." I paused, brandishing the word that nearly slipped from my lips away. "Someone who enjoys music for the art."

The inquisitive smile dropped. His eyebrows bowed together. "*So young*," he filled in for me.

My heart sank in my chest. "I didn't say that."

Liam rubbed a hand across the back of his neck, his eyes penetrating my soul. "But you thought it." He let out a little sigh and backed away from me. "Why does my age make you so uncomfortable?"

I looked down, searching the floor for the right answer. Unfortunately, it didn't have one. What was it about this man? It wasn't like me to struggle for words. I always had a dozen one-liners waiting at the tip of my tongue. I thought quick and acted quicker, but with Liam only the truth seemed to come to mind. So, instead, I said anything. Everything. Nothing at all.

"I wish I knew."

"I wish you did, too."

He sounded so sincere. If only I could tell him that it was more than his age that made me uncomfortable. It was everything about him. The way he stood tall and straight. His charismatic smile. The simple innocence of how he answered an unexpected question in an interview. Or the manner in which he entered a room, bringing it to life in an instant. It was the way his dark hair had grown out, falling flat against his forehead. The sound of his laugh and the brush of his hand against my back when we walked down the hall together. It was how a single text message from him could make my day. Or how I dreamt about him at night. He consumed my thoughts. When I wasn't with him, I wanted to be and that unnerved me.

"What I do know is…"

What was it that I knew? I knew he was special. Aggravating. Infuriating. And funny as hell. I also knew the intense longing I had to kiss those damn lips of his. To tug them between my teeth every time he pissed me off. I knew his body was hard in all the right places. I knew I could imagine licking the water off his abs instead of him drying off after that shower.

Dammit. Stop thinking about him naked.

My shoulders dropped. "What I do know," I started again, my voice a little less shrill this time, "is that I believe you can win this election. Together we'll accomplish great things."

A somber smile eclipsed his mocking tone, "There's no doubt about that." As the words fell from his lips, the ice that formed between us started to melt. Liam took a step toward me, closing the distance between us. "Actually, I have a small confession to make."

The trickster had returned.

If it had been anyone else but Liam, I would've gone on high alert by those words. Those words screamed scandal, but with Liam I had an inkling he was toying with me.

I straightened my back, ready to play along. "Anything

I should be concerned about?"

Liam shuffled his feet, a wry gleam appearing in his eyes. "You'll have to be the judge of that."

My hand extended to the two chairs that sat in front of my desk. He accepted my offer and we both sat down. I dampened my lips with the tip of my tongue. "Okay," I smacked, "lay it on me."

He leaned back into the chair, crossing his leg over his knee. His fingers wrapped around his ankle, causing the cuff of his sleeve to rise, revealing the black metal watch he wore. "I've known for some time now you're not an eighties girl."

"Is that so?"

He nodded, his mouth drawn into a frown. "And this isn't the first time I've eavesdropped at your door to listen to the music."

That caught me by surprise. "Really?"

"Yeah," he hummed. "It's always after hours. And always after Brandy's left for the night." He scratched his jaw. Dark stubble from the day had started to appear on his tanned skin. It was rather sexy. "But once they're all gone, I sit on the floor outside your office and listen with you. It's nice to know someone who has good taste in music and knows how to listen to it properly."

A small laugh gushed from me. I couldn't help it. His mannerisms were shy and sincere. This was the opposite of the Liam I was accustomed to. It was quite endearing.

"I'm flattered. But you know you don't have to sit on the floor, right? You're always welcome to come in and listen with me."

Danger! Danger! What the hell was I saying? I just

gave Liam a pass into my office. At night. Alone. With me! Bad idea. This was a really bad idea.

My near panic must have manifested itself on my face. Liam leaned forward, his foot dropping to the ground. Our knees almost touched and his long fingers brushed along my kneecap.

Had he done that on purpose?

I tried not to think about it, but the fire in my belly wasn't about to let me forget how that single, tiny touch consumed me.

"Really? That's not going to break any of your rules?"

I pushed my fingers against his chest, a weak chuckle emerging from me. "We work together, Liam. I think we're safe."

No we're not! That was a lie! A big, fat, ugly lie that excited me in a way it shouldn't.

Catching my wrist, he held my arm suspended between us. "Is that why you avoid being alone with me?"

"I...I..." I couldn't think. The heat of his hand was setting fire to my skin. My body wanted to lurch forward into his lap and claim those plump lips that were mocking me.

"You're imagining things."

"I'm no fool, Elizabeth. I see everything."

Everything? Did he notice how my pulse jumped when he grabbed me or how my body was perspiring being this close to him?

Dammit!

"Don't be silly," I admonished.

He released my hand. It fell into a limp puddle in my lap. "Not that any of it really matters. For the next few weeks, we're locked on a bus together. There's no avoiding me there."

Another challenge. And boy was he wrong. I'd avoid being alone with him. I had to.

I balled my fist, trying to regain control. "Along with the rest of your staff," I insisted.

"A limited staff." He grinned.

"That doesn't make us alone, though, but for argument's sake, at least you can learn some things about me that don't require you to stalk me from a hallway."

Liam reached out and twisted a strand of my hair between two fingers. In a slow, meticulous way, he twirled the strand around his knuckle. Not once did he tug. He applied just enough pressure so I could feel him, and with that I relaxed. Never had he touched me in such an intimate manner. I tried not to read too much into it, but it wasn't easy. "Again, it looks like we can agree on something," he teased, releasing my hair.

I shifted in my seat. "We can't make a habit of that. It'll ruin my reputation as a hard ass."

"I think your ass is plenty hard. Your reputation is safe," he snarked.

I smacked my hand over my face, groaning. "Oh that was terrible."

He cocked his head to the side, grinning. "Okay. How about this? Maybe you can bring some music along. We can spend our nights arguing over the best bands of the nineties. That way no one will think you've lost your edge and I can still get what I want."

Oh, damn. My nether regions clenched and my stomach fluttered.

"And that is?"

"To know more about you."

I laughed, shaking my head. "You might have to find another way of learning about me."

"Why's that?"

"Because," I popped off, "there's no way us being alone together, late at night, listening to Radiohead on a tour bus, could be anything but scandalous."

"Especially when one of us has seen the other naked," he smarted back.

Damn him for bringing that up.

I rolled my shoulders and leaned forward, matching his posture. This man thought he'd maneuvered me right where he wanted me to be. Game, set, but not match, because I wasn't about to let him win.

"That right there just skyrocketed this master plan of yours to a ten-point-oh on my scandal-radar. So, what do you suggest to rectify the situation?"

Liam shifted so his calves were wrapped around mine. The dark chocolate of his eyes swirled as his mind seemed to whirl. He drew in a breath, his mouth inching closer to mine. "Nothing," he purred, his voice dripping with seduction.

"Nothing?"

He looked me square in the eye, his gaze burning hot. "I think strange and interesting things can happen on a tour bus just like they do in old, drafty houses. Why would anyone want to stop those things from happening?"

My mouth gaped open. Was he suggesting what I thought he was suggesting? No. Not possible. Liam would never suggest something so casual.

Stop imagining things, Elizabeth! Too young, remember!

A knock at the door gave him pause. My natural instinct kicked in and I moved back. The chair made a loud, skin crawling sound as it scooted against the floor. Liam released a drawn out sigh, running his fingers through his hair. It was kind of cute seeing him flustered, and even cuter still to see his hair mussed after a good run through with his fingers. I turned my head to find Aaron standing at the door.

His arms were crossed over his brawny chest. A wild smirk lighted his face. "Brandy's missing from her post, so I thought I'd make my presence known. Hope I wasn't interrupting anything important."

"Nope. Nothing," I chimed.

He shifted his weight and thumbed behind him. "Good, because dinner's here."

"Fantastic!" I exclaimed, rising from my chair. "I'm starving."

I glanced down at Liam. His eyes were closed and he was shaking his head. I placed my hand on his shoulder, surprised by my own actions. "You all right, champ?"

Liam lifted his face, meeting my stare. He nodded and shifted in his seat. "Yeah," he groaned. "I'm good."

"You sure, bro? You look a little *uncomfortable*."

"Shut up," Liam hissed at his brother. He lifted from his seat and pulled it aside so we could step out together. "You heard the lady," he instructed Aaron, resting his hand at the small of my back. "She's hungry. Let's not keep her waiting."

Aaron eyed Liam from top to bottom. He lingered on

us for a moment longer before he stepped aside for us to exit.

Back in the conference room, all the campaign posters and flyers had been stacked into the center of the oval table and delicious takeout was buffeted over the surface. It'd been my idea to order Thai food. I had a hankering for some Phat si-io with jalapenos. That stuff was to die for.

When I didn't find it right away, I glanced back at Aaron. "Hey, did you not get my Phat si-io?"

"Yeah, I ordered that, too."

I opened another container, not finding my order. Then it struck me Liam had said he'd ordered the same thing. My head shot up to him. "No way!" I chortled.

"You've got to be kidding," Aaron growled.

Liam and I both snapped our gaze in Aaron's direction. The sounds of the staffers eating stopped. Everyone looked at Aaron as if the Apocalypse was about to take place. "What?" Liam and I asked in unison.

"Jinx," Liam mouthed to me.

I rolled my eyes, trying not to laugh. His tomfoolery was adorable, but a dangerous trap for me. I let my guard down once, and he'd taken over the score.

"What's wrong?"

Aaron cracked his knuckles. "We thought it was an error. A double order of Phat si-io with jalapenos. I thought only Liam ate that shit. So, we only ordered one." He rubbed his forehead. "You know what, I'll take care of it. I'll go get another order. It won't take long. I'm sorry about this, Elizabeth."

I glanced up at Liam. "It's no problem. You don't need to go back out. There looks to be ample amounts of fried rice and egg rolls here. I'll have some of that. Liam can have the Phat si-io."

"Nonsense. We can share it," Liam argued, opening another container.

"It's right here," one of the interns offered.

The package was passed down to us and Liam grabbed two sets of chopsticks. "C'mon. We shared Radiohead a few minutes ago, I think we can share some Phat si-io."

If it hadn't been for my craving of those damn noodles, I would've argued with him, but instead, I accepted his generous offer. We found ourselves a little spot at the end of the table and together we speared into the delicious meal. Surrounded by the staff, we talked and chatted as if nothing were happening, yet through it all, I knew things had changed. The dynamic between us was ebbing. Control was shifting, and it seemed to be in Liam's favor.

Score one to Liam. Game tied.

Twelve

Three days on the bus was all it took before I was ready to kill me a Congressman.

This wasn't my first rodeo. Most candidates enjoyed their privacy. They'd stay at one end of the bus and the staff and I would nest at the other. We only crossed the lines when business needed to be discussed.

Not Liam.

He was everywhere. All the time. The man couldn't sit still to save his own life. No matter where I turned he was right there wanting to know what we were working on. I couldn't wait 'til we arrived in Dallas for Kristin to join us. Maybe then I could get a moment to breathe. My only moments of solace came when he had to perform his Congressional duties or his campaign responsibilities. Congress didn't simply stop because he was on the campaign trail and there were loads of babies in Texas who needed to be kissed or reporters who needed attention.

Today was a reporter kind of day.

Off stage, the lights were dim, only bright enough for a person to see where they were going. Silent yet loud, the network crew moved about in chaotic order. Being around the media felt strangely comfortable to me. Everyone behind the scenes had their jobs and they did them well. If not for them, the person on the stage would look like a complete fool with a pretty face. Much like the way things happened in DC, although there, the faces weren't typically pretty.

I pressed my tablet to my chest and observed the makeup artist pat away the shine from the anchor's nose. Behind me, Liam paced back and forth. His hands bounced at his side as he muttered to himself. Anyone watching him would've thought he was a caged lion just captured from the wild.

He was grating on my nerves. As he started to pass behind me, I grabbed him by the wrist, jerking him to a stop. "Quit pacing," I hissed through bared teeth. My smile didn't waver but I made sure Liam heard my frustration. "They're going to start throwing meat at you soon." The sensation of touching him left me feeling weak in the knees. I dropped my hand and rubbed it against my pleated slacks.

Things between us weren't getting any easier for me. No matter how many times I reminded myself that he was too young or off limits, I couldn't get past the ache in my chest his smile caused. When we were in a room together, I felt him. His eyes. His body. The faint sound of his heartbeat. But I couldn't let him see how our flirtatious banter affected me. His competitive nature would thrive on such knowledge, and I would lose all ground I had.

"Easy for you to say," he grumbled, moving beside me. "You're not the one who's about to be on *live* television."

I chuckled, adjusting the collar of my blouse. "You're right, but then I didn't choose to be a public servant. I was smart about my political career. I stay on the sidelines where I belong."

This interview had not been on the initial Austin docket but when it opened, I couldn't turn it down. It was a local network evening broadcast and would be a fantastic plug for Liam. He needed some older viewership and this would reach that demographic. Not to mention we were on Keating's home turf. The governor's mansion was a mere five-minute drive from the station. We were practically in her backyard.

"You and your sports euphemisms," he groused. My gaze drifted from the stage to the man standing next to me. Our eyes met and the mood shifted between us. Liam inched closer to me, his arm brushing against mine. "And you can believe what you want, *Elizabeth*, but we both know you've never been on the sidelines in your life." The manner in which my name rolled off his tongue sent tingles rippling through me. He drew out every syllable like he was making love to my name.

There was no way I was going to let his sexy voice and tempting smile deter me from getting my point across, though. "Sidelines, big guy." I waved my hand around us. "Right where I belong." I pursed my lips into a smug grin.

Score one for Elizabeth.

I squinted my eyes, trying to remember my latest count.

Dammit. That tied us again.

Liam 15 - Elizabeth 15.

No matter. At least I wasn't losing.

Liam crossed his arms over his chest, stroking the tips of his fingers along the edge of my arm. My breath hitched in my chest. The warmth of his fingertips on my skin ignited that delicious ache inside me. Had I done what I wanted, I would've slapped him before jumping his bones. Neither were a viable option for me.

Determined to maintain the upper hand in this situation, I refused to look at my arm where he continued his gentle assault against my skin. My focus remained on the interviewer who'd just gone live and was making her opening remarks to the camera.

"You might be behind the scenes, but you govern the world around you like a puppeteer."

My stomach clenched at the seductive lure of his voice.

I rubbed my shoulders to alleviate some of the tension in my body. "You make me sound like some sort of control freak."

"That's because you are."

I cut my eyes to him. His expression begged me to challenge his observation, but who was I to disagree with the truth. When I chose not to respond, a small laugh pulsated from Liam. He lifted his hand, gently sliding his fingernails across my neck as he moved my hair away from my shoulder.

I choked down the scream rising inside me. Before I could smack his hand or pop off that he didn't know shit about me, the producer caught my eye, flicking two fingers.

The signal to send Liam on.

Saved by the production, I placed my tablet on some sort of equipment case, and turned Liam to face me. "Showtime, Congressman." A tug or two at his oh-so-hideous tie made me feel a smidge more in control. He'd chosen a lime green and white striped silk tie to complete the casual look we'd fashioned him in. Matched to a white shirt, black sports jacket, and pressed jeans, he could've easily been posing for a magazine cover. "Now, go out there and make me proud," I added, clapping my hands against his shoulders.

His brow did that single lift thing that drove me bonkers. "Is this where you smack my ass and tell me to win big or die trying?"

I extracted my electronic tablet from the case and smacked it against his chest. "No need. By now you should know I'll kill you if you lose," I blurted out, almost too loud.

People turned their heads to look at us and Liam let out a snort of a laugh. "And here I thought you'd be more concerned about someone overhearing me suggest you smack my ass."

At that moment the announcer called his name and the producer waved frantically in our direction. I was speechless. Not a single word left me. All I could do was stand there with my mouth unhinged, as I watched Liam make his way onto the stage.

A roar of laughter from the crowd pulsed through the gallery, but I had no clue what he'd said to make the audience laugh. My head was filled with fog. Liam had done it to me again.

Bastard.

Liam chatted with the reporter like they were old friends. Guests on the show asked him questions and he answered each one with confidence and ease. He appeared calm and collected, charming his way into her heart and the hearts of all the people watching him. To watch him was like watching poetry in motion, as cliché as that might be.

At the height of the interview, I received a call and had to step out of the building. Once I got back inside, Liam had completed his segment. He stood with Scout and Aaron near the refreshment table, chatting.

"You've never been to the music district?" came Aaron's shocked reaction.

Much to my amazement, Aaron and Scout had grown rather close. After their rocky start, I expected to have to keep them separated. It turned out that sexual tension has a way of making haters into lovers. Many nights I found them huddled up in Scout's office in a rather cozy manner. It was kind of cute to watch the budding romance develop, but I did have to warn them that if it caused any issues with the campaign, I'd hang both their asses.

"I'm not from here, Nimrod." Scout playfully jabbed Aaron in the ribs.

"Well, that settles it. We're heading downtown tonight," Liam advised. "You're coming with us, right?"

All three sets of eyes landed on me.

I placed my open palm to my chest. "Who? Me?"

Smoldering brown eyes met mine. "Yes, you," Liam replied, his pitch low and smoldering. "You can't leave me alone with these two."

A short, loud laugh burst from my lungs. "Afraid of

what they might do to you?"

"More like I'm afraid of watching them make out like horny teenagers and being accused of some pervy threesome. We wouldn't want a scandal to arise, now would we?"

"Gross!" Scout sneered.

"Horny teenagers, my ass!" Aaron protested.

"Oh, my God! Please don't say threesome so close to the microphones!" I squelched.

"See! That's why you need to be there. With me alongside these two lovebirds," he thumbed toward Scout and Aaron, "there's no telling what kind of trouble I'm liable to end up in."

"We're not in love," Scout argued. The grin on Aaron's face dropped a little, but he said nothing to deny nor support her claim.

"Whatever. I'm not going to be alone with you two while y'all are sucking face." Liam crossed his arms over his chest, casting a quick wink in my direction.

"Please tell me you two aren't actually making out in public," I prodded, doing my best to ignore Liam's little gesture.

"We're not making out!" Aaron exclaimed. "We're not even dating."

I waved my hands downward. "Shh. Keep your voices down." I looked around to see if anyone was watching. Thankfully it appeared we were unnoticed.

"So you're just fucking then?" Liam parried.

"Liam!" I hissed. "Don't say stuff like that where people can record you!"

Liam stuffed his hands in his pockets and grinned.

"Then join us and keep me out of trouble," he cajoled.

"Thanks, but I can't."

"Why not?" Aaron demanded, his arms draped over Scout's shoulder.

Liam scratched the side of his jaw. "Yeah. Why not?"

I shrugged one shoulder. "Because you really don't want an old lady tagging along. I'd be boring."

Aaron, Scout, and Liam all exchanged looks. "You're not old!" Liam barked.

"Not even close," Scout chimed in.

Aaron eyeballed Liam, who'd taken a step closer to me. It never failed, Liam always closed the gap between us, invading my personal space. If it weren't for my senses running at warp speed when he was near, I would've grown accustomed to his little maneuver by now.

"How much older do you think you are, Elizabeth?" Aaron pushed in between Liam and me, wrapping an arm around my shoulders. "You're what? Forty?" Aaron suggested.

"Forty-five," I mumbled.

"That makes you about six years older than me," Aaron noted. "Which means you're not old. As a matter of fact, you're in the prime of your life."

My eyes shifted skyward. "Fine. Then I can't go because I have work to do."

"Nope. Not buying it, Lizzy." Aaron patted my shoulder with the palm of his hand. "If you don't go, none of us go. It's that simple."

Aaron stepped back. No sooner had he moved that Liam regained his previous position. "Please. For me," Liam whispered close to my ear. "There's a bar that plays nothing but nineties rock. We can leave the lovebirds and go have some fun."

As tempting as that sounded, the idea of being alone with Liam freaked me out. It didn't matter that we'd be surrounded by his security detail. For all intents and purposes he'd proposed alone time for us. That didn't bode well for my already shattering defenses.

Overcome with the thought, I dared to gaze into those big, brown eyes. His dark hair fell forward on his forehead. Why, I don't know, but I reached up and brushed it back from his face. He released a small sigh. His lips parted slightly; full, soft, deliciously tempting. The urge to kiss him struck me like lightening. He swallowed and I noticed how his throat bobbed beneath the collar of his shirt. My whole body became electrified by that single, insignificant touch.

But it wasn't insignificant. It created tension, want, need, and desire. That simple touch sizzled with heat. It left me wanting to know more, to feel more.

Of course, that feeling didn't last. Reality came back into focus and panic set in.

Oh, God! What had I done?

How could I have allowed myself to forget our surroundings? We were in a television studio for God's sake. Cameras were everywhere. I ripped my hand back, clenching it at my side. My eyes scanned the perimeter to see if anyone noticed my moment of weakness.

Stupid! Absolutely stupid!

I forced myself to slug back the fear mounting inside me. If anyone had seen...

Forget that!

Anyone who may have been watching us would've thought I was grooming my candidate. I'd done that a million times before. Liam was no different in the eyes of the public – I hoped.

However, a full one-eighty-degree scan of the room did nothing to settle the disappointment I had in myself. There wasn't a soul in sight aside from Scout and Aaron, who both wore similar expressions of intrigue, but I couldn't shake how easy it'd been for me to cross a line, a line I'd set for myself.

A curse caught in my throat. This man's power over me was illogical.

Liam rubbed his freshly shaven jaw, a twisted little smirk lighted his lips.

Just as I feared – he was calling my bluff. There'd be no turning him down now.

I took a step back, giving myself a chance to breathe and accepting the inevitable. "Fine. I'll go. But if I drag you down, don't say I didn't warn you."

"Great! You're going." A sexy, little grin dangled at the corner of Liam's mouth. "You won't regret it."

He was wrong. I already did.

Thirteen

The music pulsed all around me to the point it almost hurt my eardrums. Almost.

Dim light shrouded the club, letting darkness reign over all who wished to utilize its cover. A long, wooden bar lined the east wall and a simple stage captured the attention of the audience. Well, at least those who weren't lost in dancing or other seedy deeds. Unlike in my younger years, there was no smoke haze to add to the ambiance of the establishment. I'd never been a smoker, but I missed the way it added character to a joint such as this.

The four of us found a round corner booth off to the side of the stage. The two men sat on the outsides, pushing Scout and myself into the center. Scout curled her legs up onto the bench, resting into the crook of Aaron's side as they listened to the band on stage belt out a slow ballad. Had it not been for the man sitting to the left of me, I might've enjoyed the group's rock-n-roll meets blues vibe. Instead, I was entranced by how close Liam was to me. The side of his leg lightly pressed into mine. Every move he made I felt.

Through the cadence of the music, I was hyper aware of him. A shuffle in his seat. Each muscle that moved with the beat. A tap of his foot kept the rhythm. Even his heartbeat rattled me. I inhaled deeply, pushing aside the rage of hormones attempting to take over. This was all in my head. I'd manufactured this silly love game and now I was paying for my imagination. I was better than this. Stronger. No one, not even my ex-husband, affected me in such a primal way. I had control of myself, even as a young woman. I could restrain my urges, and I would. No one owned me, except maybe my daughter.

Liam scooted back, resting his arm along the back of the booth, over my shoulder. Rather than shout over the music, he leaned into me to speak. "These guys are great." His whisper tickled my ear.

I swallowed down the scream trying to rip out of me. That stupid little comment had me clenching my thighs together.

I dipped in closer to him, basking in the musk of his cologne. "Yeah. It's a great cover."

That really wasn't saying much when I wasn't a fan of the original performer. Although, on the flip side, they made me like the song, and if they recorded it, I'd more than likely buy it.

A slow smile emerged on his lips. "I'm glad you approve." Something in his tone goaded me.

"What's that supposed to mean?" I shot off. My

hackles raised. Any inkling of attraction I had for him flew out the window with the appearance of that smug expression on his face.

"Nothing." He slunk further into the bench, dropping his hands onto the table in front of us.

"I don't buy it!"

Liam chuckled and glanced in my direction. "Look at them."

His abrupt change in direction caught me off guard. "What?"

He motioned toward Aaron and Scout. They were wrapped in the most intimate of embraces. For two people who claimed to not be involved, they appeared rather cozy to me.

"I'm sure in all your background checks you learned a lot about him." Liam tipped his head toward Aaron.

I rubbed my arm. "Yeah."

"I'm pretty sure if you look up the term Man-Whore in the dictionary, you'd find Aaron's picture beside it."

I bit the inside of my mouth to hold back my laughter. "That's not nice."

Liam rubbed his jaw and grinned. "But it's the truth. Well, at least until Scout." He bounced his leg, sending vibrations through mine. "She's changed him. I joke about them being together, but I know he cares for her. She's good for him."

"How are you so sure she's not just another notch in his bedpost?" It was a genuine question, and I was interested in hearing the answer.

Liam diverted his eyes back to the stage where the band was finishing their set. "Because he hasn't slept with her yet."

My head jerked toward the press secretary and the chief of staff, baffled and a bit confused. "But back at the station, you said…"

"I know what I said, in jest. But trust me, they're not sleeping together."

That wasn't possible. The way those two were twisted together, they had to be screwing around. Liam was trying to pull a fast one over me. "I'm not falling for that one."

That's when it struck me. Somehow, in turning my attention to the young couple, he'd diverted a possible argument between us. He'd played me and I let him. Score one for Liam. He was getting too good at this game, which wasn't a great sign for me.

Dark eyes pierced me through the dull light. My throat closed at the seriousness written all over him. "I told you I never lie, and I meant it."

His tone, the mere way in which he spoke with such authority that I couldn't refute him, gave me pause. I returned my attention back to Scout and Aaron, feeling a little guilty that I hadn't taken more interest in them before now. Sure, I'd noticed their little amore, but all I cared about was them not disrupting our campaign. Flings happened all the time in this business, but what Liam was implying sent my mind into overload. "Wow," I breathed, covering my hand over my mouth. "They're falling in love."

Liam shifted, bringing our bodies closer together, if that was even possible. "Possibly, but she keeps him at a distance, like someone else I know."

Warning bells sounded in my head. Danger, Ms.

Robinson, Danger!

Fuck! I really was a Ms. Robinson, drooling over this poor man. Talk about an epic face meet palm moment.

"It comes with the territory," I stated, unsure why I felt the need to explain why women like Scout and myself might not allow anyone to waltz into our lives or our bedrooms.

"I can understand that." The muscles in his jaw tightened. "But eventually you've got to let someone in. It's a lonely existence otherwise."

I crossed my arms over my stomach, my eyebrows lifted. "This coming from a man who's faking a relationship."

"I'm not faking. I've never once called Kristin my girlfriend and I never will. Besides, any faking is exaggerated by you," he deflected.

"Fine. But why her? What does she get out of this?"

"I wouldn't expect you to understand." His voice rumbled low and heady.

"Try me."

Liam rubbed the back of his neck, looking a sheepish. "Kristin and I have no secrets between us."

"Oh c'mon. No secrets at all? Is that why she isn't on the road with us?" It was a valid question, and one I'd fought with him over before we hit the trail. I still believed she should be at every event. With Liam, Aaron, and Scout joining forces against me, I lost that battle, but I didn't go down without a true fight. "Is she afraid she'll out you or something?"

His whole body stiffened. "No. Now drop it," he sneered through clenched teeth. "She does enough for me.

I'm not going to ask her to take off from her job for this."

"Right." I waved my hand in a blasé manner. "The job. Art curator." Each word I spoke was clipped to put emphasis on how I still didn't agree with her absence on the trail. "Is that code for she's in a relationship?"

He dropped his head into his hands and released an exasperated sigh. "You're relentless. You know that?"

A little pleased with myself, I gave a halfhearted shrug. "It's why I'm so damn good at what I do, and why you're leading in the polls."

"Did it ever occur to you that I'm leading in the polls because voters know I'm the best for the job?"

I bobbed my head from side to side, curling my lips. "Trust me, if you didn't have me, they wouldn't know you're the right guy for the job. Keating would've already slaughtered you."

Liam shifted to face me, his knee perched on the seat, digging into my thigh. "You're good, and I appreciate what you bring to this team, but I'm just as good. Don't forget that."

I flipped my hair over my shoulder, turning to mimic his position. Our arms crossed over the top of the bench, our knees pressed together. My blood boiled with passion and frustration. That wasn't a good mix for me, so it seemed. "You think you're so badass…"

"I am," he cut in. "And you know it, or you wouldn't be working with me."

He gripped the top of my arm, sending vibrations of heat coursing through my veins. To tell him he was wrong would be a lie, and I didn't want to lie to win. Thankfully, I didn't have to because the band stopped playing, sending a hushed silence over the crowd. Liam and I both clamped our mouths shut and turned around in the booth to present the band with a much deserved ovation.

Out of the silence, a shrill voice screeched, "Oh, my God! It really is him!"

Two armed guards jumped from their seats, as a group of young people trampled to a stop in front of the table. Liam waved off his security detail, who hesitantly obeyed, backing away but only slightly. Liam tightened his tie, and slipped out of the booth. Aaron and Scout untangled fast, composing themselves.

As Liam spoke to the young voters, I caught myself entranced by his hospitable interactions. He was energetic, completely uncaring that they'd just interrupted him during his off time. He was open to taking pictures and answering questions. They discussed everything from the band's performance to his political agenda. They'd watched his interview from earlier in the day and expressed their support for him. He was a hit.

By the time the crowd dispersed around him, Aaron was giving me a nudge. "Hey, I hate to cut this short, but I just got a call from the office. We need to head back to the bus for the night."

I glanced down at my watch, a little startled by the time. "Damn. Is it really that late?"

Aaron glimpsed at his phone. "I'm afraid so."

I reached out and tugged on Liam's sport coat. He was bidding the last of the group goodbye, and dropped his gaze back to me. "I'm sorry, Congressman," I said in my most professional of tones, "but we must head out."

Liam shifted back to the young man who'd stayed

behind after his friends had dispersed. "I'm sorry, Travis, but I need to cut this short. As I'm sure you know, Washington never sleeps."

Travis, a young African-American man with flawless ebony skin and a shaved head, beamed. "Not a problem, Congressman Baxter. I'm sorry we bothered you."

Liam shook Travis' hand. "You didn't bother me at all. And you're more than welcome to contact my office at any time. I'm here to serve you." I'd heard that line from a million politicians, but coming from Liam, I actually believed it, as did Travis. He thanked Liam once again and rushed off to catch up with his friends.

"You ready?" Liam asked, taking out his wallet and dropping cash onto the table.

As I started to scoot out of the bench, a large hand extended before me. I glanced up only to catch his eyes flicker downward. I dropped my gaze to discover an ample amount of my cleavage and bra exposed. There was a little piece of me that felt excited to see a man was locked inside the perfect persona of William Baxter. However, I quickly concealed myself because I didn't want anyone to ever accuse me of being unprofessional.

Once my wardrobe was adjusted, I accepted his hand and let him guide me from the bench. Liam tucked my hand in the crook of his elbow and started us out of the building.

Into the night, we entered. The streets were packed, even at that late hour. Winter was over, but the harsh breeze still had its reign over the great state. It rustled around us as we worked our way to where we'd left the car. We'd chosen to walk the music district so Scout could take in the sights. Not one of our brightest decisions, though I admit I argued against the idea in the first place.

Bright neon lights flooded the street as music pulsed from bars all along the way. A street performer stood along the sidewalk with an acoustic guitar, singing his heart out. Behind us, the two guards trotted, never coming close enough for anyone to notice them.

None of us said anything. It was obvious we were all tired, and the night was nowhere near over for any of us. Along the way, a huge burst of wind sliced through my blouse. My teeth began to chatter. I bit my bottom lip to prevent the racket, but that didn't stop Liam from feeling me shiver.

"You're freezing."

"I'm fine," I fibbed.

"No, you're not." He halted his steps, pulling me back with him.

Liam slipped his jacket off his shoulders and wrapped it around me.

"You don't need to do that," I disputed. "You'll freeze."

Liam rubbed his hands up and down my arms. The chill of the night disappeared only to be replaced with the warmth of lust. "I'm not cold, nor am I wearing silk. Now, slip your arms in, and let's get to the car."

My shoulders bounced with a chuckle, but I did as I was told. The sleeves were far too long, so he rolled them to my wrists. "Thanks," I muttered.

"No problem," he whispered, taking my hand and returning it to his arm.

Through the journey, I didn't think about the way his scent enveloped me from his jacket, or how his body heat had made the material warm against my skin. I refused to let my mind linger on how easy it was to walk next to him. Nor did I consider how good it felt to have my hand resting on his arm.

No, none of that entered my mind.

Right! As if I could've gotten away from any of that.

And the ride back to the bus was even worse. While there was space between us on the seat, I still felt him all around me. I could barely breathe. This man, who was far too young for me, made me crazy in ways I never believed existed.

Once we arrived at the bus, I couldn't get out of the car fast enough. Aaron and Scout beelined for the bus, neither wanting to deal with the night chill any longer. I quickly followed suit. Ready to step onto the bus, I remembered I was still wearing Liam's jacket. I stopped and turned to him, about to remove the suit coat. He stilled my actions by wrapping his long fingers around my shoulders.

"Keep it. You might need it on that drafty bus tonight."

There was nothing drafty about the bus. It was brand new with state of the art everything. And while I wanted to point that out to him, to argue that I had my own sweater on the bus so I didn't need his silly coat, I couldn't bring myself to do it.

"You know, it's my job to take care of you. Not the other way around," I teased, playfully jabbing my index finger into his chest.

He grabbed my hand, holding it by the wrist. My eyes dropped to where his touch radiated against my skin. "I'd like to think we take care of each other," he murmured, lifting his other hand to brush my hair back from my face.

My heart galloped inside my chest at the innocent but erotic caress.

Aaron stuck his head out the door. "Liam, I hate to break this up, but Marcos is holding." He waved his cell phone at Liam. "Can't keep the Congressman waiting."

Liam released me, his playful demeanor gone in a flash. He glanced over to Aaron then to me. He appeared so torn and it pained me to see him in such dire straits. "I'm sorry. I need to take this."

I laughed and shooed him off. "Go, Congressman. You've got a job to do."

As he reached up and brushed my hair back from my face, the moonlight, bright and golden, twinkled in his eyes. "Thank you, Elizabeth. I've had a wonderful evening."

Oh, shit! That sounded like a date line or something. No! This wasn't a date. He was only being polite. That was Liam's way. Always kind and polite.

I forced a smile and bowed my head. "As did I. Now get to work."

"You heard the woman!"

Liam dashed up the steps and I followed close behind. The bus doors shut behind me. I stood at the entrance and watched as he disappeared into the conference center. My cellphone rang and all non-professional thoughts fled my mind. Well, almost all. My fingers trailed the fabric of his coat as I answered the call. This evening proved to be exactly what I feared. And now, between his sly move of diversion and his act of chivalry, Liam was leading on the scoreboard.

Liam 18 - Elizabeth 15

Or was it Liam 19 - Elizabeth 15?

I was starting to lose count. How was that possible? This was a game. A game I was determined to win.

Or was I?

Fourteen

I sat at the kitchenette table, my head in my hands, with nothing but the sounds of sleep and the whirl of an engine humming around me. For the most part, everything was dark, save a dim light over the little sink and the sliver of moonlight slinking in from the oblong window. Pain pulsed through my skull, punching the back of my eyes with every beat of my heart.

My headaches were becoming far more frequent and painful. I was unsure what triggered them. At first I thought it might be from insomnia, but for the last eighteen plus years I'd survived on four to five hours of sleep a night. Sometimes less. That couldn't be the issue. No, the cause went much deeper, and if I were to be honest with myself, I could guess the culprit.

This headache struck the moment I parted ways from Liam and answered my phone. Lucky for me, it was Jordyn on the other end.

I rubbed my temples in a circular motion. Not even that alleviated my agony. And when I thought it couldn't get worse, the bus drove over what I could only assume was a pothole in the road. It jostled me to the point that I thought my head might implode.

"Elizabeth?" The sound of Liam's soft, husky voice made my already soured stomach jump. I lifted my face to find him standing in the doorway. His arms were crossed over his broad chest, his head tilted to the side. As if to tease me, his white t-shirt lifted just enough for me to see the deep lines of his abdomen angled down into his cotton night pants. "Are you all right?"

"I'm fine," I managed with a smile —at least I thought it was a smile— plastered to my face.

Liam closed the distance between us in two steps. He took my chin between his fingers, and gently turned my face, scrutinizing me from each angle. "No you're not."

I hated how easily he could read me. In an act of defiance, I pulled away from his hand and leaned back in my seat. My stomach twisted and twirled as a wave of nausea washed over me. I wanted to tell him to back off, that I was okay, but I feared what might happen if I opened my mouth.

Liam dropped his hand to his side, his fingers tapping against his thigh.

I screwed my eyes shut, the metallic taste on my tongue signaling that I was about to make a huge ol' mess on the floor if I didn't get it under control fast.

"Are you going to be sick?" he asked, his tone worried but calm.

"I'm fine," I repeated, sounding more like a frog than a human being.

Warm skin met my face, as Liam's knuckles drifted down my cheek. I opened my eyes to find him peering down at me. Deep lines buried into his forehead, his brows furrowed with concern. "Elizabeth, I'm not trying to goad you. You look miserable, and I don't like it."

I licked my lips, swallowing down the saliva coating my tongue. A small, weak sound tore from my lips as I whispered, "I have a headache. That's all."

"Have you taken anything for it?"

One nod, that was all I could muster for him.

"Do you get them often?"

My instinct was to shake my head, but my stomach thought otherwise. "Only recently."

Liam stepped around behind me. I attempted to turn my head to see what he was doing, but two hands brushing my hair away from the back of my neck stopped me. The pain was immense. Every hair follicle tingled along my scalp, but the pleasure his touch created was exhilarating. That single touch consumed me in such a way I wanted nothing more than to melt against him. His long fingers explored along the back of neck to my skull, leaving a trail of heat on my skin.

"You're dealing with stress headaches," he stated with absolute certainty.

"What are you? A doctor now?" I sneered, aggravated at how comfortable I was at being touched by him, but worse yet, how easy it was for him to touch me.

"No, but I do have some experience with this type of headache."

I twisted my hair over my shoulder, wincing at the pain it caused. "You're wrong. I don't get stressed."

Liam chuckled, his balmy breath swept over my exposed neck. "Well, something's stressing you out. From what I can tell, you carry all your stress here." He lightly pressed his thumb into my neck near my spine. I almost screamed in agony, but he moved so that both hands rested on my shoulders. His thumbs traced along the bridge between my neck and arms. "And here."

I tried to roll my shoulders, but his grip was too tight, forcing me to stay in place. "This is crazy. I'm not stressed!"

"Fine. But you do have a headache. So, let me help you."

I squirmed, attempting to escape him. Between his gentle touch and my pounding head, my body was a mess of confusion. "Like I said, I took some aspirin. I'll be fine."

"You push yourself too hard, Elizabeth. Just let me help you."

I shoved his hands off my shoulders and scooted forward in my seat, turning to face him. "I don't need your help."

Liam threw his hands in the air. The concern that once painted his expression turned into exasperation. "My God! Why is it so difficult for you to accept help?"

"Because I'm scared, okay?" A hard shiver flitted down my arms as the words flew from my lips. I clapped my hand over my mouth, instantly regretting my momentary loss of control. I couldn't believe I'd voiced that aloud. No one, not even Jordyn or Harper, had ever heard me utter those words before. So, why him? Why now?

"Of what?" he spoke slow and soft. He took a step toward me, but I was up and out of my seat before he could touch me again. I was afraid of what might happen if I felt his hands on my skin once more. He was tempting. Too inviting. And by far too dangerous to me. It was imperative that I kept my distance.

"Nothing. Forget I said anything." I moved to the small sink and rested my hands against the cold steel. Sweat prickled my skin and my pounding head became a constant throb. From the window I caught sight of his reflection. He watched me. Analyzed me. All the while he inched in closer to me, eliminating the gap I'd managed to put between us.

"What are you scared of, Elizabeth?"

Though I doubt he meant to push me, it had become a habit of his, or more like a habit of ours. The command emanating from him surged the fury inside me. I whipped around to face him, my stomach whining over the movement. "I'm scared of trusting people. People lie. They cheat. They steal. I'm better off handling things on my own so I don't have to lay my trust in someone who can or will eventually screw me over."

Whoa! Where did that come from?

I wiped my hand over my mouth, my eyes cast downward. My secret, the one I kept from everyone, was out. I didn't depend on people because I couldn't trust anyone but myself. Not that I was some jaded soul or anything. I wasn't. I'd led a satisfying life. Love surrounded me through my family, as broken as it was. But I'd seen the underbellies of power. I knew how trust could be used as a form of currency. I wanted no part of it.

"You still don't trust me," his throaty timbre rumbled through me.

The hurt in his voice made my already sick stomach churn harder. "I personally vetted you, Liam. Doesn't that tell you something?"

"It tells me you're smart and good at your job." He took a step forward. His index finger pressed beneath my chin as he lifted my face, yet I remained unable to look into his eyes.

"I'm the best," I stated, my tone a little flat.

"You are, but you've also seen too much and trust no one because of it."

"Thus is the life of politics."

Liam traced his thumb along my jaw. "Trust me now. Let me help you."

I dared a peek into those deep, dark eyes. That was my downfall. "How?"

His full lips pulled into a grin. "Sit back down and allow yourself to relax." He stepped back and patted the bench, expressing his desire for me to return to my earlier station. Reluctant, I did as I was told and slunk down onto the bench. "Now close your eyes."

My stubbornness nudged me, but I obeyed. Eyes closed, I felt him everywhere around me. The warmth of his touch, the twisting of my long, blonde locks around his hand, the way his thumbs pressed into the back of my neck. Just when I was almost relaxed, he leaned in and whispered close to my ear, "This is gonna hurt like hell for a second. Forgive me."

No sooner had he uttered those words did earth-shattering pain explode inside my skull. A large hand moved around to cover my mouth as a scream detonated from my chest. Blinding light flashed behind my eyes. My tender stomach rolled, sending me into dry-heaves. "Breathe, Elizabeth," Liam coached. "I promise if you breathe it'll be okay."

What he asked was almost impossible, but I managed to take air deep into my lungs. When I exhaled, I ripped his hand from my mouth and jerked around to him. "What the hell? You said you'd help. Not try to kill me."

Liam stepped back, crossing his arms over his chest. A jovial grin spread across his face. "Are you still in pain?"

I slid out from the bench. "Of course, I'm still..." That's when it struck me. The headache was gone. I reached behind my head to rub the place Liam had assaulted. It was tender, but the intense ache was indeed gone. "How'd you do that?"

Liam turned to the cabinet beside the window and pulled down two glasses and a bottle of whiskey. "In college I had a lot of problems with stress. Between basketball and my class load, I stayed stressed out. The team physician used to do that to me weekly, along with a scolding about how I took on more than a kid my age should." Liam chuckled as he poured two fingers into each glass and sat one down in front of me. "Needless to say, after college I learned my own pressure points. Finding yours was a cinch, since you carry your stress in the same places I do." I glanced down at the amber liquid. It vibrated with the rumble of the bus. "To trust."

I lifted my glass, but said nothing. We both downed our shots like pros.

"Now," he muttered behind the lip of the tumbler, "you want to talk about what's bothering you?"

I massaged the back of my neck, astonished at how much better I felt. "Work, I guess."

That was as close to the truth as he would get. It was Liam who stressed me out. The way he looked at me. The way he stayed so close that I often smelled his cologne on my skin long after we parted ways. But most of all, I stressed over how I wanted him when I shouldn't. I hated how one minute I wanted to rip off his clothes and the very next I wanted to scratch his eyes out.

Cool, mocking eyes zeroed in on mine. "Is it Harper?"

"Harper?" I squeaked, biting back a laugh. "Why would I be stressed over Harper?"

"I just thought..." He dropped his gaze down to the empty glass in his hand, his jaw jutted and his nose flared.

"Are you insinuating that Harper and me..." My voice trailed off.

"I shouldn't have...it isn't my place..." Liam took my empty glass from my hand and placed it in the sink next to his. With his back still turned to me, his hands gripped the small counter and his shoulders slumped forward.

"It's all right. To answer your question, no it's not Harper." I popped the knuckles in my thumbs. "And to clarify your assumption, Harper and I are not together in any capacity other than friendship." I shrugged. "Well, that and campaign funding."

Liam turned around, leaning back against the counter. His long legs crossed in front of him. "So you and Harper never...you know..." Liam's nose wrinkled.

"Slept together? God, no. Harper's like a brother to

me." Liam's shoulders sagged at my response. "What about you and Kristin? Have you two ever...you know..." I teased, using his same vernacular.

Liam shook his head. "Never. We kissed once back in middle school, but that was as far as it ever went." He paused for a moment, then lifted his chin and blurted out, "Are you seeing anyone?"

Taken aback, I slid further into the bench seat, resting my elbow on the table. My feet kicked out in front of me, crossed at the ankles, only inches from Liam's. It felt weird to talk about myself to someone, but also nice. A wry smile tugged my lips as I brushed my bangs from my face. "I haven't been on a date-date since the night I took on your campaign, and even that date had been a farce."

"Yeah, I remember you telling me about him." Liam's face burned hot in the dim cabin light. "Assholes like him are one of the many reasons why I don't mess around. Women deserve to be treasured and adored. A real man knows how to please his woman, not belittle her."

"Not all men think that way, Liam. Especially when dating in your forties."

"That's bullshit. I swear, I would've punched him for simply being an idiot. You're absolutely stunning."

Heat began to rise up my face. I covered my cheeks with my hands to hide my embarrassment. Liam had called me stunning. "It's not that big of a deal. I handled him. Quite well, I might add."

"I'm sure you did, but I still would've pummeled him on merit alone."

A sprinkle of desire fluttered down my spine. I wanted nothing more than to kiss the anger off his face. He'd come to my rescue if given the chance. He wanted to protect me, and if I cared to admit it, I wanted him to.

I lifted from my seat, and just like at the television studio, I reached up and brushed his hair back from his face. This time, all alone, I allowed my hand to linger, drifting down from his forehead to his cheek. Coarse hair scratched against my skin as I slowly drew the angle of his jaw with my fingertips. Liam closed his eyes, his breathing growing heavier as my fingers floated along the contours of his face. My touch became softer with each stroke until I went to remove my hand from his jaw. Liam's eyes popped open and he grabbed my wrist. His long fingers coiled around my arm, holding my hand to his cheek. I couldn't even begin to penetrate the hazy bubble surrounding my thoughts. The savage look in his eyes burned red hot through my veins.

Inch by inch our mouths moved closer. Already I could taste him on my lips. Sweet but spicy, and full of passion. He was decadent; a temptation.

My temptation.

When he captured my lips, I floated to heaven.

At first the kiss was gentle, almost hesitant, but then he became bolder, more confident. He pressed his mouth hard against mine, his tongue circling my lips for permission. There was no thought, no contemplation, no planning. Pure primal instinct controlled my every move, as I parted my lips.

His tongue darted inside my mouth, exploring and taking what he wanted. My hands moved to his hair, and I was suddenly thankful I'd made him grow it out. Our heart beats, hard and pounding, gave rhythm to the need that burned between us. His tongue, hot and wet, tangled with mine, but there was too much distance still between us.

A soft moan rumbled in my chest, as he pulled back, tugging my bottom lip between his teeth. He reached out and wrapped his hands around my waist, pulling me flush against him. His body felt hard and lean to my feminine and soft. I was powerless in his embrace. Even if I wanted to escape, which I didn't, I couldn't have. His arms encircled me and his tongue lunged back into my mouth, exploring every inch.

Nothing about the kiss was gentle. All my virginal beliefs about him flew right out the window by the way his fingers toyed with the hem of my t-shirt, and the carnal way he brushed the tips of his fingers along my hypersensitive skin. Liam was all man, and that man knew how to kiss.

When he broke away, we both stared into each other's eyes, breathless. Never had anyone looked at me as he did. His expression melted my heart and consumed my soul. "You have no idea how long I've wanted to kiss you like that," he murmured.

That's when my stupid brain kicked in, knocking my overactive libido out of the way. I caught my kiss-swollen lip between my teeth, unable to speak.

His smile dropped. "Elizabeth, don't."

But I did. "We shouldn't have done that."

There were no words to express how much I wanted him. It felt damn good to know he wanted me, too, but none of that was possible. He was too young for me. More important, though, he was in the middle of a campaign. He didn't need this kind of secret lurking in the shadows.

"Why not?"

I stepped back, placing distance between us.

"Do I really need to list the reasons why?"

Liam advanced forward, filling the empty space I'd created. "After that kiss you'll have to, because right now I see no reason why I shouldn't kiss you like that again and again and again."

I tried to back away but the table foiled my plans. With my ass flush against the wooden surface, Liam marched to me, his body pressed against mine as I tried to tick off the reasons. "The most important is the election," I gushed. "You don't need a scandal when you're leading in the polls like you are. And this" —I pointed back and forth between us— "screams scandal. Older woman, younger man, on top of me running your campaign!" I gasped in horror. "The media would eat it up."

"I see." Ice filled my veins at the sound of his voice. "So it's my age that really bothers you."

"No! Wait! What? No!" I stammered.

White noise buzzed through my mind. Liam's intense stare harnessed me where I stood. Not even a bump from the road could move me. As if to size me up, he dipped his head. I thought he might speak, but instead he moved so his nose brushed along my jaw. The heat of his breath jolted me to my very core. Unabashed, he pushed his hand under my shirt, circling his finger around my navel. "I'm not that much younger than you, Elizabeth McNeal."

I gulped hard. He was making love to me with my clothes on. How was that even possible?

"I know."

"Then stop worrying about how old I am."

"I'm not," I lied.

Goose bumps spread across my skin. Every nerve inside my body buzzed with anticipation. Those lips. Those fingers. Those eyes. God, I wanted him.

Further he pushed me back so that I was practically lying on the table. I gripped the hard surface, as my elbows buckled beneath the pressure. It would've been so easy for him to pull my pants down and have his way with me. His hand, skimmed lower to my waistband, teasing, but never dipping beneath the fabric. "Are you sure?"

I shivered beneath his touch, aching for him to make the final move and take me right then. "Positive," I confirmed. And this time I wasn't lying. His age was nothing when it came to the way he made me feel.

Liam pressed a kiss to the corner of my mouth. "All right. Then I'll say goodnight now, before I lose all control."

"What do you mean?"

Stupid, stupid question.

His fingers grazed along the side of my hip. "You know very well what I mean." His tongue darted out, tracing the line of my lips. I gasped as he slipped inside my mouth once again. The kiss lasted only a second, but it left me aching and hungry for more.

Liam pulled back, taking me with him. He settled me on my feet. "Thank you again for the lovely night. Get some rest. You're going to need it."

I opened my mouth to protest, but he turned on his heel and walked away. As he disappeared, I dropped back into my seat and let out an exasperated growl. Every hair on my body stood on end, and had Aaron not been sleeping in the same room as Liam, I might've thrown caution to the wind.

It'd been too long since I'd had a good, thorough fucking.

Wait?

Liam said he didn't fuck around.

Dammit! That meant no real sexy time for me.

Unless…Liam had real feelings for me.

Nah. That wasn't possible. He didn't know me well enough. And if he did know me, he'd more than likely run for the hills for fear of waking the next morning missing a testicle.

This was too complicated and my headache had returned in full force.

I dropped my head in my hands and sighed.

What have I done? What. Have. I. Done?

Fifteen

That kiss. That stupid kiss.

More like two kisses. But who's counting?

Apparently, I was.

For days I'd wrestled with the meaning behind that kiss, and for all my postulating, I remained as vexed as I had when it first occurred.

Why?

Well, for starters we were never alone long enough to discuss anything but the campaign. When I tried to pull him away, someone would pop around the corner, preventing all personal conversation. To make matters worse, Liam took to dropping little innuendos of our shared moment, knowing I wanted to discuss it and couldn't. His touches became more intimate, his voice softer and oozing with allure. He was driving me insane, to the point I did what any self-preserving woman would do in my situation. I started keeping score again.

In all fairness, I adjusted the score for my momentary lapse of record keeping, but I tried to be honest, utilizing what my memory could conjure. By my count the score was now: Elizabeth 32 - Liam 37.

Yeah, the little shit was up by five, but I blamed that on the kiss. That kiss alone was worth at least two points. More like a touchdown, but I wasn't going to be generous enough to give him that many points. Especially since teasing me had become his new favorite pastime.

Lucky for me, we were now in Dallas and momentarily off that damn bus.

Outside Liam's hotel room, I took in a deep breath before knocking on the door. Our schedule was tight for the day, and I needed my game face on. I squeezed my shoulders, cracked my neck, and donned my best smile.

The door flew open, revealing a statuesque Aaron, dressed in a well-tailored suit with his jacket unbuttoned. "'Bout time you got here."

"It's not like you didn't know how to reach me," I smarted off, adding a smack on his chest for good measure. I stepped inside and nearly jumped at the sound of the door closing behind me. It felt odd being in Liam's room. Almost intimate. Way too intimate.

"Kinda jumpy today, aren't ya?"

"Shut it, Baxter," I muttered.

The penthouse was elegance at its best. Modern yet classic, the room housed a sense of prestige becoming of a US Representative. Wall to wall windows presented a magnificent view of Dallas in all its splendor. Hardwood floors, plush furniture with a television any man would kill for, and a lavish kitchen completed the temporary abode. My suite, while beautiful, didn't hold a candle to such grandeur.

"Scout's in the living room with Liam working on last minute preps."

"Good. Good." I flattened one hand over my skirt while wringing my other around my briefcase handle. I was nervous. Very nervous. Today was monumental for our campaign. It was what we'd been working toward on this trip, and instead of thinking about what needed to be accomplished, all I thought about was feeling Liam's mouth pressed hard against mine.

"Kristin's also in there."

That stopped me dead in my tracks. Kristin. I'd forgotten she was joining us. Part of me wanted to be pissed because she would put a dampener on the game, but the other part of me was relieved. With Kristin involved, Liam would be far too busy to play and I could get back to doing what I do best — making sure he won.

"That's great news," I squeaked, my voice cracking a little too much for my taste.

"Is it?" Aaron queried, his cadence a little softer but serious.

I tilted my face upward to meet his pointed gaze, my most practiced smile drawn on my lips. "Of course it is."

Aaron's eyebrows bowed together and he shook his head. "Somehow I knew you'd say that."

A little defensive, I straightened my back. That still left me level with Aaron's chest. Damn the Baxter's and their tall genes. "What's that supposed to mean?"

Aaron extended his hand out, motioning us forward.

"It means nothing, Elizabeth."

I hated how open-ended his comment was, but didn't have it in me to argue with him.

What had become of me? Liam was turning me into a timid lamb when I was supposed to be a fighting lion.

I felt off. The world was unbalanced, off kilter.

There was a niggling in my stomach that ate at me. It had to be fixed.

But there was no correcting it, for the instant I stepped foot into the living room, that irritation became full on ire.

Liam sat on the sofa with Kristin perched beside him. Her small feminine frame melted perfectly into his strong masculine physique. She was adorable in her pink pantsuit, and of course Liam looked as dashing as ever in a black single-breasted suit. It didn't matter what Liam said about their relationship, their ease and comfort together ignited something inside me. If I had to label it, I'd have called it jealousy. But that wasn't possible. I wasn't the jealous type.

At the sight of me, Liam dropped his arm from the back of the sofa and sat up straight. Kristin uncurled her legs and twisted around to see me.

"Good morning, Elizabeth." Liam's wide, sexy smile greeted me.

"Good morning, Congressman." Fake, that's how I sounded, and I knew Liam caught it, too. I used that same tone when negotiating endorsements. Almost sickeningly sweet.

"You look lovely today," Kristin chimed in.

My gaze dropped to her and I graced her with a smile. "As do you. I'm so pleased you could *finally* break away from work to help Liam out on the trail. I know it must be a great sacrifice for you." Bitterness darkened my timbre. From the corner of my eye I noticed Liam stiffen. He didn't care too much for me going on the attack. Always protecting his precious Kristin.

Well, too bad. He'd have to deal, because Eliza-bitch was out in full force.

Kristin scooted back into the sofa, compacting herself. *You're still not invisible, darlin'. No matter how much you cower.*

"Are you all right, Elizabeth?" Scout questioned.

"Just peachy," I sang, my voice escalating with each syllable.

Aaron dropped down onto the arm of Scout's chair where he leaned in and stage whispered, "She's crabby today." He crossed his arms over his chest with an amused smirk spread across his face.

"No, I'm…"

Scout tucked a red curl behind her ear. "Why are you crabby? Sleep okay?"

"I'm not…"

"You look tired. Don't you think she looks tired?" Aaron nodded in Kristin's direction.

"Stop, I'm not…"

Kristin moved further away from Liam, wrapping her arms tighter around herself. "I really don't know her well enough to say."

"I'm fine!" I bellowed. "Now can we get to work?"

Liam sat, unmoved, staring at me.

I ignored him and proceeded to get down to business.

I reached into my briefcase to retrieve my tablet. "So fill me in on everything," I barked.

Scout scanned her notes, her nail clicking against the glass as she scrolled. Liam lifted from his seat. He slipped his fingers into the waistband of his slacks and adjusted his pants on his hips. I blinked back the memory of his fingers brushing along my warm skin and his mouth dominating mine. Liam buttoned his jacket and started to pace the floor behind the sofa. Because I wanted to maintain distance, I floated into the empty armchair, dropping my briefcase at my feet.

"We've already done a round of prep. I thought it was best if he sticks to the environment instead of going into education reform." Scout was being smart about the talking points. One of the many reasons I valued her.

"Agreed." I whipped my stylus out and began checking notes on my tablet. "But we need to be careful. I don't want him to be caught in a fracking debate. We need natural gas to keep backing us."

"Yes. I'm fully aware of that," Liam snapped.

"Good. We stick to the basics," I continued without pause to prove his little attitude didn't bother me. "Your intentions are to open viable water sources for cities affected by the drought. Leave anything to do with drilling out of it."

Liam stopped. He popped the button on his jacket and perched his hands at his hips. "I know that. I helped draft the bill."

"Of course." I graced him with a polished grin.

"Are we calling them or are they calling us?"

Scout jumped at the sound of my voice. Aaron twirled a strand of her hair around his finger.

"Focus," I bit, "The call?"

Scout maneuvered away from Aaron, her face turning as red as her hair. "They're calling us."

I glanced down at my watch. "Shouldn't they have called by now?"

Scout scrolled through her notes. "They said they'd call five minutes 'til. We still have ten more minutes."

Oh, great. Another ten minutes of this mess. I'd run out of things to discuss. Liam stopped behind the sofa, spread his arms out, and leaned forward. His dark gaze settled on mine, making me wish I were more like Kristin and could disappear into the seat cushion. His stare unnerved me. I dropped my eyes, and opened my score card. I had to do something to keep my mind off of the man who was once again pacing.

Each step he took became louder and louder in my ears. If he didn't stop, I couldn't promise I'd hold my tongue. I needed to get out of there. If only to recollect my thoughts and come back in strong and ready. Just as I was about to excuse myself to the restroom, a knock came at the door.

Thank God. A diversion.

"Um, are you expecting someone?" Aaron asked me.

"I'm not," I answered, sounding almost defensive.

"Liam?" Aaron directed to his brother.

"No, but will you go see who it is?" Liam adjusted his tie and nodded to Aaron, who jumped from his perch to answer the door.

A few seconds later, a familiar face appeared in the living room. "Howdy, y'all." Harper strolled in wearing his usual Wranglers, brushpopper, and boots. A black cowboy hat covered his head.

"Harper!" I exclaimed. I bounced out of my seat, tossed my tablet into the vacated spot, and met Harper for a friendly hug. "It's so good to see you. I wasn't expecting you until tomorrow."

"I have some business here today so I figured I'd stop by. Possibly treat y'all to supper later if you're available."

Harper slung his arm around my neck and turned me to face the group. Instantly my eyes found Liam. He'd taken my seat and was holding my tablet. My stomach curdled. I'd forgotten to set the screen lock. If he looked at my "Liam file", I was screwed. He'd find every photo I'd ever saved of him, including the pictures he'd sent to me of him in nothing but boxers and a tie.

Did I close the scorecard?

Shit! I couldn't remember.

I wanted to scream out for him to hand it over, but that sounded far too juvenile, even in my own head. In truth, our current standoff was puerile, but since I started it, I had to finish it.

I patted Harper on the back. "That sounds amazing. You're welcome to tag along if you want. You can keep Kristin company when she's not on stage with Liam."

"On stage?" Kristin screeched at the same time Liam squawked, "Absolutely not."

I smirked, chalking a new point to my count. "Why not? You too looked rather *cozy* together. I think it'd be a great plug for you. The prodigal *girlfriend* returns."

Liam stood up and dropped my tablet back onto the cushion. He marched toward Harper and me. I could see the fury burning bright behind those chocolate orbs. My hackles were up, ready to take him on, and this time I wouldn't back down. I'd win.

"You know she's not my girlfriend, and if you think..." Liam was cut off by the sound of the phone ringing.

"It's the station. It's time," Scout announced.

Damn. I was looking forward to his outrage. It meant I had control.

Liam stepped back, his face and neck red with rage and a vein pulsed in his forehead.

Liam adjusted his hideous purple paisley tie, and I decided that was the moment to go for the kill.

"And I also think you should lose that tie for the rally. Maybe go with something more suitable, like a nice blue tie." I pursed my lips, daring him to challenge me, but he couldn't. Scout thrust the phone into his hand and he had no choice but to answer.

As he made his greeting, I marched back to my seat and collected my tablet. Everything looked the same as how I'd left it, making me feel a little more at ease.

Liam paced the floor, burning the tension coiled inside him. I couldn't help but revel in my achievement. I was closing in on his lead now.

Elizabeth 34 - Liam 37.

Harper cocked his head toward the bedroom. I glanced in the direction of the room, my tablet clutched to my chest. Lord only knew what Harper wanted to talk about. "I'll be right back," I told Aaron and Scout. As I was about to say something to Kristin, I discovered she'd actually disappeared. The devil on my shoulder bounced with hope that she was in the bathroom puking her guts up at the thought of being on stage in front of thousands of people. I guessed the devil tied the angel on my shoulder up, because that bitch was silent.

I strolled toward Harper, but instead found myself face to face with Liam. The enormity of my emotions hit me straight in the chest as I met his eyes. His voice held a practiced joviality. The skilled tone of a true politician. But his face was marred with anger. Or was it jealousy? I rolled my eyes, pushing that thought aside, but my intuition refused to let it go. I wasn't a fool. I knew the man was interested in me, as I was him. That didn't change our circumstances, though.

I stepped to the side, bypassing Liam and headed to the bedroom. The instant the door closed behind us, Harper exploded. "Mind tellin' me what the hell is going on out there?"

I raised my hands in defense. "Whoa! What are you talking about?"

Harper swung his arm back and forth between me and the door. "I'm talking about this crap between you and Baxter. The tension is so thick you could cut it with a knife. We can't afford the two of you at each other's throats. It's bad business."

I wandered to the bed and sat down. "It's nothing to worry about, Harper. We simply had a misunderstanding. These things happen." I dropped my tablet beside me, this time checking to make sure my screen was locked.

Harper crossed his arms over his chest, shaking his head. "Not to you, Bet. You're always in control. But right now you're not, and I want to know why."

Liam Baxter might get me rattled, but I knew how to handle Guy Harper. I rose from the mattress, leaving my tablet, and approached Harper, slow and steady. "I assure you, I'm very much in control."

"Are you fucking him?" The tone of his voice was soulless, lifeless, so much that at first the question didn't register in my mind. When it did, I took a step back, shocked, but maintained my composure.

"I beg your pardon?"

Harper lifted his hat, running his fingers through his graying hair. "Fucked. As in had sex. Engaged in coitus." Still, no modulation in his voice. His stance, his mannerisms screamed defensive to me, but the forced way he managed his emotions felt wrong. I was missing something, and I couldn't quite put my finger on what it was.

"Why would you even ask me such a thing?"

"Answer the question, Bet."

I was stunned. This wasn't the Harper I knew. It was like someone had replaced my friend and left me to face off against a madman. We'd had confrontations before, but never had I seen him so callous. So disconnected.

My breathing accelerated. Fury burned through me. "How dare you question my ethics. Of course I'm not sleeping with the *kid*. I thought you knew me better than that."

Just saying those things left me feeling nauseous. If I'd had the opportunity the other night I would've slept with Liam. I would've crossed that line. Now it was evident to everyone, including Harper, that I harbored feelings for Liam, all because I lost control of my emotions.

That was bad business.

Damn Liam and his stupid kiss.

Harper's shoulders slumped in relief. The old Harper I knew seemed to reappear almost instantly. The ever southern gentleman emerged — smile, swagger, and all. He shoved his hands into his pockets. "I'm sorry, Bet. You're right. It was a stupid question."

I waved him off, chuckling. "It's okay. You were right in questioning. You have a lot of money invested in him. No harm done."

Harper gave me a quick wink and produced an endearing grin. "I see this man going places. I really do. I think with your help he can go all the way."

"I think he can, too. He's green, but smart."

Harper opened his arms to me. A little hesitant, I accepted his embrace. "Not smart enough if he's ruffling your feathers."

I patted his back and tried to pull away from the hug. "I can handle him. He's no match for me."

Harper tightened his grip around me, mussing my hair with his knuckles. "Now that I believe."

I smacked his hand away, squirming free. "Dammit, Harper!"

Harper belted out a hearty laugh, seemingly proud of himself. I reached around him for the door handle. "I need to get back out there. The interview should be nearing a close."

Harper smirked. "Are you really going to make him change his tie?"

I opened the door. "Nah, but it was fun busting his balls."

"That's my girl." Harper attempted to wrap his arm around my waist. I dodged his move, catching a glimpse of my reflection in the mirror adjacent from the bedroom. My hair was a mess and my blouse was rumpled from my encounter with Harper. I brushed my fingers through my hair and flattened my shirt as I rounded the corner, only to stop dead in my tracks at the sight of Liam nearing the door.

"Baxter," Harper marked.

"Liam." I grimaced, unable to take my eyes off him.

Liam cocked his head. His expression turned from dejected to irritated. "Elizabeth."

"Um. Is everything all right?" I questioned, locked in a motionless dance with Liam and Harper.

Scout shrugged. "The interview was perfect."

"Great. Wonderful," I blathered.

"I knew our boy could do it," Harper claimed, moving in closer behind me.

Liam tugged at his tie, loosening it around his neck. His chest puffed out and his focus burned on Harper and me. "Are you finished with *my* room?" It was rhetorical question, one he never intended on us to answer. "Good. I need to get ready," he rushed. "Apparently I need to change my tie to something more *suitable*."

Liam brushed past me, then clipped Harper's shoulder on his way to the room.

I pivoted around to catch the sight of Liam slamming the door behind him.

"What the hell's his problem?" Harper growled.

"I better go talk to him." My body lurched forward, ready to follow Liam, but Aaron's large hand reached out, grabbing my arm. I looked up, meeting his big green eyes. He shook his head, but said nothing. I nodded to his silent heeding.

It was my turn to feel like a caged lion. I had to escape. "On second thought, it's probably best to give him a chance to recoup from his interview. We need him on point today." I walked over and grabbed my briefcase, extracting my phone from the pocket. "You know, I need to make a few calls. I'll be down in the car whenever Liam's ready," I announced, making my way to the door.

Son of a bitch! I left my tablet on Liam's bed.

It irked me to leave it behind, but I really didn't need it at the moment, and since I knew the screen was locked this time, my secrets were safe. I'd grab it later.

As I opened the front door, I called out over my shoulder, "Oh, and Kristin, I changed my mind. It's probably best you don't appear on stage with Liam since you've already been absent for most of the trip."

"Thanks, Elizabeth," Kristin mumbled.

I nodded and slinked out of the room. This was supposed to be our day. The big one. Interviews, local coverage in his district, filming footage for his new campaign ads, and a major rally. I lived for days like this, but there I was, lost and confused. Things were messy, and I hated messy. I wanted to clear the air. To fix things.

Instead, I walked away — all in the name of politics.

Sixteen

Even with all the bullshit going on between us, never had I felt as proud of Liam as I did during the rally. He stood behind the podium, so tall and assertive, keeping his wit about him. Bold, honest, and on point, Liam inspired the crowd. He was the politician I'd waited my whole life to find. A true political unicorn. I watched, with a prideful grin, as he discussed the issues.

Since we'd left the hotel, the tension between us had mounted to unimaginable heights. We spoke, but it was clipped, calculated, and not once did he attempt to touch me. I never thought I'd fall apart over a man, and I wasn't about to do it now. However, if I allowed myself to linger on the divide between us, I might've found I could indeed lose my head over the situation at hand.

Good thing I had work to focus on. My job, his campaign was all that mattered.

Liam lifted his hand to adjust the tie at his neck. I cringed at the sight. I thought the purple tie was bad. In comparison to the one he wore now, the purple tie was a royal treasure. I wasn't a fish girl to begin with, but this tie made me detest fish. It was blood red with the face of what could only be described as a salmon at the tip. I was furious when he got into the limo wearing that hideous thing, but I refused to verbalize my complaints. He was goading me.

But I wouldn't fall into his trap. With his jacket closed and standing behind the podium, no one could see the ugly thing. From a camera angle, it appeared as if he were wearing a plain red tie.

Somewhat of a win for me.

Not really, but I'd take what I could get.

He leaned forward and rested his hands on the sides of the podium. "There is no denying we've disagreed on all aspects of these issues," he started. "Both parties have fought tooth and nail over this, but it goes deeper than mere politics. What it boils down to here is whether or not we, as a country, are willing to stand up and meet the challenge the next generation has presented us."

A roar of excitement rippled across the crowd. Banners reading "Vote Baxter" and "A Fresh Start" rose above the audience.

Oh, if only it wasn't considered bad sportsmanship to throw a fist in the air and whoop and holler, because I would've over that one. My boy just blew that shit up! He had them eating out of the palm of his hand.

My boy.

A smile tugged at the corner of my mouth, but was gone before it started. He wasn't mine and he wasn't going to be. The more I thought about things, the more determined I became. I needed to step back and not let my attraction to Liam get in the way of what was important. He was meant for great things and I'd be fooling myself if I thought I could fit into that picture as anything more than his consultant. I, who slung mud for a living, didn't deserve to bask in the light of a man like William Baxter.

"He's killin' it," Aaron whispered to me.

"He's on fire tonight." Pride exuded from my pores.

"Maybe you should rip his heart to shreds before every rally."

My head wrenched up to find Aaron's profile locked on Liam. "What's that supposed to mean?"

Aaron dropped his gaze to mine, his brows raised and a twisted smile warped his mouth. "The tie. You really pissed him off about the tie."

I swallowed and clutched my tablet to my chest. Liam had been kind enough to return it to me when they'd joined me in the motorcade. "I wish I hadn't mentioned it. I can only imagine what Stephen Colbert is going to say about this one." The talk show host had been on a rampage regarding Liam's ties from day one. So much for watching the Late Show tonight.

Aaron gave a hushed laugh. "Oh, he's going to have a field day with this one."

"Where does Liam find those things?"

"You'll have to ask him that."

Off in the distance, I heard my name. I turned my head to see who was calling me. It was one of Liam's recent contributors. A rich, old Texas oil man Harper had put in touch with me.

"Go," Aaron pushed. "I'll keep an eye on our boy."

I nodded and trotted off to make nice with big money. All for the win, I told myself.

All for Liam.

An hour later the rally ended, but that didn't mean my job was over. In fact, mine was only beginning. I was fielding calls, talking to constituents, and pretty much selling the shit out of my client. After this, he had secured himself as a major contender for the Senate seat.

Once the rally ended, I congratulated him, and walked away. That single handshake was more than my heart or mind could bear.

I didn't have time to deal with muddled emotions. So I compartmentalized.

Those feelings for Liam were put on the backburner, which meant avoiding him like a plague.

And that's what I did.

But it wasn't easy. I fluttered about the university auditorium, mingling with people but all the while I felt those intense, molten chocolate eyes on me. I'd catch a glimpse of his plump, smooth lips, or the way his dark hair fell across his forehead and my heart would tighten. His delicious skin, those long fingers, sculpted arms — everything about him beckoned me. But I wouldn't give into the temptation. Our little scuffle today proved my point. The professional boundary was imperative, no matter how much I wanted to throw caution to the wind.

Outside the auditorium, surrounded by college classrooms with their doors closed and locked, I shook hands with a straggler who was now on board with Team Baxter. Farewells and smiles bade, I watched as they exited the building. In need of numbers, I pivoted around to begin my search for Aaron or Scout.

There, at the end of the hall, standing outside the auditorium, stood Liam. I froze, locked under his spell. My heart jetted into overdrive. My breath hitched at the simple way his tongue darted over his lips.

The hall was empty. Not a single soul in sight.

Dammit!

That wasn't good. It left me vulnerable.

I had one of two choices. I could woman up, which meant ignoring his intense stare and acting as if this were any other day with any other client.

Easy enough, right?

Wrong.

That look in his eyes was lethal. At least to my ovaries.

Or I could make a run for it and pray no one noticed me being a chicken-shit.

My ovaries chose the latter.

I tucked my hands in my pockets, and as casual as possible, I turned my back on him and dashed around the corner. With no one in the halls, the clacking of my shoes seemed louder than normal, reverberating off the walls. I cringed with each step. It seemed the lighter I attempted to walk, the louder my steps got, but I kept moving.

I glanced over my shoulder to make sure I wasn't followed. When I was certain the coast was clear, I slammed my back against the lockers and covered my face with my hands. I fought back the burning ache in my chest. I was being silly, sure, I knew that, but I was allowed a moment of temporary insanity. And it was justified by my desire to save our careers from total annihilation.

I flattened my hands against the cool metal of the lockers. With my eyes closed, I breathed in deep through my nose.

Control. That's what I needed. Liam had been in control since the night of our kiss, and I hated him for it. I hated that I'd allowed myself to get caught up in the rush of the moment and given up a piece of myself in the process. Order. Precision. Power. Control. These were the things I understood. I must have them back.

Determined to regain my level footing in this relationship, I shook my hands at my side, and bounced a little at the knees. Calmed, I shoved off the lockers and tiptoed to the corner. A quick glance confirmed he wasn't there.

All clear.

Relief, and a little agony, panged inside me at his absence, but it was for the best.

"Looking for someone?" His deep voice rumbled from behind me.

I tried hard not to show any reaction, but he'd startled me. The man had stealth moves. He came out of nowhere!

Grr. All that military training of his was biting me in the ass.

I didn't even have to turn around to know he was in my personal space. The smell of his cologne enveloped me. I twisted around and just as I expected, he towered over me.

I lifted my face, faking poise. "Liam," I managed, sickened by the whimper in my tone. That wasn't my voice! Where was the fight? I pushed myself up, squaring my shoulders. So what if he caught me. I could handle this.

At least, that's what I thought until I felt the sweet caress of his breath on my face and basked in the aroma of peppermint and eucalyptus.

"Yes?" he rumbled, deep and throaty, causing me to tremble all over.

I pushed air out of my nose, forcing the girlish whims back. I would not fall prey to his charms, no matter how those eyes of his burned into my soul.

I tried to position myself so I seemed unfazed by his sudden appearance. He reached up and tucked my hair behind my ear. His touch was slow, deliberate, and lingering. I jutted my chin, fighting the desire to lean into his gentle caress.

"You wouldn't happen to be looking for me, would you?" he murmured.

"I, ah, um…" My jaw juddered with each grunt of my incoherent assembly of words. I dropped my gaze from his, shaking my head. "Ah, no. No." I tried to sound confident.

I failed.

"Look at me, Elizabeth." The command dominated me, and like the fool I was, I obeyed. I tilted my head, lifting my eyes to his. I opened my mouth to say something, anything, but nothing came out. I couldn't speak. I could barely breathe. All I could do was stare into the eyes of the man lofting over me.

"So I guess that means you're avoiding me then? After all, you're the one ducking around corners."

"I have no idea what you're talking about." I sounded off, but at least I held my wit.

He took another step toward me. "You've been avoiding me all night, Elizabeth."

My brain was on overload. His close proximity was killing my resolve. I pushed back against the very thing I wanted the most – to simply give into my desires. The pragmatic side of me took over, scratching and clawing to regain control.

"Congressman, if you haven't noticed, I've been busy doing what you hired me to do."

"I did hire you for a job. And I've been satisfied with you, until today."

"I beg your pardon?" I gasped. "I've just spent the last several hours selling you like you're God himself. Not to mention all the hours I've invested in this campaign."

"All of that's true, and I thank you, but at this moment I don't really care about the campaign. I want to know what happened today."

"I'm not sure I follow."

"You know exactly what I mean," he growled, his face dropping another inch closer to mine.

I did, but if he had to explain it to me, I took control of the situation. "I'm afraid I don't."

He chuckled, taking a step forward, forcing my back against the lockers.

I hit the metal with an oomph. My hands flattened against the cold steel. My eyes darted to the left and then to the right. This was bad. So bad. I began to freak over what our little standoff might look like to the media.

"Liam, we can't do this here. What about the media?" I tried to push him back, but his large form wouldn't budge.

"I don't care," he stated intensely.

"But I do. After tonight's rally..."

The corner of Liam's mouth quirked upward. "Forget the rally or the media. I want to know what happened."

An escape plan whirled inside my head. I had to get out of the cage he created around me. If not for me, then for him. He might not think about it now, but he would later when this was posted on every blog and television station across the nation.

"You were jealous of Kristin this morning," he thrummed deep in his chest.

I cocked my head to the side. "And what makes you think that?" I spouted off.

He dipped his head, his lips brushing the shell of my ear. "Because it's exactly why I reacted to Harper the way I did. Tell me that asshole didn't touch you in *my* room."

I withered at the feel of his tongue flicking my earlobe. All control was gone now. Kaput. Vanished. I was falling apart in his arms, which was the complete opposite of how he appeared to be. He seemed calm. Collected. Confident. Even while admitting he was vulnerable.

"You...you were jealous of Harper?"

"Yes," he breathed. "Insanely jealous."

I struggled with that concept. There was no reason to be jealous of Harper, then again there was no reason for me to be jealous of Kristin, and I was. "But why?"

Slow kisses trailed down my jaw. "Because of how you came out of my room all disheveled."

Teeth grazed along my neck, a flick of his tongue followed. A small squeak and a heavy gasp expelled from me. My hands reached around his back, digging into the fabric of his jacket.

"Nothing...nothing happened."

"Good," he growled. "Now, tell me why you're avoiding me."

"Because I can't resist you anymore."

Damn him for being able to pull the truth out of me.

"Then don't."

"But I must..." I mumbled as his mouth captured mine in a kiss that could ignite heaven and hell into a flame of glory. Earth would bow to such a kiss. The angels would sing.

His tongue slipped inside my mouth, exploring every inch, taking what was his. If my mind was working right, this kiss would've resulted in high alert, panic mode. Had someone from the media or a voter with a phone rounded the corner we'd be exposed. But I couldn't think. All I wanted was to taste him, to touch him, to claim him.

Drunk on his kiss, I felt lightheaded when he pulled back, his forehead pressed against mine. "This game stops now, Elizabeth. No more pushing me away. No more avoiding me. No more keeping score. Do you understand?" His hands slid up my sides, pinning my hips to the lockers. "Tell me you understand."

"Yes," I whimpered.

His brown eyes bore into mine with such intensity that any coherent thought escaped me. A playfulness in his devious grin tickled my insides. He reminded me of a cat that caught the mouse. Liam hooked his arm around my waist, pulling me flush to his body. His mouth once again captured mine.

My mind whirled with the feeling of his warm tongue exploring my mouth. My hands slipped into his hair, tangling into his soft locks. Liam's hand pressed into the small of my back, forcing my body to conform to his. Engulfed in his embrace, surrounded by all things Liam, I was lost to logic and reality.

Until he pulled back for a breath. That's when it hit me. "Wait? What do you mean no more taking score?"

Liam didn't move. He held steady with my gaze, his nose wrinkled and his eyes danced. "You have a file on me."

I clasped my hand over my mouth. "You invaded my privacy?" I shrieked. "How dare you?"

Liam shrugged a shoulder. "You vetted me. I was curious what you'd found. The tablet was there and I saw a file with my name on it. I wasn't expecting to find what I did, though. You're going to have to tell me how the scoring works."

"Damn you!" I tried to shove my way out of his arms, fury burning through me.

His grip tightened around me. "No. Don't you dare try to push me away again. I didn't know what I was looking at until it was too late. Had I known it was your personal stuff I wouldn't have looked."

"But you did!"

"And I loved what I saw!"

"What?"

Liam raked his fingers through his hair, streaming a long breath. "I loved that folder, Elizabeth. It means I get under your skin as much as you do mine."

Embarrassed, I dropped my gaze. "That's private."

"And I'm sorry for invading your privacy, but with the whole Harper thing and how you were acting this morning," — he touched his fingertips to the side of my face and let out a sigh — "I'm sorry. My jealousy got the better of me. Forgive me? Please."

How easy it would've been for me to slap him and march off. Had it been anyone else, I might've, but it was Liam. And I believed him. So, I gave a single nod.

"Good. Now, let's find the others and get out of here." His hands dropped from my body, slipping into mine. The clickety-clack of my heels reverberated through the halls as he rushed me toward the auditorium. "Wait. We can't go in there looking like this."

I pulled back, bringing us to a halt.

"Like what?" he asked, a little confused.

"Like this!" I exclaimed, pointing between the two of us. We were both beyond disheveled. His hair was rumpled, and his jacket askew. Liam glowed with this just been kissed flare. I reached up and combed his hair with my fingers. I adjusted his jacket and tie, snarling at the hideous thing. "Just so you know, I'm burning this tie."

"Why?" he balked. "This is an amazing tie."

"No. It's not."

He pulled the knot and slipped the tie from around his neck and tucked it into his pocket. With a flick of his fingers, he popped the top button of his shirt and grinned. "Better, Ms. McNeal?"

I nodded and smiled. "Much. Now, how do I look?"

"Absolutely stunning." He leaned in and pressed a soft kiss to my lips. "And I love how kissed your mouth looks right now"

I gasped, covering my mouth. "Oh, God. What if someone notices?"

Liam kissed the tip of my nose. "Let them notice, Elizabeth."

"Absolutely not! For all intents and purposes, you're with Kristin."

"I'm with you," he proclaimed.

"You're with me?"

A radiant smile lighted his eyes. "If you want me to be."

I did want him. I wanted him so bad, but this was stupid and risky.

I opened my mouth to speak, but Liam stopped me. "Don't, Elizabeth. Don't over think this." He cupped my face in his hands. "It's a simple yes or no. If you want me, I'm yours. If you don't, I'll walk away and we'll go back to being nothing more than a candidate running for office and his handler."

A sudden burst of numbness struck me. "Could you really walk away?"

"It wouldn't be easy, but if that's what you want, I'll do it."

"Then you're stronger than me."

He leveled me with his gaze, as he dropped a tender kiss to my lips. I closed my eyes, caught in the wake of our kiss. Where all the others were passion filled, this one was different. His soft lips caressed mine causing my heart to ache. There was no rush, no push, only sweet truth in his actions. The truth that neither of us could fight this, even if we wanted to. When he finally broke free, he brushed his knuckles along my cheek. "Not so strong, I'm afraid." He tapped the tip of my nose. "Now, let's go see a man about some grub. I'm starved."

"What about Harper? Shouldn't we call him? He did offer to take us to dinner."

"Fuck Harper."

"Nah. He's not my type."

Liam laughed deep inside his chest. I liked the sound of his laughter. There was a sense of home about it. He touched his knuckles to my cheek. "C'mon, you silly woman. Let's get out of here."

We set off to find the remainder of our staff. Liam, respecting my need for discretion, walked beside me, his hand hovering over the small of my back but never touching. He'd done this a million times before, but this time was different. We were different. And I liked it.

I hated when our Texas trip came to an end. Liam and I had taken to meeting up in the middle of the night on the tour bus to make out. It damn near killed me every time he put on the brakes. I often felt like the man of the relationship, telling him we'd wait until he was ready, but damn if I didn't have to take care of my lady-boner after every make-out session was over. I never quite understood the term *rub one out* before now, but thanks to Liam, I was doing a lot of rubbing.

The hardest part of returning to DC was facing reality. On the bus, it was just us. Back home it was the campaign, constituents, and bills in constant need of our attention. Liam spent most of his time on the Hill while I busted my ass at headquarters. His lead in the polls was growing in ways we'd never anticipated. I didn't have to come up with any kind of dirt on Keating to help him. Not that I didn't have a stockpile on her already. The woman was the epitome of a dirty politician.

I was pouring over the new mailers Brandy had dropped on my desk when my cell phone rang. I glanced down to find a text message from Jordyn.

Jordyn McNeal: Where are you?

I looked at the clock. It was half past eight. Shit! I'd lost track of time. I was supposed to have met Jordyn for dinner over an hour ago.

Elizabeth McNeal: I'm so sorry. On my way.

Her response came back rather quick.

Jordyn McNeal: Not at the restaurant. Picked up pizza. See you at home.

I collected my things and hightailed it out of the office, but not before glancing out my window at the Capitol. Liam was up there pulling some last minute votes. A smile appeared on my lips at the thought of him, but no matter how much I loved spending time with him, there was always this little nagging voice in my head telling me I was being a fool. I was too old for him and he couldn't afford a scandal.

That didn't mean I listened to the voice. Much.

An hour later, I pulled into the driveway, shocked to see two cars parked in front of my house. One was Jordyn's little blue Volkswagen Beetle she had to have on her sixteenth birthday. The other I knew all too well from its usual spot at HQ — Liam's.

A plethora of quandaries passed through my mind all at once. From *how on earth did Liam get my address* to *oh, God, he's in there alone with Jordyn*. No one, not even Jordyn, knew about Liam and me. It was safer that way.

I parked my car by the curb and checked myself in the mirror. This was one of those rare days I allowed myself to dress casual for work. I donned a Vote Baxter for Senate t-shirt that the volunteers wore, jeans, and sneakers. My hair was pulled up into a high ponytail, which I quickly tugged down and combed my fingers through. I applied a fresh coat of lipstick and slipped out of the car.

I found the front door unlocked. Once inside, I heard two voices floating from the kitchen. I dropped my briefcase at the door and padded down the hall, following the delicious aroma of pizza and the peals of laughter. My legs halted at the door of the kitchen, my chest struck at the sight before me. Liam and Jordyn sat across from each other, half eaten pizza plated in front of them, and both grinning ear to ear.

Most women probably would've soared with delight over their daughter and their...whatever Liam was to me...getting along, but to me all I could think of was how natural they looked together. From the start I'd fought how I felt for him because of our age difference and now, seeing him and my child together, it hit me like a ton of bricks.

I chewed my cuticle, watching them for a few minutes. From where I stood, I had a clear view of Jordyn's face, and Liam's side profile. I tried not to dwell on how strong his jaw looked with a couple of days' worth of stubble. He must've been sleeping on the Hill. His shirt was fresh, but the crease in his slacks was a little flat and, lucky for me, he lacked a tie.

"But seriously, Congressman, Pipe was phenomenal," she gushed. "I've never felt such a rush."

"I told you, call me Liam, and yeah, I know what you

mean. But you really could've hurt yourself during that wipe out. You've got to be careful." A low chuckle rumbled from him. "As if I have any room to talk. I've wiped out too many times to count out there."

"That's so awesome!" Jordyn sunk her teeth into her pizza. "But do me a favor, don't tell Mom. She'll flip out."

She wasn't kidding. I was freaking at the thought of her wiping out on the Banzai Pipeline. It was one of the reasons I'd struggled letting her go to Hawaii in the first place. The other was a boy, but that was a whole other story. To know she could've been hurt, it took everything I had not to barge in and give her a piece of my mind.

"I can't make any promises," Liam stated, picking up his slice. "If for some odd reason your mother asks me, I'll tell her. I won't ever lie to her."

"Ugh! She scares you, too. Damn you politicians. You realize she's not God, right?"

Liam chuckled through a mouthful. "You sound just like her."

"Don't say that!" Jordyn screeched.

Liam dropped his slice of pizza on the plate. "You should take it as a compliment. Your mother's an amazing woman."

Jordyn sucked cola through a straw. "She is pretty awesome."

I couldn't help but smile, but I did feel a little guilty for eavesdropping on their private conversation.

A lull of silence ensued between them. I was about to step in when Jordyn swallowed down her bite. "You like Mom, don't you?"

Liam had taken a swig of the beer I assumed Jordyn

had offered him. At least it wasn't my underage daughter drinking. "Of course I do. She's the best consultant in the business."

"That's not what I mean," Jordyn stated matter-of-factly.

"You talk around things just like she does, too."

"Then let me be frank. You have feelings for my mother."

Damn my child and her keen senses!

My heart rate ramped up in my chest. My palms began to sweat. I couldn't believe that Jordyn would raise such a question. I swallowed down the thick lump that formed in my throat, hanging on what he might say next.

Liam linked his fingers and pressed his locked knuckles to his mouth. A slight smile appeared on his full lips. "Yes."

There was no pretext, no subterfuge, it was simple yes. Nothing more.

"She likes you, too, you know," Jordyn noted.

I damn near choked on my own spit.

Liam leaned back in his chair, scratching his fingernail along the edge of the plate. "Has she told you that?"

Jordyn laughed hard. "You know my mother, Liam. Do you think she's told me anything?"

He chewed the inside of his cheek, then joined in her laughter. "What makes you think such a thing?"

"Because never have I seen her as happy as she's been since you two returned from Texas."

"Are you sure she's not excited that I have a hefty lead in the polls?" he joked.

But Jordyn turned rather serious. "I know her political

game face. That's not what she's sporting. She blushes. She giggles. My mother doesn't giggle, and she certainly doesn't blush."

Liam snorted. "God, you really are your mother's daughter."

"Psh!" Jordyn motioned him off with a roll of her eyes. "Joke all you want, but I'm right."

"What makes you think it's me?"

Jordyn shoved the pizza crust in her mouth, chewing methodically. "Because" —she swallowed down her bite— "you're the only man in her life besides Uncle Harper, and I know for certain it's not him. Besides, it's always your name she blushes over."

I wanted to yell out at her, *I don't blush!*

"You're observant like she is, too."

Jordyn leaned forward, meeting Liam's gaze. "That I am, and I'm warning you, if you hurt her, I'll make it my mission in life to see your political career rank down there with Hoover or Bush."

"Which Bush?" Liam popped off.

"Take your pick. They're all shit."

Liam dropped his head back in laughter. "And they're all Republicans."

On that note, I had to break up the little party. After I exhaled a deep, cleansing breath and plastered a polished smile on my face, I stepped into the kitchen.

"Hey there, you two," I chirped.

Liam jumped up from his chair and turned to me, but Jordyn slinked down further into her seat. Her smile widened as she crossed her arms over her chest. "Nice of you to join us," she cooed with a wink.

So she knew I was there. Go figure. My sneaky little girl.

I'd taught her well.

"Good evening, Elizabeth. I hope you don't mind my being here. I stopped by and your lovely daughter let me in," he rambled.

"Actually, he was sitting outside when I got here. I felt kind of sorry for him."

Liam narrowed his gaze at Jordyn and I couldn't stop the bout of laughter that bounded out of me. "I completely understand. He's kind of like a stray puppy, isn't he?" I teased, stepping around to the fridge and grabbing myself a beer. "You can't help but want to rescue him." I popped the metal cap off the bottle and took a long swig.

Liam tucked his hands into his pockets. "Great. Two McNeal woman giving me shit. I've entered the ninth circle of hell."

"With Mom, I'd say more like the second, but what do I know of ancient texts," Jordyn razzed.

"Isn't that the lust circle?" Liam probed.

I smacked my hand over my face. Damn college kids and their literature courses. "Jordyn, how about another slice," I interceded before she could answer.

Jordyn popped up from her chair, giving Liam a pat on the back. "Nah. I gotta head out." She collected her empty paper plate from the table, but I stopped her before she could dispose of it in the trash can. "Wait? You can't leave now. I just got here."

She side-stepped me and deposited her plate into the trash. "That's why I wanted to do dinner at seven. I have an exam tomorrow that I gotta study for. I'll stop by your office afterward for lunch. Is that okay?"

I brushed her soft red hair away from her face. She'd inherited that trait from her father's Scottish heritage. Or at least that's what I always assumed. "Yeah. That's fine. I'm sorry I lost track of time at work today. I'll make it up to you tomorrow."

Jordyn pulled me into a hug. "I know you will, Mom. I'll see you tomorrow. I love you." She pressed a kiss to my cheek and then thrust a hand at Liam. "And it was a pleasure meeting you, Congressman. You'll be happy to know, you have my vote."

Liam graced her with a sweet smile and shook her hand. "I consider that a great honor."

"As you should." Jordyn grabbed her bag off the island and draped it over her chest. "Layta, Bitchas!" She waved.

"Language!" I yelled out after her, shaking my head.

Liam sat back down at the table, laughing as the front door slammed shut. "What are you laughing at?" I demanded.

"Only that I've heard you use much worse language than *bitchas* when a poll doesn't go your way."

I settled into the chair Jordyn had vacated and opened the pizza box on the table. Mushroom and olives, my favorite. "Just because I curse like a sailor doesn't mean my daughter should."

He scratched his ear. "I don't think you curse like a sailor, really. You have your moments, but usually you're well collected."

I sank my teeth into the cheesy goodness, savoring the flavor. I couldn't recall the last time I'd eaten today. For that matter, in the last twenty-four hours. Somehow I'd managed to survive off of English breakfast tea. I swallowed down my bite with a swig of my beer. "So, what has you calling tonight?" I grabbed a napkin, wiping my mouth. "And how do you know where I live?"

Liam laughed, chugging down the rest of his beer. "I got your address from Aaron."

"You could've just asked me for it."

"I was afraid you wouldn't give it to me."

I nodded. He was right, I probably wouldn't have.

Liam reached over and twirled a lock of my hair around his finger. He stared at me for a protracted moment, swallowed thickly, and dropped his hand. "You know what, this was a bad idea." He jumped up from his chair and rushed out of the kitchen.

A little shell shocked, I pursued him, calling his name. He didn't stop. He reached the front door and placed his hand on the knob. "Look, I'm really sorry. I wasn't thinking. I interrupted your evening with your daughter. Gah, I'm an idiot. I just thought... We hadn't really seen each other since we returned..." His head dropped. "Never mind. I'll be by headquarters tomorrow. I'll see you there."

Hesitant at first, I reached around him, taking his hand from the doorknob. In a gentle motion, I turned him to face me. His eyes were squeezed closed, his face scrunched tight. His whole body tensed. "Liam," I rasped, "look at me."

Those long lashes of his fluttered open. There, in his dark orbs, was everything he wanted to say, but couldn't seem to put into words. I touched my fingers to his stubble dusted jaw. In an instant his muscles loosened. I pushed up on the tips of my toes and pressed my lips to his. His hands gently cupped my face, his thumbs caressing my cheeks as his mouth moved in time with mine.

An eternity passed, and when he released me, wave upon wave of emotions rolled over me. This wasn't like making out. There was meaning behind this kiss, a power that had manifested itself inside me without me even realizing it. This was the same feeling I'd experienced after the rally.

He stared into my eyes, searching. Whatever he was looking for, I was certain he found it as a smooth smile settled on his freshly kissed lips.

"I've missed you so much. It's killed me not being with you."

"I've missed you, too," I concurred.

Liam traced the lines of my face with his fingers. His movements were slow and intimate, causing me to wither beneath his touch. As his hand slid down my neck between my cotton clad breasts, he whispered, "I've ached to touch you. I want you so bad that I've dreamt of what it would feel like to make you mine."

God help me, I wanted him, but this was risky. On the bus, it would've been clean. No one but us would know. But now he was parked outside my house. There was a reason why I wouldn't have given him my address. If the media ever caught wind of his car parked outside — all night — it would certainly make the headlines.

Up next on the ten o'clock news: Senate hopeful, William Baxter, caught in sex act with his campaign manager.

I cringed at such a thought.

With that in mind, I knew I had a choice to make.

Either, I could fulfill the hunger that was burned inside me and throw caution to the wind, or send him away and save us both.

There was only one answer to my dilemma.

"Make me yours."

The last syllable was barely off my tongue before his lips came crashing down on mine. His hands dropped to my waist, pulling me tight against his hard body. I wrapped my arms around his neck, yearning to be closer. His mouth was hungry, desperate to be sated. Everything inside me waited for him to put on the brakes. He always did when we came this close, but it didn't happen. Not this time.

His tongue coaxed my mouth open, sliding inside. Intensity mounded between us. Each stroke of our tongues expressed a sense of urgency that neither of us could fight against. The flame of desire was no longer an ember, it was a forest fire, burning wild and out of control. I was consumed by my unwavering need for this man.

Without warning, Liam pulled back. His face was wild with passion. His hands moved to the hem of my shirt, bunching the soft cotton beneath his fingers. Questioning eyes smoldered, giving me one last chance to back out. But there was no escape for me. I was in it, lock, stock, and barrel.

"Take me," I breathed.

"With pleasure," he growled.

Eighteen

Our mouths collided. It didn't matter where he touched me as long as I felt his hands on me. In one swift move, he shoved my back against the cool wood of the door, pinning me between it and his rock hard body.

In my arms he came to life. Wild, ferocious, and unrestrained. All this time he'd held back. Always the perfect gentleman on the bus, but now my caged lion was freed.

I almost screamed when he stopped kissing me, certain he was about to put on the brakes yet again. He pulled back, his mouth parted, panting. He pushed my hair back from my face, staring into my eyes. Lust and longing transformed his features from a man of power to a man of carnal prowess.

He lifted an eyebrow, a smirk turning his lips. He

gripped my waist, and pushed his knees between my legs. "I see it in your eyes," he purred. "How you want me to fuck you right here against this door."

My insides clenched tight. He'd pegged me right.

"I'm not going to, though."

What!

He gripped my hair in his fist, twirling it several times around his hand. I gulped back a yelp when he yanked my head back against the door. "Instead, I'm going to show you how a real man can make you feel." He dragged his tongue down my neck, tasting me inch by inch, until he reached the hollow of my throat. "You've never been fucked the way I'm about to fuck you." His smooth confidence convinced me without so much as feeling him that I was in for the ride of my life.

My eyes widened and my mouth gaped as he ground his pelvis into me. I tried to move my hands between us, wanting to expose what I was feeling inside his pants, but he wouldn't have it. He released my hair as he grabbed both my hands and pinned them against the door, securing them beneath his oversized palm. He shook his head, his eyes scolding me for my insubordination as he drove his erection into me.

"What do you think you're doing?" he demanded, squeezing my wrists.

I pursed my lips. This was a challenge, and I loved a challenge.

"Why, Congressman, you're not the only one with moves." I dropped my eyes to his crotch, smirking at the twitch in his pants.

I leaned forward and flicked my tongue along the

smooth surface of his mouth. He growled and parted his lips, allowing me to taste his sweet tongue against mine. I reveled in my success, however my momentary control of him was merely an illusion. He circled his hips against mine, and sucked my tongue deeper into his mouth. In that single action, I was defeated. All power lost. And I loved it.

Liam released my hands, stepping back from me. He toyed with the hem of my shirt and his eyes bright with mischievousness. "Arms. Up."

Lesson learned the last time, I did as I was told. He curled his fingers into my shirt and yanked it over my head, tossing it aside in a heap on the floor. He traced the tip of my bra with his finger, causing goose flesh to explode across my skin. Liam lowered his head, his eyes honed in on mine as he captured my silk-covered nipple between his teeth. My whole body pulsed while he sucked and rolled my hard, sensitive pebble with his tongue. I inched my hands out to touch him only to be met with a warning glare. I pounded my fists against the door, hyperaware of his dominance over me, but aching to touch him.

A sultry grin pursed his lips. "Don't make me go out to my car to get a necktie," he warned.

My fuzzy brain was lost on that one, and he didn't mind clarifying. "To tie you up with, Lizzy. Good and tight, so you can't move or see."

Oh!

"You wouldn't."

"Try me," he dared.

My mouth dropped at his insinuation. He captured my untouched nipple between his teeth, repeating the same torture. I clenched my fists, withering against the hard wood. Brazen moans tumbled from my lips. I wanted to feel him, everywhere. I needed to feel that hard body, naked and hot, plummeting into mine. I thrust my pelvis forward, utilizing the seam of my jeans to gain some much needed friction. All those make-out sessions on the bus never prepared me for this.

Liam released my nipple and gripped my hips. "Not yet. I've waited a long time for this, and I'm going to take my time. Do you understand?"

He'd waited a long time? Jesus! Fuck! If the US Military wanted to torture a woman for information, this was the perfect way to do it. My panties were soaked through and he still had me practically clothed.

"But I need you," I shamelessly whined, puckering my bottom lip into a pout.

He clamped down on my lower lip, sucking it hard between his teeth. He released my tender flesh with a pop and grinned. "I need you, too, but I want you every which way I can have you. I'm going to lick, bite, suck, and tease you until you're on the brink of madness. And when you think you can't take anymore, I'm going to do it all over again. I'll keep doing it until you finally give yourself over to me...completely."

Oh, those words. Those sexy as fuck words. If I hadn't already been drenching wet, I would've been with those words. Liam pressed his palm in between my legs, rubbing me with the hilt of his hand. I cried out at the much needed pressure. "You like that." There was no question. He already knew my response. This was no inexperienced boy. This was a man to whom I was helpless to struggle against.

"Yes."

He took two fingers and pushed upward into my jeans. His mouth grazed my jaw. "Imagine how good it's going to feel when I'm pumping them hard and fast inside you. I will know your every moan, whimper, and cry. I will memorize the way you shudder as you come for me. Now, tell me, where's your bedroom?" His low growl resonated deep into my core.

I blinked. "Um, upstairs. First door on the left."

Liam stepped back from me, grabbed my hand, and dashed us up the stairs.

At my bedroom door, he swung me around to face him, crushing his mouth to mine. He managed to push me backward into the bedroom while fondling the button of my jeans. By the time my knees hit the back of the bed, I'd kicked off my shoes and he was dragging the dark denim down my legs.

I stood before him in nothing but my bra and panties. Much like my uncustomary wardrobe for the day, my lingerie also wasn't my typical. My very wet bra was silvery silk and my panties plain white cotton. I was embarrassed that he didn't see me well put together. He hooked his thumb into the waistband of my panties, his long fingers slipping down and curving into my heated center. "Better than I imagined," he purred. "Very sexy."

My knees buckled as his fingers explored beneath my cotton undies. He watched me, squirming against his fingers and just as I thought I might explode, he pulled his hand back, catching me around the waist before I fell to the bed.

"I'm not ready for you there," he rasped.

My wobbly knees shook as he held me close to his still

fully clothed body. I pressed my hands to his chest, tapping the buttons of his shirt. A single blink of his eyes granted me permission to remove it. I popped each button, pressing my mouth to his warm skin as it became exposed. All the way down my tongue flicked against his sinewy muscles, tugging the fabric from his body. When it was fully open, I slipped my hands underneath and pushed it down his arms, slow and steady.

"Better?"

"Not quite. I want to see all of you," I beseeched, reaching for his belt.

Liam placed a finger under my chin and tilted my head back. "You've seen me naked. It's my turn to see you."

"But..."

His mouth crashed into mine, stopping my rebuttal.

Slowly, his hands moved to unhook my bra. He slipped the silky material from my body and dropped it at my feet. He grazed his teeth over his bottom lip, his eyes moving down to my naked breasts. "And I thought seeing my name plastered across your amazing tits was a beautiful sight to behold. God, I was a fool."

Okay, that made me blush. He'd noticed my unusual apparel. Apparently he also approved. Most of all he enjoyed my breasts.

Eat that, stupid plastic surgeon!

He brushed my cheeks with his knuckles and gave me a quick wink before sliding the backs of his fingers down my chest, between my breasts. My nipples were hard as rocks, arching toward him, almost begging him to claim them. He graciously obliged, taking each one into his large palms, and tracing circles with his thumbs. I hissed at the sweet yet torturous sensation.

But he didn't stay put for long. His hands passed down the plains of my stomach until he reached the waistband of my panties. Liam dipped his fingers below the fabric, slowly pushing them down my legs. As my panties inched down, Liam dropped to his knees before me. I stepped out of my cotton bikinis and watched as he threw them aside. He looked up at me, licked his lips, and grinned.

My knees buckled the instant his tongue tickled along my delicate skin. I rested my hands in his hair, thankful that he didn't protest. All I could think of was lying back on the bed, but his arms held me up, refusing to let me go.

The earth shattered into a million pieces with each flick of his tongue. I bucked my hips and yanked his hair. Oh, the delicious sounds he made and the way they vibrated against me almost sent me over the edge. Sensing my imminent release, Liam eased his pace. Each lick was soft and kept me teetering, but for me it wasn't enough. I thrust my hips forward, trying to force him to suck me harder.

Instead he released me. "Uh huh," he murmured, nudging his nose along my pelvis. "Not until I say."

My stomach was so tight that I found it difficult to breathe. I scraped my nails along his scalp and cried out as he flicked his tongue in all the right places. His warm breath coursed over me as he swirled and lapped, relentlessly tasting me. When I crumpled, unable to maintain my position, he released me and allowed me to fall back to the bed.

Liam stood up, his focus honed in on my body spread out before him. I wiggled against the duvet. "I can't," I pleaded, kneading the soft cover. "I need…"

Nothing made any sense to me. This man, this gorgeous man had my body shaking without having entered me. I'd never experienced anything like that in my life. Sure, I knew what an orgasm was. I'd had my fair share, but this, this was unlike any orgasm I'd ever experienced.

Liam reached down and touched his fingers to me. As his fingers slipped inside, I quivered and shook, rocking my hips against his hand.

So close. Oh, so close. I was there. Ready to fall off the edge when he pulled his fingers away from my body.

I looked up, dying inside yet never having felt more alive. Liam pursed his lips and unbuckled his belt. I panted for air as he unzipped his pants and released his hard length that had been straining beneath. "I have all night to play with you," he growled. "Seeing you lying there, I can't take it anymore."

I slammed my fists down on the bed, and cried out in relief, "Finally!"

Liam howled in laughter, stroking his impressive length in his hand. "How often have I invaded your dreams, Lizzy?" His hand coasted down his shaft. "Me, taking you like this?"

I chewed on my bottom lip, enraptured by his hand moving where I wanted my body to be wrapped around. "Since the first time I saw you," I admitted, a little embarrassed to be giving voice to my dirty, little secret.

"You liked what you saw that night?"

No words escaped me as he inched closer to the bed, pressing his knees against it. He smirked, and rubbed his thumb across the tip.

"I love what I see now."

I opened myself wider to him, ready for him to take all of me, when suddenly he stopped. A deep line buried itself into his forehead. "Shit," he snarled.

I leaned up on my elbows, fearing he might've changed his mind. "What's wrong?"

"I don't have a condom." He ripped at his hair, growling in anger. "I only wanted to see you. I wasn't planning..."

I sat up and met him at the foot of the bed. Emboldened, I pressed a kiss to his stomach, wrapping my hand around his erection. "That makes this even better."

Slowly I started to stroke his smooth, hard length. He closed his eyes, savoring the pressure of my hand on his pulsating need.

"But we can't..."

"Down the hall, second door on the right. In the nightstand you'll find a package of condoms." I circled my thumb around him, smirking at the way he pulsed in my hand.

"Really?"

I nodded. "It's Jordyn's room."

"How do you know your daughter has condoms in her room?"

I wiggled my brows. "Because I'm the one who bought them for her. I personally believe if a girl's in a relationship she should be prepared to take care of herself."

Liam pressed a kiss to the tip of my nose, while unhooking my fingers from around him. "God, you're an amazing woman."

I wrinkled my nose and laughed, smacking his firm

ass. "Go get the condoms."

He was gone in a flash. By the time I'd moved to the top of the bed, Liam was back in the room with the box in hand. He slipped the rubber over him, and knelt down on the end of the bed. The mattress shifted under his weight as he crawled up toward me. He settled between my thighs, his tip pressed into my aching need.

Somewhere between his departure and him slipping on the condom, the mood between us changed. The dirty man who claimed to torture me until I was falling apart morphed into the sweet man I knew so well. His face transformed and his eyes softened. He pushed my hair back from my face, my heart was racing so hard I was certain he could feel it against his chest.

"Beautiful," he whispered.

All at once, his mouth fell to mine and his body filled me. He linked our hands together, drawing them above my head. In that moment, we were connected in every way possible. Soul to soul. Heart to heart. Body to body. Our passion consumed us. He thrust into me, our hips meeting in perfect ecstasy.

He'd teased my body so much it was instantly ready to find its release. And it did. I cried out as my climax overtook me, only to have those cries swallowed down by Liam who refused to release my mouth from his kiss. His hands locked tighter around mine and his hips pushed faster and harder into me. He was gentle, reverent even, but his movements were jagged. Again and again he plunged into me, taking what he knew was his.

When he met his own release, it was the most magnificent thing I'd ever witnessed. He wrapped his arms around me, holding me close to him. His whole body shook. His moans were deep and sated. There was something about the feel of him losing control in that brief moment that brought about another climax for me. Together, we reached the stars of intimacy.

Liam gently kissed my lips. "God, I wanted to last longer than that," he groaned, his forehead dropping to mine.

I wrapped my hands around his face, pulling his head back so I could see into those deep, soulful eyes. "Round one, or are we out for the count for a little while?"

He chuckled. "Oh, sweetheart, we've only just begun."

I squealed as he grabbed the covers beneath me. He ripped them down and pulled them over our heads, thus beginning round two.

Nineteen

More times than I could count, Liam claimed me. When he said he would torture me until I submitted myself to him, he wasn't kidding. And while my body buzzed with energy from his mastery of sex, my favorite moment was waking up in his arms, just before sunrise.

That was also my least favorite moment, for it was then he had to leave me. If I'd had my way, we'd have stayed locked up in that room and forgot the world existed outside, but that wasn't an option.

Politics didn't stop for sex. It might take a break, but it didn't stop.

Liam pressed a sweet kiss to my temple, his nose nuzzling my tangled locks. "Will you come to my place tonight?"

I tilted my head, kissing his chin. "Why?"

He tapped the tip of my nose with his fingertip.

"Because I need to be close to work, but I also want to be with you." He brushed his knuckle along my jaw, drawing my mouth to his. It was impossible to resist him when he kissed me like that.

"Okay. I'll be there."

He pecked my lips once more. "I have to head out, but I'll be by headquarters sometime today."

He slipped out of my arms and got out of my bed. Even disheveled from a night of naughtiness, he was still perfect. I rested on my elbow and watched as he got dressed. When he was fully clothed and ready to leave, I lifted up to join him. Liam raised a hand, stopping me. "Get some rest."

"I'm just walking you to the door."

He sat down on the bed beside me. His long fingers smooth my messy tresses. "I know if you get out of this bed, you won't get back in. I can see myself out." He pressed a sweet kiss to my lips, his palm stroking the bare skin of my arm.

"Fine. You win."

"I always do," he gloated.

"Gah!" I shoved him away, flopping back down on the mattress. His addicting laugh blanketed me.

As he started out of the bedroom, he cocked his head, glancing at me over his shoulder. "If I haven't told you yet, I want you to know how amazing you are."

"You're not too bad yourself."

"Not too bad?" He feigned insult. "Well, if that's the case I better kick it up a notch tonight."

I giggled, shuffling under the sheets. Was it even possible for him to outdo himself?

"I think you better," I jibbed.

He gave me a quick wink. "I'll see you later."

I chewed my bottom lip, as he walked out of my room.

No sooner had the front door close that I covered my face and started kicking my feet.

For the second time with Liam, I'd opened myself up to him. I admitted how much he consumed me. I allowed myself to cross the line. I lost control.

Damn him and his stupid superpower!

Last night had been beautiful to the point of perfection. So what if I allowed myself to open up to him. There were worse things that could happen.

Like someone finding out about us.

The more I pondered the ramifications of my actions, the antsier I felt. There was no way I'd find sleep with my head running ninety miles an hour. So, I got out of bed, and took a long, hot shower. Every muscle and bone in my body ached. While the shower helped some with the physical, it failed to ease my mind.

I'd slept with my client. I crossed an unethical line. Worse yet, I was officially a cougar!

Sometime later, I pulled myself together enough to get dressed and head into work.

At headquarters, I rushed to my office, too absorbed in my thoughts to even say hello to the staff. I had a headache coming on that trumped all headaches.

Once inside my office, I closed the door and dropped into my chair. My purse and briefcase landed on my desk with a thud. I dropped my head in my hands, contemplating my next move. I'd had a taste of Liam. There was no going back from that. I could end it. That'd be the smart thing to do. Then again, I never claimed to be smart. I claimed to be good. Good at hiding stuff that no one wished to be found.

That was my only solution. I'd cover up the truth.

No, I did not have sexual relations with that man.

It was official. I was losing my marbles.

A rap at the door tore me from my head. I glanced up to find Scout standing in the doorway. Her hair was piled high on top of her head and the small freckles on her nose matched the khaki blazer she wore.

"Damn, girl! You look amazing today. You're practically glowing," she complimented, as she stepped inside and dropped into the chair before me.

"I didn't get much sleep," I grumbled.

It was the truth after all.

"It doesn't show. You look fantastic. Did you do something new with your hair?"

I rubbed the back of my neck, trying to emulate the same motions Liam had used to get rid of my headache on the bus. "If you mean did I forget to brush it this morning; more than likely." I shrank back a little. "Um, hey, is Aaron here yet? I want to know if the new polls are in."

Scout shook her head. "He's on the Hill with Liam today. They should be in later. Would you like for me to call him?"

I shook my head. If Aaron came over, then Liam would follow. I wasn't ready to face him in front of people yet. My body still hummed with the memory of him pulsing inside me, and my imagination created a horrific scenario in which the whole office would instantly know we'd had sex.

"Nah. Just have one of the staffers bring the numbers

by. I've got a lot of work to do today and I can't wait on them to arrive."

"Anything I can help with?"

"Not right now, but if something comes up, I'll let you know."

Scout stood and backed toward the door. "All right, boss. I'll be here if you need me."

"Thanks," I muttered, firing up my laptop.

I was in for a very long day.

Hours passed, and before I knew it, I heard a knock at the door.

"It's open," I called out.

"Hey, Mom. You ready for lunch?" My eyes darted to the clock on the wall.

Damn, where had the time gone?

"You forgot," she grumbled, parking herself in front of me.

"I didn't. I was just finishing up here." I closed my laptop, thankful for her distraction. I'd barely gotten any work done, my mind replaying the previous night's events over and over. "How'd you do on your exam?"

"What exam?"

"The one you abandoned me to study for last night."

Jordyn stared at me for a moment. She clapped her hands over her mouth "Oh!" she exclaimed, the light bulb brightening above her head. "That exam. I did fine."

I rolled my shoulders, the tension so tight that they popped with every movement. Jordyn narrowed her gaze on me, her smile widening by the second. "Oh Em Gee!

You slept with the hot Congressman!"

I gasped in shock! "What?"

"You did!"

"Shhh!" I hissed, waving my hands at her. "What on earth gave you that idea?"

Jordyn started to laugh. "You did! You did!" she chanted. "You slept with him. Way to go, Mom!"

I buried my face in my hands, dying. "Can you say it any louder?"

She sprang from her chair and slammed the door shut. "There. We're alone. Tell me everything."

"Absolutely not!"

"He spent the night, didn't he?" she squealed, dancing about and clapping her hands. "Damn, that man must have fucked you good. Look how red your face is getting."

I cupped my hands over my cheeks, feeling the heat burn beneath my skin. "I don't blush!" I gritted my teeth. "And language, my dear daughter."

"Pssh!" She dismissed my scolding. "You're blushing right now." She plopped back down into her chair, leaning forward and resting her elbows on my desk. "Was he any good?"

"I'm not discussing this with you!"

"Wow! He was *that* good. Nice!"

"Stop it!"

"Stop what? I'm proud of you. I knew when I left you the two of you might get bizzay. I meant, the sexual tension just rolls off you."

I rubbed my temples, putting two and two together. "You didn't have a test today, did you?"

A sardonic grin colored her face. "Nope. But I knew

Congressman McHotty Pants wasn't there to talk strategy." She wiggled her brows. "And now I'm really glad I left."

"This is a disaster, Jordyn!"

"Why? I think it's amazing."

"He's my client, and he's ten years younger than me," I argued, my chest aching even as the words tumbled from my lips.

"So the circumstances aren't perfect, but his age is a moot point. It's not like he's my age. And besides, he likes you, and I know you like him. It's written all over your face."

"You don't get it. I'm on his staff. That doesn't bode well in an election. I have to end this before we get in too deep."

Jordyn leaned back in her seat, crossing her arms over her chest. "I'd say you're already in too deep, Mom, but that's not a bad thing." She released a soft sigh. "And his age and being your client really aren't the issues at hand. They're your excuses. The real problem is you like him a lot, and it scares you."

"What are you talking about?"

She pulled a sticky note from my desk and started to fold it into triangles. "I'm talking about you having real feelings for this guy."

"No more than I do for any other client."

"Bull shit. Since Dad, all you've ever had were flings. It's why I pushed you to start dating after I moved out. You'd sleep with some staffer or aid and discard them after an election. You refused to settle down because it scared you. I always figured it had something to do with me. All my life you've put me first, so dating wasn't an option. A quick bang cured the itch. Right, Mom?"

"Jordyn Marie!"

"Whether you want to admit it or not, it's the truth." She pointed at me, circling her accusing finger in the air. "Liam scares you because he's not a quick lay."

I edged forward, resting my elbows on my desk. "You don't know what you're talking about."

"You can't fight what you feel for the man."

"I'm not fighting anything," I lied.

"I know you, Mom. The moment he left this morning you went into clean up mode."

"Clean up mode?"

"Yeah. You know. When you discover one of your clients has screwed up so you move in to clean up their mistakes. You think through every scenario and come up with the best solution to fix the issue." She smirked that *I so busted my mother* grin.

I growled and threw my hands in the air. "Fine. Since you seem to know everything today, what do you suggest I do?"

Jordyn stood and marched around to me. She perched on the edge of my desk and took my hands in hers. "You allow yourself to fall in love, that's what you do."

"And how do you propose I do that?"

"Well," she giggled, "for starters, you stop worrying so damn much. Just enjoy the man for Christ's sake. Have some fun."

Being with Liam was fun. He made me laugh, and in between our romps in the sack, we really did enjoy talking with each other. He challenged me and he didn't take shit from me. I liked that about him.

"Wow! Look at that," she breathed. "I don't think I've ever seen you smile like that."

I pulled my hands from her, shooing her away. "Oh, stop."

"This is amazing," Jordyn chirped, bouncing and clapping. She rested against the window sill, crossing her legs in front of her.

"Are you sure I'm not some sick cougar who's preying on a younger man?"

Jordyn snorted. "Are you kidding me? That man pursued you." She snapped her fingers. "He showed up at your house. Not the other way around." She started smacking the air with her hand. "And then he gave it to you good."

"Oh, Jesus!" I rolled my eyes and grabbed my purse. "Where're we going for lunch?"

Jordyn grinned, glancing down at her watch. "How about Siroc? And afterward you can go see Congressman McHotty Pants on the Hill."

"He's busy." I glanced out the window toward the Hill, and smiled. "But I'll see him tonight."

Jordyn squealed and pushed off the sill. She wrapped her arm around my shoulders, and pulled me in close to her small frame. "Now, we're talking. Let's skip lunch and head home. We have to find you the perfect outfit to wear for your date tonight."

"It's not a date!"

"Mom, trust me. It's a date."

Nerves sparked inside me. She was right. It was a date. I'd never felt nervous over a date before.

"You know what. I have a better idea." I clicked my

tongue to the roof of my mouth. "Let's go shopping."

"Well, all right." She clapped me on the back.

The intercom beeped and Brandy's voice squawked through. "Elizabeth, Mr. Harper's on line two for you."

I slipped around my desk and pressed the intercom button to respond, "Tell him I'll call him back later."

Jordyn's smile flattened into a straight line. "When are you going to tell Uncle Harper about you and Congressman McHotty Pants?"

I rummaged through my purse for my keys. After Harper's insinuations back in Dallas, I had no intentions of telling him anything. "I'm not."

"That's a bad idea, Mom."

"It's none of his business. As a matter of fact, it's no one's business. This is between you, Liam, and me. At least until after the election. Got it." I found my keys and dangled them around my finger.

Jordyn linked her arm into mine. "You know I won't tell anyone, but remember, you're the one who told me there are no secrets in politics."

I sighed in defeat. Just as I was about to give in to my heart, my daughter had to remind me of my logic.

"Stop that, Mom."

"Stop what?"

"You're going into cleanup mode again. Liam's good for you and I refuse to let you talk yourself out of a good thing. I only wanted to point out that it would be best if Harper heard about this from you, okay?"

While I felt she was right, I also knew the damage telling Harper could cause. I did the only thing I could do to settle the conversation. "Okay."

As we left my office, I sent Liam a text message. I didn't want him to think I was dodging him if he showed up at headquarters.

Elizabeth McNeal: I'm going shopping with Jordyn, so I won't be in the office this afternoon.

My phone buzzed in my hand within seconds of me pressing send.

William Baxter: Have fun. See you tonight.

I slipped my phone into my purse and smiled.

You sure will, Congressman. You sure will.

Twenty

Nine o'clock.

I parked my car in front of Liam's townhome. All day long I was a bundle of nerves. Our encounter the night before had been spontaneous. This, however, was premeditated. The political guru in me cringed at my lack of rationale, but the woman inside me hungered for the man inside that house.

One last glance at myself in the mirror and I got out of the car. Glancing over my shoulder to see if anyone noticed me, I found the streets devoid of life. The moon was nonexistent, almost as if it were staying hidden just for me. I thanked the man in the moon for vailing my secrets.

At the door, I buttoned my coral jacket over the ivory satin camisole Jordyn insisted on me wearing. To be honest, I wasn't too sure I was dressed appropriately. Normally on a first date I'd sport a little black dress or something in burgundy. Dark colors were my niche. Jordyn swore with my hazel eyes and blonde hair, lighter colors and distressed skinny jeans were the right way to go.

God help that kid if she was wrong.

I rubbed my lips together, my hand mid-air ready to ring the doorbell. This was the moment of truth. Butterflies in my stomach, I pressed my fingertip to the pearl button. An odd feeling swirled inside me as the chime broke through the silence. It wasn't anxiety. It was more like anticipation.

From behind the door, I heard the padding of feet followed by the twist of the lock. It creaked opened, and there before me stood a relaxed Liam, wearing dark wash jeans paired with a gray collared shirt under a black pullover sweater.

A slow smile bloomed over his face. "I was beginning to wonder if you'd stood me up."

I rested a hand on my hip. "As if I could. You know where I live."

"You're catching on quickly."

"Not quick enough, it seems."

"Faster than you think." Liam rushed his fingers through his hair, pulling it back from his forehead. For the first time since the night I'd met him, I noticed the scar above his left brow. I stepped toward him, tracing the small but prominent scar.

At the realization I'd touched him so intimately before we were behind closed doors, I dropped my hand and clenched it at my side.

Liam slipped his fingers under my chin, tilting my face upward. Light haloed around his head shining through each strand of his dark hair. "Stop worrying. I won't let anything bad happen to either of us."

"You can't promise that," I rasped.

"I just did."

Warm tingles shot through me as the power of his words sank in. He was committing himself to me. There were no gimmicks, no coups, just a simple promise of what was yet to come.

All my life I'd put my daughter and my job ahead of romance. I didn't need a man to dictate how to live or who to be. I came and went as I pleased, but with Liam, things were different. By walking into that house I was giving myself to him beyond sex. Beyond politics. I was giving him everything.

Without hesitation, I stepped inside.

As the door closed behind us, I circled my arms around his neck, and planted a kiss to his lips. He complied, pulling me flush against his taut form. A tender greeting turned sultry in seconds. He cupped my ass as his rich, warm tongue probed my willing mouth. Even as close as we were, locked in this smoldering kiss, I wanted more. Needed more.

My hands moved down his chest, stopping at the button of his jeans. Liam caught my wrists and pulled away from me. "Not yet," he panted. "I have dinner all set."

"Dinner can wait. I want you. Here. Now."

"You have me." He brushed his knuckles down my cheek. "And we have all night together. So, let's not rush things."

I furrowed my brow taking in his light yet serious expression. Liam tilted his head to the side, waiting for me to respond. I pushed up on my toes and pressed a kiss to his square jaw. "Okay. No rushing things." I took a step back and smirked. "It's not like I haven't already had you naked in my bed or anything."

Liam licked his lips, his eyes glinting with mischievousness. "Or walked in on me getting out of the shower."

I clapped my hands to my hips. "I think hot and heavy sex trumps naked shower time."

"I can't argue there." He gave me a wink and wrapped his arm around my waist. "Now, no more sex talk until after we eat."

I had to bite my tongue on that one. Oh the sexual innuendos I could conjure from that comment.

Liam directed me through his tastefully decorated home, filled with bright colors and bold prints. Liam's affirmation for all things bold seemed to surpass his taste in neckwear. Spacious and open, it carried the feel of a bachelor pad but with an elegant flare.

"So, how was shopping with Jordyn?" Liam inquired, as we entered the kitchen. He pulled a bottle of wine from the fridge and showed it to me. I nodded my approval. The man did have good taste. He uncorked the bottle and began to pour.

"You tell me. Was my trip successful?" I did a little turn in the middle of his kitchen before sliding onto a bar stool. Before me sat two lidded plates. A brown paper sack rested in front of the plates, all rolled and crumpled. It seemed like an odd centerpiece but I could roll with it.

My eyes darted to Liam, who smirked. "I'd say it was successful. You're stunning."

He slipped a glass into my hand. I took a sip of the sweet wine to hide the heat I felt rising in my cheeks. I'd been told I was beautiful many times, but there was something about Liam saying it that made me feel warm and fuzzy inside.

Damn him for making me blush.

Liam took his place beside me at the bar. "I hope you don't mind. I'm not really a formal kind of guy. I thought it might be more comfortable to eat dinner here rather than in the dining room."

I swirled the wine inside my glass. "This is perfect." I glanced at the odd centerpiece again. Maybe he was trying to ripen avocados or something. My mother did that when I was a kid. I tilted one way then the next trying to decipher what could be in the bag. There were no indicating marks, so my curiosity got the better of me. "Okay," I pointed to the centerpiece, "I must know, what's in the sack?" I placed my glass on the counter. "Please don't tell me it's shit some pissed off constituent left on your doorstep."

Liam snorted and sputtered on his wine. "God, no. I've never had that happen. Knock on wood." He rapped his knuckles against the bar.

"That's Formica," I pointed out.

"Close enough." He gave me a quick wink and pushed the bag toward me. "This is for you to take home with you in the morning."

"You got me a gift?"

Liam shrugged. "I wouldn't call it a gift. Believe me, I thought about buying you something, like flowers or chocolates, but I knew that really wasn't your style."

"I never realized I was so hard to buy for," I joked,

tugging the sack open. I stuck my hand inside and pulled out a box of condoms. "Talk about your wrong choice of words."

Liam took the box from me and placed it back into the bag. "That's to replace the box we stole from Jordyn last night."

I grabbed the sack and peered into its depths. "But there's more than one box in there!"

Liam lifted his hand, resting it on my cheek. "Last night you told me you believe a woman in a relationship should always be prepared. Well, I believe a man should be as well. So, I bought a box to keep in your room and one for mine."

I shifted to the edge of my seat and kissed his sweet wine-flavored lips. "That's sweet, but please tell me you didn't buy these yourself. I beg you to tell me that I shouldn't be on the horn with Scout right now preparing for an onslaught of candid photos of you in a drug store buying multiple boxes of condoms."

Liam kissed the tip of my nose, laughing. "I sent Aaron, because I knew you'd have a meltdown."

I wasn't sure which was worse — some random person seeing him buy condoms or his brother buying them for him. "I guess that means you told Aaron about us?"

"And you didn't tell Jordyn?"

I drummed my fingertips against the counter. "She guessed."

"As did Aaron. Apparently, I was *glowing* this morning," he stated with a hint of amusement tinging his tone.

I clasped my hands over my mouth, laughing. "Oh my

God! Me, too!" My laughter soon died as I considered what this meant. "We need to talk about this."

"Agreed." I turned to face him. He did the same, straddling his knees around mine. He took my hands in his and smiled. "So, my dear handler, how do we move forward?"

My head bobbed of its own accord. He was making light of the situation, but I felt the nervous tension in him. "It might be best for us to keep our relationship under lock and key until after the election."

He rubbed his thumbs along mine. "I expected that and agree, but wouldn't it be prudent to let Scout in on our little secret?"

Scout. Shit. No, I didn't want to tell Scout. I didn't want to tell anyone. Little secrets turn into big scandals, and the more people in on the secret, the bigger chance there was of it getting out.

"You want the truth?" I flipped my hands over, threading my fingers through his.

"Always."

"If I stepped back and pretended I was talking to another client, the first thing I'd do is tell him to get the hell out of the relationship. No piece of ass is worth the potential loss." Liam's mouth popped open. I released his hand and pressed my fingers to his lips, stopping his near tirade. "I'm not saying I'm a piece of ass. You've made your intentions very clear."

He kissed the pads of my fingers. "It's good to see you were listening."

I slid my hand to his cheek, unable to hold back a smile. "I have been, but you must understand, I know what women like me can do to men like you. You can't afford a scandal like me."

"You're not a scandal." He was so serious that my heart ached. Yet I knew he was wrong.

"I am, whether you want to admit it or not. But, with that said, and knowing that neither of us is willing to walk away, I agree it's imperative we tell Scout. Not that I like it, but it's the responsible thing to do."

Liam hummed in agreement. "Spoken like the class act I hired."

"I'm sure it'll be a relief to Aaron. I bet he's about to explode with this little tidbit on us."

Liam pulled my wrists to his lips, kissing my pulse lines. "It is, but it's fun to watch my brother squirm."

I smacked Liam on the chest, laughing. "You're so mean to each other."

"That's what brothers are for!"

I rolled my eyes and turned toward the counter, tapping my fingers on the lid of the plate in front of me. "It's settled. Tomorrow I'll call Aaron and Scout in for a meeting and we will discuss our," I paused, the word *relationship* on the tip of my tongue, instead I detoured, "situation."

"Sounds like a plan, but I do need to increase our list of confidants by one."

I frowned. "You realize the more people who know the more chances we have for a slip up, right?"

Liam took a long drink of his wine. "I do, but I also know this person would rather die than betray my confidence."

"Kristin?" I guessed.

"Yes. She's my dearest friend in the world, and I feel it's best she knows what's going on."

I toyed with the napkin beside my plate. I understood wanting to keep a best friend in the loop. There once was a time I would've run to Harper with my good news, but his reaction in Dallas was enough of an indicator that he wouldn't take the news well. The pragmatist in me would've agreed with him.

"If you think she needs to know, I understand. But please stress to her the importance of keeping our secret."

"Kristin knows how to keep a secret," he stated with fierce authority. "She's proven that time and time again."

That same feeling I had when I first met Kristin struck me. I almost asked what they were hiding, but knew I'd get the same answer he always gave. I'd bide my time. Eventually, I'd get to the bottom of the Kristin mystery.

"I know she can."

"So we can put this part behind us?"

"I think so. We have our tight knit circle and that's where we stay until after the election."

"Until after the election," he agreed. "Now let's eat."

And that's what we did, along with spending the better part of our evening simply getting to know each other outside of the campaign. I learned so much about him, things that no amount of vetting would have ever uncovered. Beneath that political façade laid the heart of a philosopher and poet. Being with him, the man, not the candidate, was interesting and enjoyable. He could quote Nietzsche, Heidegger, and Plato with ease. We argued about the greatest musicians of the nineties, and when he suggested that The Offspring were better than Metallica I damn near had an aneurism.

By the end of the night, we were in his bedroom doing things that would make the headline news sing with scandal.

That part I tried not to think about.

In the early morning hours, I woke in his arms to the sound of his cell phone ringing. Liam rolled over, releasing me from his warm embrace. "Yeah," he grunted. "I was afraid of that." There was a pause. "Okay. Give me twenty minutes. I'll be there."

I rolled over, the room dark save the light from his phone. "What's wrong?"

His hand slipped under the covers, gliding along the curve of my hip. "I have to head into the office."

"Okay. No problem." I shifted in the bed, ready to make my departure.

"Where do you think you're going?" Liam protested.

I stopped. Not being able to really see his face left me unsure how to respond. "I, um, I figured since you were leaving, I should, too."

"Absolutely not! I asked you here tonight because I thought something like this might happen. I wanted to be close to the Hill and still be able to find you in my bed when I returned."

"Really? You're not worried about me being alone in your house? What if…"

"Stop right there. No one but Jordyn and Aaron knows you're here. You don't need to worry about a leak. And it's not uncommon for a consultant to visit her client in the middle of the night, is it?"

I shook my head, as if he could see me in the dark.

"I want you here, like this, when I get back. Okay?"

My heart panged at his sincerity.

"All right. I'll stay."

"Good. Now, go back to sleep. I shouldn't be gone long." He placed a sweet kiss to my lips and slipped out of the bed. A light flickered on from the closet and then dimmed through a closed door. In the distance, I heard Liam padding around getting dressed. Moments later, the light was gone and so was he.

I curled up on the bed, drawing his pillow in close to my face. It smelled like him — warm, woodsy, and all male. I smiled and snuggled in, waiting for sleep to take me, but it never did. No matter how hard I tried, I couldn't fall asleep without him beside me. My body yearned for him. My heart longed to be with him. So, I did what any normal, red-blooded American woman would do. I got out of bed, slipped into his discarded shirt, and began to snoop.

My first stop was his bathroom. A small piece of me felt guilty for looking through his toiletries, but I enjoyed smelling his aftershave and discovering what products he used. This was like my own little window into William Baxter. No one but me would know these details about him.

CK One? Really?

I didn't even realize they still made that cologne. Go figure.

After exploring the bathroom, I moved to his closet. It was a magnificent space, organized and clean. An OCD person's wet dream. All of his ties hung neatly on a motorized tie rack. Suit jackets dangled from the top rung of the closet and his shirts on the bottom. To the right, all of his slacks and pants hung, creased to perfection, reminding me he was once part of the military. I tried to imagine Liam in uniform, all stars and stripes forever.

"I bet you looked sexy as fuck in that uniform," I purred, stroking the crease on one of his jackets.

Curious to see how extensive his collection of ugly ties went, I pressed the button, turning on the tie rack. The whole damn thing was color coded by the rainbow. Every bright color imaginable circled past me. I stopped the motor as it landed on yellow. A mustard yellow tie with sun yellow paisleys rested on the hanger.

Hideous!

I shook my head and turned around, only to come face to face with an amused Liam.

A scream tore through me. I slapped my hand over my mouth. "Jesus! Don't sneak up on me like that!" I clutched my chest, my heart racing. "Give a girl some warning."

Liam shrugged a shoulder and inched forward. "I'm back."

I gave him an exasperated look. "I mean beforehand."

"I wasn't sneaking, but it sure does seem like you were. Did you find anything interesting?"

Oh the humiliation of being discovered. "I, uh." I shifted my weight, dropping my eyes from his expressive gaze. "I'm sorry. I couldn't sleep, so I got up—"

"I see you found my ties." He stalked toward me, his body tense.

"Yeah. I still want to know where you find these ugly things."

A wicked smile curled his lips. "They're not ugly, they're unique. Just like me."

"Is that your excuse for wearing them?" Another step

forward. With no means to escape, Liam trapped me inside the closet.

"I don't need an excuse, but if you must know..." He reached around me and slipped the mustard colored tie from the rack. "I figure since I already stand above the rest of the crowd, I should give them something interesting to look at."

He wrapped the tie around my neck, drawing me to him. Our mouths collided in a sensual kiss. My stomach clenched as his lips molded to mine with that perfect mix of passion and control. Slow and deliberate, he moved his mouth down my jaw, tasting my skin just below my ear. "By the way, you look good in my shirt."

My head fell back, a gasp of ecstasy on my lips. "It was on the floor, and I..."

His hand slid up the length of my neck; his long fingers tangling in my hair, as he cupped the back of my head. "Don't explain. You're welcome to wear my clothes anytime." His free hand slipped down my hip and dipped under the fabric of the shirt, cupping my bare bottom in his palm. "In fact, I insist you wear my clothes more often." His mouth once again captured mine, enveloping me in a precious kiss.

The closet light flipped off. Liam's arms slipped beneath my legs. He lifted me off my feet and carried me to bed, where he rested me on the mattress.

In the dim morning light, I was whisked away to the world of ecstasy that only William Baxter could bring. If his leaving me alone meant I'd be greeted this way every time he returned, I could handle him going away. At least for a little while.

It was official.

I was hooked.

Happily addicted to all things William Baxter.

And rehab wasn't an option.

Twenty-one

I glanced up at the clock on the wall.

Fifteen minutes to wait 'til Aaron, Scout, and Liam were scheduled to join me in my office. My legs bounced with nerves. No matter how I tried to spin the situation in my head, I had only one outcome produced every time — Scout freaking out and demanding to have my mental faculties checked.

And I wouldn't blame her one bit.

Rather than ponder on something out of my control, I diverted my thoughts to work.

Work was always good.

It wasn't long after I turned on my computer and checked my emails that a series of raps came at the door. Liam poked his head inside. "Hey, Lizzy."

"Liam!" I hissed, heralding him to enter. "You can't say things like that here."

Liam stepped into my office and closed the door behind him. "No one's here yet, and besides, they're not going to think twice about me calling you Lizzy."

"You don't know that for certain. A nickname suggest familiarity."

"Oh-kay." He pressed the lock on my door and stalked toward me. "I'll refrain from calling you anything but Elizabeth."

Like a beacon around his neck, I was drawn to the mustard yellow tie he was wearing. It was the same one he'd wrapped around my neck the night before. The bastard had the audacity to wear it into the office.

"You've got to be kidding me," I screeched. "How could you wear that one? Today!"

Liam glanced down to his chest. "It's just a tie, *Elizabeth*."

"That's not just a tie!"

He inched closer to me. "It's not like I tied you to my bed with it...yet."

I squirmed in my chair. "No, but we had sex on that tie."

"Technically not on it. It was on the floor this morning, which is why I wore it."

My instinct was to go all girly and cover my face with my hands. Instead, I stood up and met Liam on the other side of the desk. In my most stern, authoritative voice, I explained, "You can't do shit like that. We have to be careful."

"It's a tie." He rolled his eyes with a flutter dramatic enough to make Jordyn proud. "You're paranoid."

"Maybe, but I refuse to be the reason you lose this

election. And if I get squirmy over a freaking tie, well, I, ah," I paused to collect my thoughts. "I don't want to give us away."

Liam braced my shoulders between his palms. "Does that mean I can't kiss you right now?"

"Absolutely not! No kissing in the office. No public displays of affection. Period."

Liam dropped his hands from my arms. His head started to bob then it turned to a nod. "You're right. I promised to protect you, so we'll play this safe." He brushed his knuckles down my cheek. "I want you to always feel comfortable with me."

I placed my hand to his chest, calmed by the steady beat of his heart. "I am comfortable with you, but as much as you want to protect me, I need to do the same for you. This is the only way I know how."

Liam rested his hand over mine, the heat of his palm burned wildly against my skin. "I understand. I really do. You're a good woman." He leaned in close to my ear, whispering ever so softly, "Lizzy."

I pushed him back with a laugh. "You're terrible."

"I know." He grabbed my wrist and brought it to his lips. Every time he did that I melted.

"You know you make it hard for me when you do that."

"I'd say I'm sorry, but I'd be lying."

I slid my hand from his, and wandered back behind my desk. "I wouldn't have believed you anyway."

He gripped his chest, a feigned shocked expression plastered on his face. "You wouldn't believe me? Me? Honest, Liam."

I tapped my knuckles against my desk. "You forget; I know you better now."

Liam drifted along my bookshelf, checking out my album collection. "Doesn't make me a liar."

"Never a liar. Only a man who knows how to use his tongue."

Liam's eyes gazed at me from over the album jacket he held in his hand. "Elizabeth McNeal!"

"If I were still keeping score, I would've gotten a point for that one," I teased.

"Score one for Lizzy."

I snapped my fingers at him, playfully gritting my teeth. He chuckled and slid the album back in its place.

"Did you talk to Kristin?"

Liam extracted my Band of Horses record and held it up to me. "Great album."

"Liam?"

His shoulders slunk as he shoved the record back into place. "I called this morning."

"I take it she's upset." Which I expected. She knew the damage we could cause.

"Not really upset. Just disappointed. She feels I'm putting my career in jeopardy."

"She's right, you know."

Liam's slack form straightened to his full height. "I don't see it that way."

"I know," I whispered.

Liam glanced up at the clock. "Aaron and Scout are late."

My gaze wandered upward to check the time. "That's not like them."

Liam unlocked the door and slid it open. He glanced around and shrugged. "I'm sure they had to deal with traffic." He roamed back to my shelf, perusing the music again.

It bugged me that Kristin wasn't happy for him. A deep seated instinct rose inside me, pining to protect him. I was causing him suffering already, and about to make it worse by revealing our affair to his closest staff. Bile rose in my throat, knowing even if I wanted to put on the brakes, he'd refuse.

"Knock, knock," Aaron's voice resounded at the door, his knuckles tapping against the frame.

"About time, bro!" Liam snarked, a jovial glint sparkled in his eyes, as he slipped the record back on the shelf.

"Sorry. It was my fault," a frazzled Scout announced, following Aaron into the office. Her shirt was partially tucked into her slim pants and her hair in an unruly ponytail. "I had to have my triple soy latte this morning or there was going to be hell to pay around the office today." Scout chugged on her large coffee and maneuvered to close the door.

"No sleep?" I quipped.

"Not with Rambo the Sex Fiend, here." She thumbed toward Aaron.

Hmm. Must be a family thing.

That also meant that Aaron and Scout had finally crossed the sex boundary. Maybe this wouldn't be so bad since she'd also given into her own Baxter brother.

Who was I kidding? She was already pissy.

I was screwed. Not in a good way either.

Aaron glanced around to the chairs and sofa in my office. "Speaking of which. You two haven't…" He started making noises that I could only imagine were meant to emulate the sound of a bed squeaking. "…in here, have ya?"

Liam rammed his fist into Aaron's bicep. "Show some respect!"

"What?" Aaron punched Liam back in the shoulder. "I just want to find out what surfaces are untouched so I can sit there."

"Wait? What?" Scout bleated. "Are you two?" She wrenched her head around to Aaron. "You knew about this and didn't tell me?"

Aaron lifted his hands defensively. "I wanted to, but I was sworn to secrecy."

Scout snarled and growled.

"You have no idea how hard it's been for me, babe," Aaron whined. "He made me buy condoms."

"Condoms? Jesus!" Scout's face paled. She pulled a long swig of her coffee. "I'm going to need something stronger than this today."

Scout's reaction was exactly what I'd expected. It was the same reaction I would've had if I was on the other side of the desk. It was the same response that still tried to creep up inside of me, distorting my happiness like the clouds hugged the sun outside my window. And I didn't, for one second, blame her for such a reaction. Her instinct was the reason I demanded her on our team. Scout would handle this professionally and with couth, but she'd also be a voice of reason.

I geared myself for what was surely yet to come.

I stood from my desk and waved my hand around the

room. "For starters," I glared at Aaron, "no, we haven't had sex in this office. Nor will we.

"And yes, Scout," I diverted my attention to her. "Liam and I are...involved."

Scout tapped the lid of her coffee. "I can't say I'm surprised. You two have had a certain chemistry from the get go."

I glanced to Liam who stood in front of the couch, his hands tucked into his pockets. Aside from that tie, he was gorgeous. Black suit, crisp gray shirt, and polished shoes. Everything a well-pressed politician should be and more.

"I wish I had your foresight. It hit me like a load of bricks," I chuckled.

Liam graced me with a coy wink. Aaron pursed his lips but said nothing.

With a simple smile, Scout teased, "I'm not surprised by that, either. Business before pleasure is the McNeal creed, after all."

"You can say that again," Liam retorted.

"Hey, now! I was hired to do a job. I'm good at what I do."

Aaron chortled. "From the look on Liam's face, I'd say you're really good."

I cast a stern expression in Aaron's direction. "Go ahead. Get it all out. Because once you leave this room, you're never to say another word about Liam and me again." I tapped my foot. "I'm waiting."

Aaron, as big as he was, slinked at the brass of my challenge. "I think I'm good, for now."

"Your call."

"Okay," Scout interrupted, "I'm happy for you, you

know that, but…" She took another drink of her coffee, before letting out a little gasp of satisfaction. "I guess what I'm asking is how do you want us to handle this? Would you like me to hold a press conference to address this with the public? Are we to take a poll to see how he will be perceived with someone as…" She stopped.

"Someone as old as me," I finished for her.

A little sheepish, she nodded. "Well, yeah."

I loved Scout for her brutal honesty, but damn that hit hard below the belt.

Liam straightened, his feet spread apart, ready for a fight. "She's not old!"

Aaron patted Liam on the back. "Calm down. No one's saying she is. What Scout's trying to convey is how the public will perceive her."

"Who cares? Elizabeth's what I want. And I don't need a poll or some know-it-all constituent telling me she's not right for me simply because she's older than me."

"Liam," I intervened. "It's all right."

He gritted his teeth. "No, it's not, but I'll shut up."

I chuckled and shook my head. He was endearing.

"Everyone, please sit down." I waved to the chairs and sofa.

Scout scooted into the chair in front of me, placing her cup on my desk. She reached across the wood surface and grabbed a pen and legal pad. Aaron and Liam took a seat on the sofa, while I stood, leaning against the corner of my desk, my legs crossed in front of me. The room was silent, everyone waiting for me to speak. I clamped my eyes shut and pinched the bridge of my nose.

"I realize this is a difficult situation. It has scandal

written all over it." I took in a deep breath. "And under normal circumstances I'd advise my client to nip things in the bud before they're made public...well, I can't do that in this situation. So, there will be no polls or press conference. I want this to stay as close to home as possible."

"But..." Scout started to protest.

I waved my hands. "Only the people in this room along with Jordyn and Kristin are to know about us, and it will stay that way."

"You're not telling Harper?" Scout questioned.

"No. I don't see the need."

"I'm confused," Scout stated, the pen in her hand smacking against the legal pad.

"We tell no one. Liam's killing it in the polls, and we don't need Keating or the media getting wind of this. We've based his entire campaign on his clean persona. They would run wild with this story and we'd lose our edge."

"So you think Harper would leak this?" Aaron questioned.

I was appalled at such an accusation. "Absolutely not. I simply feel it's best we not put him in a bad situation. He's done enough for us. Let's show him some respect."

That was true, after all. It was because of him we were all in that room.

Aaron straightened up, the boyish grin now gone from his face. In its place was Aaron Baxter, Chief of Staff for Congressman William Baxter. "Sorry. I meant no disrespect. I like Harper, and you both know I want you to be happy, but can't you wait until after the election? Wouldn't that be safer for all of us?"

"We discussed that option," Liam replied. "But imagine how you'd feel if someone asked you to stay away from Scout for a few days let alone months."

Aaron crossed his legs, clasping his hands around his knees. "I see your point, I really do, but slinking around in the shadows is no relationship. It'll weigh down on you both and end up leaving you vulnerable."

"Believe me, Aaron, I've considered that. You know me," I sighed. "This is my reputation on the line as much as it is Liam's. If I thought I could stay away from him, I'd do it."

Liam flinched at my words. "You'd really do that?"

I nodded. "If I could, but I can't. Hence this very awkward conversation."

"Yes, yes," Liam muttered.

I cringed at his pained expression. "I didn't say that to hurt you, Liam. I'm admitting how selfish I am when it comes to you. I'm putting us on the line for my feelings. I've never done that before. No one has ever made me feel the way you do; to the point I'm potentially damning both our careers for my own selfish needs."

Liam lifted from his seat, and crossed the room to me. His hands encased my neck, as he pulled me in for a kiss. I should've protested him kissing me. Even behind the closed doors of the office was dangerous and off limits, but I couldn't stop him. He pulled back too soon, leaving me breathless.

"You're not selfish. I am. I've brought us to this point and if anything were to happen, it's all on me. You understand?"

There he was again. Liam, my protector.

"We're being selfish together."

Liam kissed the tip of my nose. "Together."

"Wow," Scout sniffled. I tilted my head to see her wiping a tear from her eye. "That was beautiful. There's no going back from that. So, we do our best to keep things under wraps. No smoochie smoochie or anything that could be misconstrued as possible flirting. You'll have to maintain your typical relationship, which pretty much means keeping each other on edge. Do you think you can handle that?"

Liam wiggled his brows. "I think we can handle that. We'll consider it foreplay."

I smacked Liam's chest. "Oh, you're bad."

"Score one for Liam?" he ribbed.

I laughed at the lighthearted countenance he sported. "If we must."

Aaron shifted forward, planting his feet on the floor. He clapped his hands together, his face drawn into a grimace. "Okay, I hate being the Negative Nancy here, but what do we do if the media catches wind of the two of you?"

My momentary happy bubble burst. A solemn visage darkened Liam's face.

"We'll cross that bridge if we come to it," I declared.

Scout glanced down at her watch. "Okay, one last thing before I head off to my conference call. I really think we need to make an announcement clarifying that Liam and Kristin are only good friends. If anything does come out about the two of you, it will keep Liam from coming off as a cheater."

I rubbed my hands together. "Too risky. Neither have

claimed they're in a relationship, so if we make an awkward announcement like that now, the media will smell blood in the water. We don't want to give them a reason to snoop."

Scout brushed back her hair. "You're the boss, but I must stress I think not publically announcing them as only friends is a bad idea."

"Noted," I stated with finality.

"Okay, well my conference call starts in twenty minutes. I need to head out of here."

"I think we're done, anyway. I cannot stress this enough, please keep this between us. That's all I ask."

Scout bounced up out of her chair and swiped up her coffee. "You got it, boss." She patted me on the shoulder and strolled to the door. "And for what it's worth, it's good to see you happy."

She turned the knob and exited the room.

Now that the door was open, Liam took a step away from me. While I hated any distance between us, I appreciated him abiding by our agreement.

"I agree with Scout. It's nice to see you really smile, Elizabeth," Aaron noted.

"Thanks," I muttered, a little embarrassed.

"Now stop it. Everyone will know something's up." Aaron barked out a laugh.

I rolled my eyes and waved him off. "Don't you have work to do? Get out of my office."

Aaron rose from the couch. "Yeah. Actually, Liam, we need to head to the Hill."

Liam groaned. "I'll be so glad when we pass this damn thing."

"You and me both," Aaron growled.

Liam turned to me. "I'll see you tonight?"

I dropped my head and lowered my voice. "Your place again?"

He grinned. "Eight o'clock."

"Okay."

Once the two men left my office, the smell of Liam's cologne lingered in the air. I closed my eyes and breathed in deep. I hated knowing this could end in disaster. My only solace was knowing I'd put together the greatest political team money could buy, and if things did head south, they'd hit the ground running.

Twenty-two

William Baxter: You like Bilbo Baggins?

"Bilbo Baggins?" I mouthed, staring at my cell phone, scratching my head.

Life had become a whirlwind of work and Liam. Every waking hour we had free from work we spent together. While we texted off and on throughout the day, we kept things clean — one could never be too cautious — yet there was always an undertone to the conversation that left me tingling all over.

In this particular text, however, we'd been talking about food. He'd mentioned he was starving and I replied the same. Next thing I knew, he was asking if I liked a hobbit. Talk about coming out of left field.

I puckered my lips from side to side. I wasn't much of a *Lord of the Rings* fan, but Jordyn was. She'd forced more midnight showings on me than I cared to count. So, if I were to choose a hobbit, I'd probably pick Bilbo. At least he seemed prepared for anything. However, I preferred the dwarfs. They knew how to get the job done.

Elizabeth McNeal: Sure. He's great for a hobbit.

Seconds later, I received his reply.

William Baxter: I'm talking about Bilbo Baggins on Queen St. Meet me there at seven for dinner.

My heart rammed itself into my throat. Was he crazy? A public meal. Alone!

I took in several deep breaths. This was a bad idea. A really, really, *really* bad idea. I'd been there a few times. Hello, I had a kid who was a *Lord of the Rings* enthusiast. It was pretty much a tourist attraction, which I was sure was why he suggested that location. It was unlikely anyone would recognize him there.

Smart, but still stupid.

Against my better judgement, I replied to his message with an affirmative.

At seven o'clock, I arrived nervous as hell. If anyone were to see us together they would more than likely think we were having a simple business dinner, however, I couldn't shake the feeling we were pushing the envelope a bit too far. This was a dangerous game we were playing with some seriously high stakes.

I walked in the door and smiled. The smell of savory dishes and sweet wine floated in the air. A beautiful rustic decor with lots of greenery and stained glass windows created a simplistic yet tasteful establishment.

My eyes roamed around the room in search of Liam. I didn't have to look very far. At a table in the far back corner, he waited, partially concealed from a somewhat noisy crowd. Our eyes met, and a slow smile bloomed across his face. I wondered if anyone noticed his smile the same way I did. His teeth weren't perfectly straight, but those crooked bottom teeth added to his charm.

I started toward the table, lost in the sight of him. Early that morning, I'd watched him dress in a sexy as hell three-piece suit, matched with one of my favorite shirts, and a tie that was unspeakably ugly. Almost as if to appease me, the monstrous tie was gone but so were the jacket and vest. What was left was a comfortable man, wearing a button-up shirt with his sleeves rolled to show his strong, tanned arms, and a black metal watch. Needless to say, he made me weak in the knees.

"Hey, you." Liam stood up and maneuvered around the table to pull out my chair for me. While his gesture was endearing, I looked around for spectators.

"It's fine," he whispered close to my ear. "No one's watching. I promise."

"I know. I know." His actions were so sweet and there I was tainting them. "I'm sorry."

"Don't be. I understand. It's not like we've never been seen in public alone before. Just act natural."

Natural! How the hell was I supposed to act natural when every nerve in my body was firing simultaneously? I pushed down the panic inside me. It was foolish of me to be so overly concerned. Liam was right. No one would think anything of this. He was a candidate having dinner with his campaign manager. Nothing more.

I smiled, slipped into the chair, and permitted him to help me tuck it under the table.

"I hope you haven't been waiting too long."

Liam waved toward a waiter, as he settled back into his seat. "I just arrived myself."

"What made you choose this place?"

"It's close to your house," he leaned in and whispered, "which is where I intend on this night ending."

"Oh?" My eyes widened at his insinuation. "Oh!"

Air crackled all around us, charged with wanton expectation. I draped my napkin over my knees, forcing myself to maintain my composure.

"Rather confident in yourself, don't you think?"

Liam cracked his knuckles. "Damn right I am."

The waiter arrived and we placed our drink orders. Or should I say, Liam ordered for the both of us. Under normal circumstances I would've tore into a man for being so presumptuous. No one but me knew what I wanted, but with Liam I had no sudden knee-jerk reaction. His chivalrous nature comforted me, which was odd, because I was a woman set in her ways. I'd shied away from romance for so long I'd forgotten it even existed. I viewed the world through scandal-colored glasses, always looking for an angle in every situation. Yet all my prickly, stubborn edges didn't frighten him away. Instead he smoothed and polished them.

I fidgeted with my silverware, straightening each piece.

Liam's hand slipped across the table toward mine. Out of instinct, I yanked back.

"Are you nuts?" I growled. "We're in public."

Liam leaned back in his chair, clenching both fists against the table. "You zoned out on me. I was trying to get your attention."

My shoulders dropped as I exhaled. "I'm sorry. I did it again."

His balled fists relaxed against the surface. "It's okay. I get it."

I shook my head. "No, you don't."

He tilted his head to the side, his eyes full of compassion. "Then explain it to me."

I wiggled my fingers, shaking my hands in front of my chest. "I don't know how to do this, Liam."

"Do what?"

I jerked my hand out toward the restaurant. "This."

A glimmer of a grin appeared on his lips. "Have dinner?"

"Gah!" I hissed. "No. You. Public. Dating without dating."

His gaze rested on mine, a forlorn grimace harrowing his brow. "All I wanted was to spend an evening with you that didn't consist of us being stuck inside the house or at the office. It's not like I'm going to make out with you here."

My eyes grew wide. "You better not!"

Liam straightened his back and lifted his brows. "Are you trying to challenge me, Elizabeth? We both know how I handle a challenge."

I gulped, my knowledge quite extensive on what a challenge with Liam entailed. "Do you want to commit political suicide?"

Liam's foot brushed up along my calf, hooking behind my knee, and pulling my leg between his. "No, and I'm being careful, but you can't blame a man who wants to enjoy the company of his girlfriend in public."

My heart swelled inside my chest. I closed my eyes, unable to contain my smile at his words. *"Girlfriend?"*

"Yes." His hand slipped beneath the table. I fought to remain still, as his finger circled my knee. "You're my girlfriend, Elizabeth McNeal. My strong, smart, independent, gorgeous girlfriend. And once this is all over, I intend on spending many nights holding your hand and kissing your sexy lips, in public."

Elation. Pure joy pulsed through my veins. I rubbed my foot along the back of his leg. "Is that a promise?"

"It's more than a promise. It's a...oh, shit!"

Quick as a flash, Liam's hand disappeared from my knee and the warmth of his leg was gone from mine.

Panic surged inside me. "What?"

I followed Liam's pale stare. My stomach plummeted at the sight of Gerald Samford entering the restaurant with a large party.

"You've got to be kidding me!"

No sooner had those words left my mouth did the rich old fart notice us. He waved his frail hand and grinned.

I tucked my hair behind my ear. "Okay. Keep calm."

"I am calm."

"I was talking to myself," I hissed.

"Well, then, keep coaching yourself, because he's coming this way."

No problem. I had this. I'd charmed and lied my way out of many ugly situations. We were safe as long as neither of us lost our shit.

Fine. As long as I didn't lose my shit.

"Congressman," Samford's wavering voice came from behind me. "And the lovely Ms. McNeal."

I turned in my chair and plastered on my most polished smile. "Gerald Samford! What a pleasant surprise. How are you?" I stood up and shook hands with the old man. Liam followed suit.

"Not as good as our dear boy," Samford boasted.

"You flatter me, sir."

Samford wafted his hand. "Pish posh."

Liam and I returned to our seats, but not before Liam did the unthinkable and held my chair for me. I tried to gauge the look on the old man's face, but it remained unfazed. He probably thought nothing of it. After all, he did come from a generation where men held doors for ladies.

Ah, the good old days.

A lull of silence ensued. Then, as courteous as ever, Liam extended a hand. "Would you care to join us?"

"Thank you, but I can't. Tonight's my great granddaughter's birthday. This is her favorite restaurant. I should probably get back to them."

"Wish her a happy birthday on our behalf," Liam beseeched.

"Will do." The old man's eyes bounced back and forth between us. A wild, full grin appeared. "Unless Ms. McNeal would care to accompany me as my date."

I tittered. "That's sweet, but the Congressman and I have much to discuss."

"I'm sure you do." He gave Liam a wink. "You're a lucky man to have such a beautiful woman by your side."

Liam folded his hands under his chin, resting his elbows on the table. "I tend to agree."

"You remember what I told you at the party?" Samford hinted.

"I do, sir. And do you recall what I said?"

The two men shared a defiant stare before they laughed together. I was lost as to what the hell they were talking about. Samford patted my shoulder with a quaking hand. "He's the real deal. A rarity in this town." His bony fingers squeezed into my flesh.

"That he is."

Samford released his grip on me. "Try the duck. It's delicious." He glanced back at his party being seated. "I must go. Call my office next week, Ms. McNeal. I'm sure there are things we need to discuss."

My cheeks rose again with my cultivated grin. "Of course."

Once the old man stepped away, Liam groused, "I really hate that smile."

Insulted, I glared at him. "You hate my smile?"

"No. I said I hate *that* smile. The one you use when dealing with constituents. I love the smile you share with only me."

And that very smile exploded across my face. "I love the one you share with me, too." I glanced over my shoulder at the old man. "I have to ask, what were you two talking about?"

Liam rubbed his hand along his jaw, chuckling. "I probably shouldn't tell you."

"Tell me!"

Liam pressed his knuckles to his lips, holding back his grin. "You remember the party at Harper's right after we met?"

"Of course I do."

"Well, Mr. Samford informed me that there was

nothing sexier than having the woman above you, beneath you."

I gasped and jerked my head to look at the old man again. "No! He didn't."

"He did. He told me that if I were smart, I'd whip you hard and show you who was boss."

"Oh my God! He's a dirty old man!"

"Pretty much."

"Where the hell was I when he said this?"

"Standing right next to him."

"No!"

"Yes. I was shocked when you said nothing. Then I noticed Victor and realized why you didn't."

Laughter bubbled in my chest. "I would've died had I heard him. What did you say?"

"I informed him that behind every good man was a great woman and that I'd lucked out, because you're better than great. You're the best. And I'd be a damned fool if I thought about whipping you."

A skewed smile arched at my lips as I brushed my bangs away from my face. "You mean there are no foreseeable spankings in our future?"

Liam's playful grin turned to a smoldering one. He bowed his head, his eyes molesting me as he dipped his voice low and seductive. "My dear, Elizabeth, I promise I'll never whip you into submission. I love your spunky nature too much for that. But I also promise to spank that tight ass of yours until it's cherry red before fucking you so hard you won't be able to walk straight for days." Confidence radiated from him.

Goodbye appetite. Hello drenched thighs and an ache

between my legs.

There was no way I could maintain my composure after that. We had to get out of there and fast or I would pounce him, right there, for the world to see.

"Let's go."

"We haven't eaten," Liam protested.

"Forget food. I want you. Now!"

Liam waved down the waiter and paid for our drinks. We were out of the restaurant as quick as a flash, and at my house even faster. Neither of us cared to see if Samford was paying attention to our abrupt departure. All we knew was we needed each other right then. Appearances didn't matter. Especially when Samford proved to be a perv.

Millionaires. Go figure.

Twenty-three

Surrounded by darkness, except for the illuminating glow of the running projector, I struggled to maintain my wit about me. I shifted in my seat, my body tense and my breathing shallow. No matter where I moved Liam was there. His warmth, his scent, the sound of his breath were all amplified by the darkness. My blood sizzled, aching to be skin to skin with him, but that wasn't an option.

Not here.

Not now.

Instead, I was stuck in this boiling hot conference room, watching the latest television ad. If I was to do my job, I'd scrutinize every word, every color, every frame of the reel, but no. My mind wasn't on work. I was focused on the way Liam's knee brushed against mine under the table.

God, those muscular legs of his. Thick. Manly. Leading up toward...

As I thought about a naked, sweating Liam hovering over me, his body entering mine, connecting us beyond time and space, a shiver ripped through me.

Since our little near-miss at the restaurant, I'd been on high alert. Liam attempted to convince me that I was overreacting and that we were only setting ourselves up for failure by staying in the shadows, but I refused to listen. Between raging libidos and deep, dark secrets, I feared I couldn't trust myself past the strain of the work day. On the days Liam ventured into headquarters, my bitch-o-meter skyrocketed from its typical four-point-eight to an alarmingly high nine-point-oh. And when Liam was in a particularly teasing mood, I broke the scales. But I had to admit, I looked forward to our evenings after a day such as that.

Today had been one of those days. From the moment he entered the building, we'd been at each other's throats. The staff thought nothing of it. Liam and I, on the other hand, were well aware of the strain we were placing on ourselves.

Liam adjusted in his seat. Where his knee had once touched mine, his long fingers were in its place. My mouth was dry. My throat thick with want. Every inch of me quivered with desire. No amount of Kegels could compress the ache between my thighs.

Inch by delicious inch, his hand slid under my skirt. Knowing he couldn't push the envelope too far, but just enough to drive me wild, he was in no rush with his torture. His hand on my inner thigh felt cold as ice and hot as hell, confusing my senses.

The room was full of people. On either side of us sat

Scout and Aaron. The rest of the table included various members of the staff and the film's director. This was the worst place to lose control, yet the animal inside me roared for release.

I narrowed my eyes to Liam. On the outside, he appeared calm and cool, but I knew that look in his eyes. He was crazed on the inside. Driven by want. He was as consumed by the buzz of passion between us, just as I was. We were both on the brink of breaking when the lights flipped on.

"Well?" Both of us exhaled at the same time. At the end of the table, the director looked at me with expectation. "Elizabeth? What do you think?"

I had no clue what I thought. The commercial was a blur of Liam tantalizing me. I rolled my shoulders and pushed back from the table, forcing him to drop his hand. Typically, I was a quick witted, think on my toes kind of gal. Not this time. My head was all mush. But I had to do something before we exposed ourselves.

I stood up and walked around toward the screen where Liam's slogan was plastered in shades of red, white, and blue. My hands bounced against my thighs, as I stared at the wall. "You can't tell me this is the final cut."

The director hissed a curse under his breath.

I about faced, glaring at him. "Really? This was your idea of a final. I should fire you right now for such impudence. I told you I want bold. Young. Expressive. You gave me old fashioned, boring, and tired." I flung my arm toward the screen. "We're trying to sell to the younger voters while playing on the heartstrings of the older ones. They're supposed to fall in love with him. See him as new and refreshing. The breath of life our state and country need. What you gave me was another politician using the same old antics."

"I did what you want—"

I lifted my hand, stopping the director mid-sentence. "No, you didn't. Try again."

"I didn't think it was bad," Liam piped in.

I tilted my head to Liam, dragging my fingers along the length of my ponytail. "Really? And you have so much experience in this area of campaigning, do ya?"

Liam lifted from his chair in a fluid motion. "You're right. This isn't my area of expertise—"

I pointed to him. "Ha! Exactly! But it is mine."

"As you've told us all a million times," he sneered.

Perfect. He'd picked up on my cue. Time to keep up appearances.

"Excuse me?" I challenged.

Liam raised an eyebrow, staring me down. The crackle of desire electrified between us. It was a miracle no one noticed. Well, almost no one. Aaron and Scout's eyes bounced back and forth, neither saying a word, as they followed along with our ruse.

"Unless you're going deaf, I believe you heard me."

"I've had just about enough of your crap today!" I yelled.

"Oh really? Because I happen to disagree with the great Elizabeth McNeal?"

Gasps and whispers filled the air around us. He was really putting on a good show.

"That's it. My office. Now."

Aaron rolled his eyes. Scout shook her head and began

messing with her cellphone.

Liam took a step toward me, almost prowling. "You're not the boss of me."

"Maybe we should give you two a moment," one of the writers suggested, perched to stand.

I lifted my hand. "No. You stay here and fix this mess. I think it's time for me and our *candidate* to have a chat."

The staffer dropped back into his seat, clamping his mouth shut.

Smart kid.

Liam straightened to his full height, which would intimidate even the boldest of men, and adjusted his neon green tie. I tried to mimic his authoritative attitude, knowing that I didn't carry the same command in my stance as he did. I stepped back around the table to my abandoned tablet and snapped it up.

"If you'll excuse us," Liam stated to the room, following me out.

Not a single word was uttered as we marched toward my office. Everyone who saw us moved quickly to get out of the way. All of our previous disagreements throughout the day had created the perfect subterfuge.

I plotted how we could escape the building. We could have a huge fallout that everyone might be able to hear. One of us could storm out, followed by the other. We'd meet at his place and scratch this itch we'd created.

Yeah. It was a perfect plan.

If only we could execute it.

We passed Brandy typing away on her phone. She glanced up and her face blanched. My expression must've given her an indication that Liam had balked against me...again.

"Hold your calls?" she asked.

Her big, blue eyes moved to Liam, filled with pity for the man.

"Please. We're not to be disturbed."

"Yes, ma'am." She nodded to Liam. "Congressman."

"Brandy," he replied, duplicating her salutation.

We entered my office and I closed the door behind me. "Okay. Here's the plan."

Just as I passed my thumb over the lock, Liam grabbed my tablet from me and tossed it aside. He twirled my ponytail in his hand, pulled my head toward him, slamming my back against his chest. "You liked exerting control in there, didn't you?"

Oh my heart. The pounding was so loud that my ears felt as if they might explode. I loved this side of him. Aggressive. Feral. Wanton.

Bye-bye plan. Hello wingin' it.

His nose skimmed along my jaw. "Yes-s," I dared to answer.

Liam cupped my breast in his hand while tugging my hair tighter with the other. He ground his pelvis against my back, giving me a taste of what I was in for. The feel of his erection pressed against my butt was too inviting. I reached behind me, yanking on his belt.

Liam released my hair and flipped me around, pinning my shoulders to the door. "In here, I'm in control. Got it."

Yep. I had it, and I loved it.

He licked his lips, staring into my eyes without so much as blinking. I nodded my understanding of his command. "Now, what to do with you. You've been particular about no office interaction."

"Fuck that rule." I bent my elbows, reaching for his belt. "I want you naked, on my desk, and in my mouth."

"My dear, Elizabeth." He smirked, wrapping his fingers around my wrists. "I like your thinking." He raked his teeth over his smooth lip. "But no. I don't think I'll let you have your way this time."

I let out a gasp, yanking at my arms. I wanted to touch him. I squirmed and wrestled to free myself, but the more I moved, the tighter his grip became. Liam leaned down, capturing my mouth with his. His tongue pushed between my teeth, taking the very breath from my lungs.

Enraptured by his hungry kiss, I didn't even realize when he'd slipped his tie from around his neck and wrapped it around my arms. The knot was loose to escape if I needed to, but tight enough to hold me as he desired. Liam moved his mouth to my ear. "Right now," he breathed, "I want to fuck you. Hard."

I mewled at the thought, willing to let him have me however he wished.

He moved his hands down my waist and under my skirt. I took the chance to circle my linked arms around his neck. He pushed my skirt up until it hugged my hips. He glanced down at my panties. His finger traced along the waistband. "Do you have any special connection to these?"

"They're panties," I noted, a little dumbfounded.

"So they're not like your favorites or anything?"

"No."

A sensual crooked grin tugged his lips. "Good."

He twirled his long fingers into the fabric. With very little effort, he shredded the material against my skin. It stung slightly, but I was so turned on by the action that a little pain meant nothing to me. He tossed the mangled fabric aside, not caring where it fell. His large palm moved between my legs. He pressed the heel of his hand against me, applying pressure where I needed him. I hissed through my teeth at the sensation, my head falling back against the door.

Liam tsked at me. "No, no, Sweetheart. No getting comfortable for you. I'm only testing the waters and they feel quite warm."

He ducked out from under my arms, and pulled me away from the door, digging his fingers into my bare hips. His lips crashed into mine, clashing our teeth against one another. Showered in hungry, aggressive, yet somehow sweet kisses, I purred with excitement. Liam walked me backward through my office. I didn't care where he was taking me, all I wanted was the hard fucking he promised.

He came to an abrupt stop, ripping his mouth from mine. His dark eyes were even darker with lust and want. He twisted me around so that my back was to him once again. Before me laid my favorite view of the Capitol. The night sky shone bright with evening lights and the moon played peek-a-boo behind the clouds, almost as if it knew what it would soon be witnessing.

I caught Liam's handsome reflection in the glass. He appeared wild, crazed with lust, but my heart shattered into a million pieces at the look in his eyes. There was happiness in them. Contentment. It was the most beautiful thing I'd ever seen.

Behind me I heard his belt unbuckle and his pants unzip. My eyes turned upward to meet his through the reflection. He grinned at me. "You have no idea how many times I've imagined taking you against this window."

My heart jumped into my throat. Political Elizabeth, with all her infinite logic, reared her ugly head, screaming this was dangerous, but with my heart in my throat, her voice of reason was choked down.

Right on cue, Liam whispered in my ear, "We can stop this right now if you're uncomfortable."

That was when I should've said, okay, let's stop. But instead, "Take me," fell from my lips.

"As you wish."

Bound by his necktie, my palms pressed against the window. Liam pushed my shoulders forward while pulling my backside flush against him. A small yelp rushed from my chest at the feel of his body entering mine in a long, hard thrust that practically lifted me off my feet.

Liam yanked my ponytail, forcing me to tilt my head to the side. His teeth raked over my exposed skin, nipping just enough to tease but never to mark. When I squirmed, he tugged, never allowing me any control. He twirled my hair tighter around his hand, forcing my face upward where he met my mouth in a devouring kiss. I felt him. All around me. He pumped and pushed, thrust and pulled, drowning me in the spirit of desire, lust, and passion. Yet, underneath those things, something bubbled inside me. Something so clear but muddled it confused me.

What was I feeling?

I shoved the thought aside and focused on my imminent climax. I pushed up further on my toes, trying to give myself the leverage I needed for him to increase his speed. He took my cue, digging his fingers deeper into my flesh, driving into me hard and fast. He grunted the sexiest sound in the world, which let me know he was getting close. Each thrust became more rigid. His teeth grazed my earlobe, the sound of his breathing, quick and heady, filled my ears. Tingles rippled over my skin. My stomach burned from the intensity of his sexual assault.

He reached his hand between my thighs, pushing me over the brink. I clamped down on my lip, biting back the scream building inside my chest. Every pent up emotion; my need for him, the fear of being caught, and even the love I carried for this man, poured out of me in that moment.

Wait! Love? Where the hell did that come from?

Did I love him?

I cared for him deeply. Of that, I was certain. But love? Preposterous.

I didn't do love. Love was messy. Uncontrollable.

But wasn't that what Liam and I were. We were everything wild and chaotic.

Liam pressed his face in my shoulder. "Fuck," he rasped.

As he thrust once more, his body jerked, finding his own release. I rested my forehead against the cool glass, looking out at the Capitol buildings, lost inside my head.

I caught Liam's reflection in the window. His brow knitted tight together, as he slipped out of me. He reached around and released my hands from his tie. The mood between us changed from passion to uncertain.

I didn't like it.

Liam turned me to face him, cupping my chin between his fingers. "What just happened?"

"Nothing," I fibbed.

"No. You were into this, but then…" His face scrunched up. "I don't know. Something's wrong."

I shifted my skirt back down my hips and teetered on my toes, pressing a fiery kiss to his lips. "Nothing's wrong. I promise."

Liam searched my face, seeking answers he wouldn't find. My head was reeling with my new found knowledge.

Sure, Liam said he didn't do casual, but that didn't mean he loved me. What if I was in love with him and he wasn't with me? It would hurt, but I could handle that. I'd simply have to find the strength within myself to walk away once the election was over. But what if he was in love with me? He'd want things that a young man in his position should want. A wife. A family. I'd done those things. I didn't think I could do them again. Being a wife didn't work out so well for me the first time and I already had a beautiful, grown daughter. I'd be stepping backward, not moving forward.

I forced a smile and touched my fingers to his forehead. Lines rippled across his usually smooth skin. He really was the most handsome man I'd ever met. Not to mention the best sex partner I'd ever had. He understood me as I did him. So, if he did love me, would it really be moving backward to give him those things?

Gah! My head hurt. This was all too complicated.

"That was amazing," I cooed, pressing a chaste kiss to his half-opened mouth. His shoulders relaxed some. "You're amazing."

Liam adjusted his pants, concealing his slight nudity. Had anyone told me that night at Harper's, when I walked in on him getting out of the shower, that I'd actually enjoy the pleasures created by that body, I would've laughed in their face. Now, here I was, toying with the notion that I was in love with this man. Madly, deeply, head over heels in love with him.

I couldn't help but smile at the thought, no matter how much it frightened me.

He returned the smile, drawing the worry away from his face. "As are you."

Liam latched his belt and I turned back to the city view, submerging myself in my emotions.

I was in love with William Baxter.

Liam rested his hands on my shoulders. "Are you sure you're all right? You have me worried. I didn't mean to push you too far. You know I have nothing but…"

I whipped around, pressing my fingers to his lips. "Liam, please stop. You did nothing wrong. I'm happy. That's all. Now, you better get back out there before someone starts suspecting we're doing more in here than yelling at each other."

Liam gauged me. He was no fool. He felt the shift in me, but how was I to tell him that I was freaking out over discovering I was in love with him?

Finally he nodded. "Okay," he muttered against my fingertips. "If you say so."

I brushed my fingers along his kiss swollen lips. "I do. Now, go."

Liam staggered toward the exit. He paused to use the mirror by the door to return his tie to his neck. He scratched his forehead after adjusting his tie, his eyes honed in on mine. I plastered a smile to my face.

"You're wearing the wrong smile," he muttered.

My smile dropped. Tears burned at the corners of my eyes. "I'm just tired, sweetheart."

"Do you want me to stay home tonight so you can get some rest?"

"Are you crazy? I sleep better when you're next to me. Besides, we leave for Texas in a few days and I'll be forced to keep my distance from you. I need my Liam fix before then."

A true smile spread over my face. One in which he returned.

"I need my Lizzy time, too."

"Good. Now go!" I repeated.

Liam released a tight laugh. "Fine. I'm going."

He popped the lock on the door and left my office, once again greeting Brandy on his way out.

I sat down at my desk and dropped my head in my hands. I had no idea how to handle myself with him now. After today, nothing would ever be the same again. Maybe it would be a good thing we were about to be back on the tour bus. It might give me a bit of clarity.

Or more like a little distance to come to terms with the truth.

I loved him. I really, truly loved him.

So basically, I was screwed!

Twenty-four

So much had changed since I was last at Harper's ranch that it felt strange walking back into that place. Not that the house was anomalous. That never seemed to change. It withstood the pillar of time. The differences were within me.

The last time I was there, I was alone and content to be so. I believed my life was perfect and thought the two most important things in my life, Jordyn and my job, were all I needed. I had money. I had success. I had power. I had it all.

Everything but love.

While I carried the secret of my love close to my heart, I somehow felt free.

When Harper offered for us to stay at the ranch rather than on the tour bus, I jumped at the chance. I'd still have to mind myself with Liam, but at least I would have a soft, comfy bed to sleep in.

Before we left, we made the painful decision to keep our interactions, even in private, as professional as possible. We'd already taken enough risks with our little office stunt. It was best to simply put on our political game faces and buckle down until the end of the race.

No sooner were we off the plane when that plan failed.

In the main hall of the Lone Star Ranch, Liam and I stood awaiting our gracious host. Upon entering, Ivory took our luggage, which gave Liam free hands.

Never a good thing with him.

He slipped in as close as possible, ghosting his hand over the small of my back. Touching without touching made my skin hum.

I glanced up at him, raising my eyebrows in warning. It was times like this where I envied him most for being able to scold me with a single brow lift.

Cocky and smug, he pretended not to notice my silent reprimand, making no move to separate from me.

"Bet!" Harper's deep voice called from the staircase.

Liam let out a groan and dropped his hand.

"Harper!" I sang, extending my arms out toward him as he approached us. "It's so good to see you." Harper pulled me into a hug, lifting me off the floor in the process. I squeaked, a little embarrassed by his actions. It wasn't like him to make such a scene. "Put me down!" I smacked him against the chest. "Have you lost your mind?"

Harper settled me on my feet, laughing. "Maybe. It's been too long since you were last here."

I took a step back, adjusting my skewed blouse. "I saw you a month ago."

Harper tucked his thumbs into the waistband of his overly starched jeans. "But that was in DC. It's always nice to have you back home."

My mouth set in a grim line, I eyed him in askance. He was acting rather peculiar, even for Harper. "You mean back in Dallas, right?"

His jaw flinched, but he smiled. "Of course that's what I meant. Home in Dallas."

Liam moved from behind me. "How's it going, Guy?" He extended his hand to Harper.

Harper grasped his hand, hard. I could feel the strain in Liam's arm as they shook. "Congressman, welcome back to Lone Star."

"It's always a pleasure to be here." Liam's cadence was polite but formal. That was his business tone. I glanced up at Liam and then back at Harper. They both were grinning but it was forced, and in Harper's case, a little eerie. The two men released each other's hands but neither moved. I felt stuck. Caught between a rock and a hard place.

"Yes," I piped in. "Thanks for inviting us to stay here. It's very generous of you."

Harper dropped his gaze to me and grinned. "Anything for you, Bet. You know that."

Liam stepped in closer to me. I side-eyed him. There was an intense, predatory look on his face. I shook my head slightly, silently telling him to back down.

He didn't listen.

"Will Aaron and Scout be joining you?" Harper inquired, oblivious to what was going on.

I brushed my bangs back from my face, tucking my

hair behind my ear. "Those two lovebirds decided to stay in a hotel."

"Afraid the whole house will hear them?" Harper chortled.

"I don't even want to think about it." I feigned a dramatic shudder. "And I'm certain Liam wouldn't wish to listen to his brother get his groove on down the hall."

"The Congressman looks like the kind of guy who likes things a little…" Harper wrinkled his nose then wiggled his eyebrows, "*rough.* I doubt he'd mind."

My mouth popped open. "Harper!"

Warning! Warning!

I nudged back that red light going off in my head. This was Harper. He liked to get a rise out of people.

He lifted his shoulders. "The Congressman knows I'm joking. Right, Liam?" Harper clapped Liam's bicep. Liam looked at Harper's hand then moved just enough to free himself.

"Sure," Liam hummed. His hand flattened against my back. My head shot up, giving him yet another warning look. "You know, we've had a long flight," Liam crooned, refusing to meet my eyes, "will we be in the same rooms as last time?"

His eyes crinkled with amusement, Harper stretched a hand toward the staircase. "You are. They're all set up for you. I'll show you the way."

Liam marched out in front of me, blocking Harper from stepping any closer. "No need. We know the way, but thank you for your hospitality."

Wordless and a little annoyed, I stared at both men with my mouth hanging open. At any moment, I expected one or both to start throwing punches. Knockdown, drag out fights were commonplace in the political arena and these two had the telltale signs of a battle brewing.

"It's no trouble at all. You're a guest in my house."

"She's more like family, wouldn't you say, Harper?" Liam bounced back.

"Fellas," I stepped in. "We're tired," I informed Harper, "so please forgive our rudeness. Your hospitality is greatly appreciated, but we can show ourselves to our rooms."

"Well, all right." Harper took a step back, but not before catching my hand. "We're still doing our dinner at the Palm tonight, right?"

Shit! I'd forgotten. Every time I came to Dallas, Harper and I had a standing dinner date. I rubbed the back of my neck, shifting my weight from one foot to the other. "Harper, I have a lot of work to do. Raincheck?"

Harper's shoulders slumped, and his smile fell. "Seriously? I already got our usual table reserved. C'mon, Bet. It's tradition."

There was that damn rock and hard place thing again, because I could feel Liam's eyes searing holes into the side of my head. And damn Harper for using those pouty blue eyes on me. I huffed in frustration. "Okay. Fine. I can put off work for a couple hours. It's not like I can turn down a Palm steak."

Harper clapped his hands together once, the sound reverberating through the great room. "Perfect. Our reservation's at eight. Car will be ready at seven." He inclined his head to Liam. "I'd invite you to join us, but this is a family engagement. I'm sure you understand."

I gaped at him. "What the hell, Harper? That was rude."

Liam placed a hand on my shoulder. "No. It's all right. I'd never interfere with family."

"I'm sorry, Bet. I wasn't trying to be. I can change the reservation if you'd like."

"Really, no need," Liam insisted. "If you'll excuse me." He stepped around me, and stormed up the stairs, taking two steps at a time.

I stifled a groan, frustrated to no end. "Fine. I'll be ready by seven." I pointed toward the staircase. "I think I better unpack and get a little rest if I'm to be awake for dinner."

Harper bowed his head and tipped an imaginary hat. "By all means, madam." He glanced at Liam's back, a slow, smug smirk curling his lips. "If he changes his mind, let me know. Otherwise, I'll see you at seven." He placed a kiss on the top of my head and disappeared.

I trailed my palm along the bannister as I ascended the staircase, taking my time. When I reached the top, Liam was nowhere to be found. At my door, my hand rested on the knob. I cocked my head toward Liam's room, wondering if I should go down there instead. Since the door was closed, I assumed he didn't want to be disturbed.

A little annoyed by both men's behavior, I twisted the doorknob and stepped into my room. Out of nowhere, two large hands grabbed me at the same time my bedroom door slammed behind me. Sweet, hot, kissable lips pressed hard to mine. Liam lifted me up off the floor, wrapping my legs around his hips and carted me toward the bed. I didn't have time to think. My body simply reacted to the man I loved.

His long fingers kneaded my ass, as his tongue hungrily caressed mine.

He laid me down on the bed, crawling on top of me. I gasped for air when he released me from his kiss. "I've been dying to do that since we got on the plane." His fingers drew down the column of my throat.

"Is that so?"

"Very much so." He ticked the buttons of my shirt, one by one, popping them open. I arched my back toward him, moaning softly as his hand slipped inside my blouse and under the silk of my bra. "Seems like you feel the same," he teased, rolling my hard nipple between his fingertips.

"If I didn't know how thin these walls were, I'd tell you to take me. Right here. Right now."

A coy smirk widened across his face. "We can be quiet." He moved his hand down the plain of my stomach to the waistband of my black slacks.

"No. It's too risky. Harper'll hear us."

Liam unbuttoned my pants, gliding his hand into the recesses of my panties. I hissed at his hard but gentle touch. "Let that old coot listen. He might learn something."

My blood ran cold. "Excuse me? Old?" I scooted out from under Liam. My body already fighting against my mind. Let it go, my body screamed. I need him to touch me, it pleaded. My mind on the other hand was suddenly pissed. "Harper's only four years older than me, Liam."

Liam realized what he'd done and instantly tried to pull me back to him. "That's not what I meant."

I stiffened, refusing to let him budge me. "Then what did you mean?" I pulled my shirt back over my breasts, clasping the pearl buttons together.

He threw his arms up over his head, defiance written all over him. "I don't like the way he looks at you. Okay."

"And how does he look at me?"

"Like he wants to eat you. And frankly, I'm the only one who gets to do that."

Be still my ovaries. Even angry, the thought of Liam's face between my thighs made me instantly wanton.

"Stop exaggerating. He doesn't want to eat me, Liam. He's my oldest and dearest friend. You know that."

Liam sat up and pushed to the edge of the bed. "No, what I know is my girlfriend is going to dinner with a man who wants to fuck her every which way from Sunday while I'm stuck here, unable to protect her."

Thus the pissing contest. I should've known.

I sidled up next to Liam, cupping his face in my hands and pressing a long, hard kiss to his lips. "I'm yours. You know that."

"Yes, but he doesn't."

I planted a kiss to the corner of his mouth. "It's tradition. And when I get back, you better be here, in this bed, naked and hard."

"Why? I thought you were afraid of him hearing us."

His little pouty face was kind of cute. "He'll be asleep."

"You're contradicting yourself, you know."

"Maybe, but it's my prerogative as a woman to be contradictory."

A quirk of a smile lighted Liam's face. "So stay with me. Don't go to dinner with him tonight."

I traced the line of his lips with my thumb. "I can't do that. He'd only end up staying in, sulking."

"At least you wouldn't be alone with him."

"I'm going to be in a crowded restaurant. That's not alone." I bowed my head, kissing along his neck. "You could go if you want. He did invite you."

"Reluctantly," Liam huffed, but tilted his neck as my kisses progressed along into the collar of his shirt. "Damn him. Why did we agree to stay here again?"

"Appearances." I moved my hand around to the back of his neck, slowly scraping my nails along his hairline. "So be a good boy and learn your speech for tomorrow."

Liam grabbed my hips and pulled me to straddle him. "On one condition."

"Name it."

A hint of mischief crossed his face. "I want you in the shower, tonight."

"What?" I gasped. "Are you crazy?"

"Maybe, but I do think turnabouts fair play. You saw me naked getting out of that shower, now I want you naked in it."

I cut him a scandalized look. "You're playing dangerously. You know that, right?"

"I am. But that's how you like me."

I laughed and smacked his shoulder. "Your ego is too big for this room."

"You've never complained about my ego before." He grabbed my hand, placing it on his crotch. He was hard. Very hard. Which made my whole body weak with want.

I began to rub my hand along his length, aching for him to be inside me. "And I never will."

"Good. So, shower. Tonight." He leaned in, sucking my earlobe between his teeth.

I squirmed as he pumped his hips against my hand.

"Fine," I caved. "But if we're caught..."

"We won't be, and what's he going to do if he does catch us?"

"Pull your funding for starters."

"This late in the game. Not gonna happen." Liam's mouth found mine. I melted against him. "Besides, if he did that he'd also be hurting you," he murmured against my lips. "And he wouldn't hurt you. That much I'm sure of."

"You don't know that."

"Trust me, I do."

"If you say so," I mumbled.

Liam fell back on the bed, pulling me on top of him. I allowed myself to get lost in his touch. His kiss. His passion.

Hours later, I was downstairs in Harper's car, heading to a dinner I really wasn't interested in attending. Upstairs, naked and sated, rested the man who held my heart.

Was it stupid to have sex in Harper's house? Yes. Very stupid. But worth it if it meant the man I loved was a little less stressed and happy.

And at least with his kiss still fresh on my lips, I could enjoy my dinner, too.

At least that's how I rationalized everything. And you know me. Ms. Rationality.

Twenty-five

Diversion was a wonderful tool to have in a communications arsenal, and tonight it came in handy.

For the most part, Harper and I enjoyed idle chatting during the hour long drive from Lone Star Ranch to downtown Dallas. We spent most of our time talking shop or about Jordyn. Anytime he tried to sway into my personal life, I found a loophole to divert him. It worked, but there was a constant nagging at the back of my mind that something was off. There seemed to be a weirdness hanging between us. We laughed and talked like old friends do, but it wasn't the same. I chalked it up to me being different and Harper somehow intuitively feeling it. Or maybe it was all my imagination. Either was possible.

Inside the restaurant, we ordered our favorite meals with a bottle of wine. As promised, he arranged for us to sit at our usual table. I loved this spot because it gave me full view of the restaurant while granting me privacy from the rest of the patrons. This place was a hotspot for celebrities, politicians, and those of wealth, many of whom were honored by having a caricature of their face painted on the beige walls.

"So," Harper mumbled through a mouthful of baked potato. "You and Baxter seem rather chummy lately." He gulped down his bite.

I slowly chewed my asparagus almost moaning at the buttery flavor. "I hate that word," I deflected.

He wiped the corner of his mouth with his napkin "What word?"

"Chummy." I sliced into my steak, cutting a small bite and stabbing the tender beef with my fork.

"What's wrong with chummy?"

With a little shrug, I proceeded to chew my food. "You know how some women don't like moist or pussy?" Harper nodded. "Well, those words don't bother me. You could say cunt, twat, or snatch all day long and I'd think nothing of it. But you say chummy and I get this shiver down my spine." I rolled my lips upward, wrinkling my nose. "Maybe it's because it makes me think of salmon and those fish are nasty."

Not to mention that ugly ass salmon-faced tie of Liam's. God, I hated that tie. So much, in fact, that I stole that hideous thing and shredded it in the industrial shredder at HQ. Never again would he wear a tie with an ugly fish face on live television.

"Fine. Instead of chummy, how about friendly?"

I sipped my wine. "Friendly's good."

A lull of silence hung between us.

"Well?" he pushed.

I glanced up at him over my glass. "Well, what?"

Harper dropped his fork on his plate. He rested his elbows on the table and templed his fingers in front of his mouth. "You. The kid. Friendly."

A hint of anger flared inside me. It was really none of his business. Besides, he'd never pressured me about men before. Well, except Russell, but that was his best friend and happened a long time ago.

I took another bite of my delectable meal, sadly not savoring it this time because of Harper's inquisition. "Of course we're friendly," I finally stated. "He's my client. There has to be some semblance of normalcy between us if we're to win an election."

"Normalcy?"

"Friendship? Comradery?" I snapped my fingers, droning. "Comradery might be too much."

Harper took a bite of his overly rare steak. I snarled. How he could eat the thing while it was still mooing was beyond me.

"You know you can talk to me about anything, Bet."

That made me feel a little guilty, but not enough for me to spill my secrets to him. "I know." I took a sip of my wine and glanced toward the door. "Oh good Lord!"

My wine glass hit the table with a loud clink. I slinked down into the bench seat, wishing I could disappear into the dark wood and the green vinyl upholstery. My hand slapped over my face, I peered through my fingers to see if I'd been noticed.

What was it with me, restaurants, and unwanted appearances? Geez!

"What?" Harper whipped his head around, trying to see what I was staring at.

"Don't look!" I hissed, waving my free hand at him.

Harper turned back to me, flabbergasted. "How can I see who's there if I don't look?"

"You don't need to...shit! He's coming this way."

"Who's coming this way?"

"Elizabeth?" The somewhat forced southern drawl of Dr. Jack Gamble sent chills down my spine. "Elizabeth McNeal?"

Fuck me!

Not literally. Please never try to fuck me literally!

I plastered a grin on my face and sat up straight. "Jack Gamble," I schmoozed.

Harper lifted an eyebrow, mouthing, "Who is this?"

I slightly shook my head. Harper, the ever relentless, wasn't satisfied. He drummed his fingers on the table, as if he were expecting me to just blurt out that this guy was the prick I'd ripped apart for insulting me.

Jack leaned forward and gave me an awkward hug. "It's so great to see you. You look amazing."

That's not what you thought the last time, asshole. Grr.

Everything about this guy sent me into a murderous rage. He was easy on the eyes, which explained why I agreed to go out on a date with him in the first place. His dark black hair and ocean water eyes were a tantalizing combination. However, I would never forget his arrogant, self-righteous indignation. It infuriated me to think he'd pulled that shit on other women. And I'd have laid money down most of them would've fallen prey to his high and mighty shit.

"Thank you," I said, neglecting to return the compliment. No need to fuel his ego further.

His cocky grin faltered a bit, but one look at Harper and it returned in full force. "Hi," he greeted Harper. "I'm *Doctor* Jack Gamble." Harper accepted his handshake and I almost snorted. Jack appeared in pain by Harper's strong grip.

"Guy Harper."

"Pleasure." He turned back to me. "So, Elizabeth, what brings you to Texas? The last time I saw you, you said you were heading back to Washington."

Really, douchebag? You're going to try to make conversation with me?

I swirled my finger around the rim of my wine glass. "I'm running Congressman William Baxter's campaign for Senate," I bragged.

"Is that so? So, do you always go on dates when you come to Dallas?"

Harper pretended to cough, but I could see those damn eyes of his dancing. Bastard.

I laughed, almost sick at Jack's insinuations. "Harper's one of Congressman Baxter's *major* contributors."

Maybe I glossed over my relationship with Harper, but this douchebag didn't need to know any more about my life than he already did. Although, by the look on Harper's face, I might've said the wrong thing. What did he expect? For me to proclaim he's my lover?

"I see." Jack tucked his hands into his pockets. "So, are you seeing anyone?"

My eyes bulged out of their sockets, and I damn near choked on my own saliva. Was this guy really trying to proposition me after how I left his ass the last time?

"I...ah..."

Harper leaned forward, waiting for me to complete my sentence. Jack's mouth twisted in a smirk, his perfectly plucked eyebrows raised in anticipation.

"I stay rather busy." That wasn't a lie.

Harper fell back against the seat in a huff. Jack nodded. "Same here. Speaking of which, I should head over to meet my party. I've kept them waiting long enough."

"What? No busty blonde bimbo on your arm tonight?" I spat. Call me bitter, but I couldn't let him walk away without taking a jab at him.

Jack's teeth clamped together and his blue-green eyes flashed red. "I beg your pardon?"

"Oh, I apologize. I'm simply curious about your dating life since you're so interested in mine."

"I'll have you know the last blonde bimbo I went on a date with was you," he seethed.

I snorted. "I hardly classify as a bimbo according to what you said the last time we met. Besides, I know how to eat with a fork and don't require my tits to carry my leftovers for later."

Harper barked in laughter. I gave Jack a wink and waved him off. "Now, go on to your party. I'm sure they're dying to be entertained by your small penis...I mean mind."

"You're a bitch, lady."

"And you're a douchebag. Are we done stating the obvious?"

Jack stormed off and I dropped back into my seat, laughing with Harper. "God, that felt good!"

"Tell me what you really think of him."

"Does twatnugget cover it?"

Harper banged his fist on the table, rolling in laughter. "Damn, Bet. That's cold. Who is he, anyway?"

"Remember that night you called me to meet Liam?"

Harper stared at me for a moment, then twisted his head around to the direction Jack trampled off to, and then back to me. "That's the guy? The one who thought you needed work done?"

"That's him. Asswipe!"

"That guy's got some balls." Harper tossed his napkin on the table and waved to the waiter.

I shrugged and finished off my wine. "More than likely he gave them to himself."

"Oh, you're cold, Bet."

I tossed my hair back. "Just honest."

Moments later Harper paid the check, and I slid out of the booth, antsy to get back to Liam. There was a shower calling my name.

I leaned forward to grab my clutch and pea coat. From the corner of my eye, I caught the profile of the last person I'd expected to see — Bonnie Keating. She was engaged in conversation with someone and it appeared quite animated.

Already riled up from taunting the douchebag, I decided to kick the hornet's nest for a little fun.

"Hey." I nudged Harper. "Check it out. It's Keating."

He took my jacket from me, helping me into it. "Hmm. So it is."

I straightened my pea coat along my hips and buttoned the center button. "I'll be right back. I'm going to say hi."

"Haven't we had enough impromptu meetings for one night?"

I patted his shoulder. "Don't be such a pansy. This'll be fun." I marched in the direction of Keating, my chest puffed with pride. When I came close enough to see her dinner partner, I stopped, all my haughtiness knocked out of me.

Dark eyes met mine and a twisted smirk disfigured Victor Knolls' face.

What the hell was he doing with Keating?

My confusion had to be written all over my face. At least I assumed it was, because when I turned to see if Harper was witnessing the same thing, I found he'd stopped dead in his tracks and his face had paled.

At least I wasn't the only one who found this disturbing.

Unable to stop myself, I descended on Keating and Knolls. "Governor Keating," I greeted her.

Two large men, whom I'd expected, since the governor would be a fool to go anywhere without her security detail, jumped up and headed toward me. Keating waved them back, inclining her head to me. Her bright green eyes glistened in the light. She tilted her head so that her crooked nose made her small eyes seem even beadier. "Why, Ms. McNeal. How ya doing?" She lifted her hand for a lady-like shake.

"Well, thank you," I responded out of habit. "And you?"

"Good, good." She extended a hand toward her dinner partner. "You know my old friend, Victor Knolls, yes?" He rushed his fingers through his almost transparent hair.

"Yes, ma'am. How are you Victor?"

A wicked smile burned across his cheeks. "Fantastic."

Harper managed to pull himself out of his stunned state and joined me. "Good evening, Governor."

"Guy Harper, what a pleasant surprise." Her tone was so candy coated I was getting cavities just being near her. She looked out past us then focused in on Harper. "Would you care to join us for dinner?"

"Thank you, ma'am, but we just finished," I answered. "I only wanted to stop by and wish you well on this weekend's debate."

Bonnie's gray bob bounced when she laughed. "Thank you, Ms. McNeal. The same to Congressman Baxter."

I nodded once. "I'll make sure to pass the message along."

Victor sort of snorted and coughed at the same time.

Bonnie cut him a stern look. He straightened right up.

There went my warning bells. My head whirled with the possibilities of what these two were up to. Whatever it was, it wasn't good.

The Governor turned her smile back to me. "The Congressman has his interview with Masters tomorrow, yes?"

I shook my head. "Not until Thursday evening. How about you?" Not that I wasn't well aware she'd just finished hers. Corgin Masters was a well-known journalist and debate mediator. It was customary for him to perform a live interview with each candidate individually before the big debate. Usually he liked conducting them back to back, on the same day if possible, but I worked it so he couldn't interview Liam until the night before the debate. That way Liam would be fresh on everyone's mind. All part of my strategy.

"Actually, I just finished." She signaled the waiter. "So, I'm treating myself to good food and old friends."

Victor shifted in his seat and that's when I noticed a large envelope tucked under his leg. Just as I suspected. He had dirt. But what kind of dirt was the question.

While she was Liam's opponent, Bonnie Keating was still the Governor of Texas. I had to maintain a certain level of respect, even for her sleazy dinner companion, no matter how much I wanted to question what was in the package.

"How wonderful. I'll have to catch the highlights later."

"You should."

"We'll let you get back to your dinner. Have a wonderful evening, Governor."

"The same to you, Ms. McNeal."

I could've sworn I heard Victor snicker, "You're gonna need it," but I wasn't sure, so I left it alone.

Harper placed his hand at the middle of my back. He bid his goodbyes, practically shoving me away from the table in the process.

"Hope you enjoy your evening," Victor called out after us. A laugh came from their table and my stomach dropped. Something big was heading our way, and I needed to act fast.

Out of their sight, I rummaged around in my clutch for my cell phone. I had to call Liam. For all I knew, they'd discovered Liam and me and were about to expose us. We had to be ready for anything, because mark my words, it was coming.

I dialed his number.

All I got was his voicemail. Three tries, still no answer.

I tried Scout. No answer.

Aaron. No answer.

What the hell was the point in having a bunch of employees at my whim if they weren't actually at my whim?

The whole drive back to Harper's ranch, I tried calling. Nothing but voicemails. I was physically ill by the time we pulled into the drive of Lone Star Ranch. Nothing Harper said could calm me down. And that nagging exploded into full consternation when we found Scout and Aaron's rental parked in front of the house.

I flew out of the car, barely giving Harper a chance to put it into park. No matter how hard I ran, my legs couldn't move fast enough. I managed my way through the yard and the front door, not giving Ivory a chance to perform his duties.

Inside the house, I skidded to a stop at the sight of Liam sitting in the great room. His head was down, his long fingers carded through his hair. Aaron sat next to him and Scout was crouched in front of him.

"Liam," I gasped.

He rolled his head in my direction, the brims of his eyes red and his face taut. Aaron and Scout both looked at me, worry coloring their expressions.

The pit in my stomach expanded from a hill to a full blown mountain. "What happened?" I demanded.

Aaron stood up and turned to face me. "There's been a…" he wrinkled his brow, "development."

"What kind of a development? Why didn't any of you answer your damn phones? Why didn't you call me?" My voice rose several octaves, causing me to cringe.

Scout straightened up. She grabbed a familiar envelope from the ottoman, and maneuvered around to me. "Sit down, Elizabeth." She presented me with the envelope. "We need to talk."

Frozen, I stared at the impeding package like it might bite me. Victor had been here.

Shit! This didn't bode well. Not well at all.

Twenty-six

"You're going to want to sit down for this," Aaron repeated Scout's initial request.

I slid my fingers into the envelope, ignoring everyone. All I could imagine were pictures of Liam and me inside that package. He'd yet to say a word. All he'd done since I walked in was tug at his hair.

My heart sank inside my chest as I pulled a stack of photographs from the package.

They were right.

I needed to sit down.

So I did.

I fell into the wing-backed chair and sifted through the pictures. However, not a single one of them were of me. They were of Liam with some busty older woman. She had legs that went for days and tits that would've made Dr. Douchebag proud. She literally would have made the perfect political trophy wife for Liam with her perfectly coiffed blonde hair and pearls. If Liam were ten to fifteen years older, that is.

From what I could see there was nothing terribly incriminating in the photos. There was one where the woman hugged Liam, but it was more friendly than intimate. Another showed Liam with his hand on her forearm, laughing. The worst was of Liam tucking her hair back as he whispered into her ear.

One by one, I scrutinized each photo. From what I could tell the pictures were dated. Liam's hair was enough of an indication of that. There wasn't a single picture of his hair grown out as it was now. I had an odd sense of relief because of that one minor detail. The other thing I noticed, however, was the location where most of the pictures had been taken.

"These were taken in one of the Congressional buildings," I mewled.

"Yes," Aaron agreed.

Harper rapped his knuckles against the wall. My kneejerk reaction led me to gather the pictures to my chest.

Harper's eyes darted around the room landing on me. "Everything all right in here?"

"Yes, Harper. Nothing to worry about," Scout stressed.

"Are you sure? You all look like Camelot has fallen?" Harper pointed toward the photographs. "What ya holding there, Bet?"

I pulled the pictures away from my chest and glanced down at the beautiful woman's face. "Just work stuff. Nothing important."

Harper scowled. "I've seen enough intel in my day to

know what those are. And by your reaction, they're not good."

"Don't worry about it, Harper. Really."

Harper took a step forward, his hand outreached toward me. "Bet."

Liam sprang from the sofa, crossing the distance between Harper and me. "She said don't worry about it," he growled.

Harper pulled his hand back, taking a step toward Liam. "I put a lot of money into you, Baxter. If you've fucked up, I'd like to know about it."

I rose from the chair and moved between the two men, facing Liam. I pressed my fists to his chest, the pictures crumpling in my hands. "Sit down."

Nose flared, the veins in Liam's temples appeared on the brink of exploding. "It doesn't matter how much money he's donated; I don't need him all up in our business."

Without thinking, I raised my hand to Liam's face, drawing his eyes to meet mine. Almost instantly his body relaxed. I smiled tenderly and brushed my thumb across his cheek. "I'll handle this. Okay?"

Liam covered my hand with his. His breathing slowed to almost normal. "Okay."

"Good. Now, please sit down."

Liam planted himself back on the sofa. I whipped around to Harper who was pretty much a deep shade of purple. "Friendly, huh? Comradery, you say." He threw his hands in the air.

"Harper, I've got everything under control. Trust me."

"I used to. That was until you started lying to me."

"When have I lied to you?"

"Doesn't matter. I'll be in my office."

I huffed in frustration, as Harper marched out of the room.

"Do you need to go talk to him?" Scout questioned.

I shook my head. "I'll deal with him later." I circled around to the three sets of eyes staring at me. "Right now, we need to get ahead of this." I landed on the couch next to Liam. "First things first, where did these come from?" I shook the photographs in my hand.

"Victor," Liam sneered.

Just as I thought. That little weasel was up to something. That envelope at the restaurant was probably a matching set.

Liam turned his head to me, his face drawn and defeated. "He stopped by here just after you and Harper left. I didn't think anything of it. Victor's an old friend."

"Not much of a friend if he's doing this," Scout stated.

"I wasn't much of one to him, either." Guilt softened his timbre.

"How can you say that?" I demanded.

"I let him go without just cause."

"Winning is just cause," Aaron balked.

"You only say that because you and Scout are sleeping together," Liam countered.

"No," I intervened before a brawl between the brothers broke out. "He's saying that because it's the truth." I tossed the pictures onto the ottoman and took Liam's hands in mine. "If Victor should have a grudge against anyone, it should be me. This isn't your fault. He's merely some old coot out for revenge.

"Now," I inhaled deeply, preparing myself for answers

to questions I wasn't entirely sure I wanted to hear, "who's the woman and what's her significance to you?"

Liam squeezed my hand. Tucking his leg underneath him, he adjusted himself so he was facing me. "The woman is Anita Cole. She's an aid in Congressman Marcos' office."

"She works for the majority whip. Great." Sarcasm melted from my tongue. This not only put this woman in a place of power, but also involved a high-powered Congressman. This could be detrimental to Liam if not handled with care.

Liam nodded. "She's also the wife of General Michael Cole."

As if it could get any worse! "She's married!"

"Yes."

"And you fucked her?" I squeaked.

Liam jumped back, his face marred by rage. "Absolutely not! I've told you time and time again I don't do casual and I certainly don't fuck married women."

I released Liam's hands and grabbed the photos. "So, what exactly are Victor's claims?"

Liam pounced from the sofa, ripping at his hair. "Isn't it obvious? Even though he knows it's not true, he's claiming I screwed the General's wife." Liam began pacing the floor, caged inside his head. "When I called him on the lie, he told me the truth didn't matter. Only the perception of the truth did."

I grabbed the pictures and sifted through them again. If spun in the right way, they could be incriminating. I rested them in my lap and crossed my hands over top of the glossy prints. "Okay. That means they have no real story, so they'll fabricate one. Since this is General Cole's wife, they'll probably let the media run wild with the allegations. Aaron," I pointed to the chief of staff, "I need you to get Congressman Marcos' office on the phone. We need to coordinate with their office immediately."

Aaron lifted from the chair, whipping out his cellphone. "On it."

"Scout, I need you to find out where these pictures originated. I want to know who, when, and why they were taken. Then I want you to get on the horn with anyone you know in the media. We need Liam in front of a camera. I want him to be open about his friendship with Mrs. Cole. A shit storm is coming and we need to prepare ourselves for the destruction."

"Got it!" Scout jumped into action, following Aaron out of the room.

Liam stood near the fireplace, his head down.

I walked over to him, placing my hands on his spine. "Baby," I whispered.

He whipped around to me, pulling me tight against his chest. "I was so afraid you'd think the worst. I was certain you wouldn't believe me. You do believe me, right?"

I brushed along his cheek with my knuckles, and pressed a chaste kiss to his sweet lips. "I do believe you and I don't for a second think the worst of you. I also don't believe Victor hates you as much as you think."

Liam seemed surprised by the remark. "He's trying to ruin my career, Elizabeth."

"He also gave you warning. He didn't have to do that."

A tiny smile lighted Liam's face. "I never pegged you as an optimist." He brushed his fingers down my arms.

"I'm not, but I'm learning."

Liam found my mouth with his. How easy it would've been for me to get lost in him. To forget everything now hanging over our heads. But I couldn't. I had to do what was right for him, for us.

I pulled away, breathless. "We can't do that out in the open like this." I glanced over my shoulder toward the open hall. "Actually, it might be best if we don't take any chances, even in private."

His dark brows furrowed. "What do you mean?"

I took a step away from him, only for him to move forward and close the distance. I sighed. "I think we need to cool things off for a while."

Liam stumbled back like a man who'd been punched in the gut. "You're breaking up with me?"

I rubbed the back of my neck, feeling a headache come on. Unable to stand due to the ache in my chest, I lumbered to the sofa and sat down. "No. That's not what I'm saying."

"Sure sounds that way to me."

I worried the inside of my cheek. "We're vulnerable." Liam opened his mouth to speak, but I stopped him. "You're vulnerable. The media's going to be on a frenzy to find more and I don't want to give them any reason to look at us."

Liam rushed to me, dropping to his knees. "I can't lose you, Elizabeth. I need you."

"And I'll be here for you. But until you're elected, I think we need to cool things off."

He placed his head into my lap. I slowly ran my fingers through his hair, comforting him. "This feels like you're leaving me."

I rested a kiss to the top of his soft hair. "I swear. This is temporary. I'll be here to help you win, but I can't be with you physically. I refuse to give them a chance to tear you apart. I believe in you too much."

Liam lifted his head, his dark eyes weighing me carefully. "You really mean that."

"With all my heart." I touched my fingers to his jaw.

"You promise, once the election is over…"

"Yes. I promise."

He nodded. "Okay. I trust you. I'm going to miss you, though."

"Not as much as I'm going to miss you."

Liam let out a humorless chuckle. "What now?"

"For starters, I think one of us needs to move into a hotel for our duration here."

"Damn. I was really looking forward to having my way with you in the shower tonight."

A soft, sad laugh resounded from me. "Do you only think with your dick when it comes to me?"

Liam pushed up on his knees, his dark orbs steady on me. There was no joking in his body language. No amusement in his expression. "No. When it comes to you, there's another organ that does all my thinking for me."

The words were there, lingering between us. Or were they?

I opened my mouth and snapped it shut. I wanted to blurt out that I was in love with him. I'd been in love with him for some time, but I couldn't. If I did, I knew I wouldn't be able to walk away, and I had to let him go. If only for a short time, it was the only way to ensure he'd win.

Liam splayed his fingers along my neck. "I'll go with Aaron and Scout to the hotel tonight. You stay here. Harper's your friend."

I tapped the tip of his nose. "So, he's my friend now."

Liam shrugged one shoulder. "I still don't trust him, but you do. And I trust you."

I leaned forward and laid a sweet kiss to his forehead. "As I do you."

"All right," Aaron returned to the room with a loud boom. "I spoke with Marcos' chief of staff. She's working on getting us in touch with General Cole. She also said Congressman Marcos will give a statement on Liam's behalf, if needed."

And like that our little bubble was burst. We both jumped into our work and later that night, more like early in the morning, I watched as Liam drove off with Aaron and Scout. It was the first time in a long time I felt like crying. I didn't, but I felt like it.

Twenty-seven

Just as predicted, the story broke hard and fast.

Senate candidate William Baxter caught in an alleged affair with General's wife ran across the bottom of the television screen in bold white letters.

I sat glued to the TV with my mouth gaped open, watching yet another early morning show bashing Liam. As a habitual insomniac, running on four hours of sleep in the last forty-eight hours was par for the course, however, for me, there was more to it than years of terrible sleep patterns.

I struggled falling asleep without Liam. It was strange. I'd never needed or wanted someone in my bed. I enjoyed sprawling out across the mattress, but with him, I yearned to feel him pressed up against my back. I felt safe with him near me.

Then there was my typical fall back for restless sleep –

there was too much work to do. For the last forty-eight hours, I'd been on cleanup duty. Whenever a small fire popped up regarding Liam, I was on it. There was no controlling media productions like the one I was watching, but I could ensure they at least had their facts straight.

And poor Kristin. The media was practically camped outside her doorstep wanting to know how she felt about all this. I had to admit she handled herself with poise and grace. My only issue with Kristin, however, was when she proclaimed she and Liam were never a couple, that he was only her best friend. True, they'd never professed to being together before, but now with such allegations hanging over Liam, the media had a good ol' time stressing the Baxter/Page connection. Kristin meant well, but that didn't keep me from wanting to strangle her for not doing as Scout and I both advised her. Simply say — no comment.

"After he's shown a blatant disrespect for authority, how are we to trust him to put the welfare of the country before his own selfish needs?" squawked the overly polished male news anchor in his gray suit and bright colored plaid shirt.

"I think you're confusing the issues here," another journalist defended.

"I don't think so. Even if he didn't have sex with Mrs. Cole, he still lacked respect for the sanctity of her marriage. I mean, look at the way he's looking at her." They flashed a picture of Liam and Anita laughing together.

I threw the remote across the couch. "Oh, c'mon. They're friends, you moron! You can't tell me you don't have any female friends." I pounded my fist on the coffee table, rattling my tea cup on its coaster.

"They do appear to be rather cozy, and since Mrs. Cole refuses to respond..." I tuned out the rest of what the reporter was saying.

I fell back in the seat frustrated, crushing my palms to my eye sockets. Unfortunately politician promises are a dime a dozen and really weren't worth that dime. Congressman Marcos backed out of speaking on Liam's behalf when General Cole refused to make a statement. Everyone on the other side of the fence was silent, which left Liam exposed. After thinking about it, I was sure Victor and Keating were betting on their silence. The General didn't want his good name dragged through the mud. Not if he ever intended on running for office. If he supported Liam now and we lost, the General would lose clout. I couldn't say if I were his advisor, I wouldn't have suggested the same thing. It simply sucked for us.

"You can't tell me that something didn't happen between Congressman Baxter and Anita Cole. I don't buy it for a second," the belittling reporter insisted.

I couldn't take any more of that reporter's nasally voice. I stretched across the sofa for the remote and shut off the television. The silence of the house engulfed me. Lord only knew where Harper was. I figured he was in his room, asleep. Not everyone was saddled with a brain like mine that refused to rest.

However, it was possible Harper was nowhere in the house. Since the story broke, he'd avoided me like the plague. It hurt being ostracize by him that way, but at the same time I understood. He believed I concealed information from him, which I had. But for a reason.

For my own selfish reasons.

But I tried to make it up to him. After the story broke, I sought to talk to him. Every attempt I made was met with cold silence and contempt. I even offered to leave the ranch and stay at a hotel. He balked at the idea, claiming I was imagining things and we were fine.

Fine.

Right. How tenth grade emo girl of him.

I circled the ring around my index finger while reaching for my tea cup. The liquid had cooled considerably since I made it, but it still warmed my body as I swallowed. There was so much I needed to do before Liam's interview with Corgin Masters and I had no idea where to start. Too many personal things rattled around in my head. Like my lack of communication with Liam. We'd spoken for business purposes only, but even that was nominal. Not hearing his laugh or seeing him smile was killing me, but it was for the betterment of the campaign.

My stomach grumbled as my tea hit it. It made me feel a little queasy, but then again, I hadn't eaten anything in a while. So, I scrambled off the sofa and hiked my way to the kitchen. As I rummaged through the fridge, I heard the doorbell ring. Ivory was on duty, so I let him handle whoever was there and found a bowl of fruit to nibble on.

I hopped up on the counter with the bowl beside me and tossed a pineapple chunk into my mouth. As I chewed the juicy fruit, Ivory entered the room. "Ms. McNeal. You have a visitor," he announced.

A little perturbed that I didn't get more than a bite, especially since my stomach was really gurgling now, I shoved the fruit back into the fridge and followed Ivory down the hall to the great room. On the sofa sat a beautiful

Hispanic woman with long, flowing chestnut hair. She stood the instant she saw me. "Ms. McNeal." She stepped forward with her hand extended out to me.

I nodded and accepted her handshake. "What can I do for you, Ms…"

"Herbert. Mariah Herbert with the Dallas Morning News."

Dammit! Ivory let the media in.

"Pleasure to make your acquaintance, Ms. Herbert. How may I help you?"

Mariah, all legs and well-tailored suit, walked over to her briefcase and pulled out a folder. She handed it to me with a flick of her wrist. "I'm here to talk to you about these."

I took the folder from her hand, but didn't open it. "I'm afraid you missed the scoop. Congressman Baxter and Anita Cole are friends. Nothing more."

Mariah twisted her lips into a dangerous smirk. "Please look inside the folder, Ms. McNeal."

My already nauseated stomach was rolling now. I flipped open the folder and damn near tossed my cookies. Page after page revealed distorted photographs of Liam kissing me in my office. The faces were clear, but not much else. The slats from my window blinds covered a lot. "Where did you get these?"

Mariah's chest puffed with pride. "An anonymous source."

"Victor Knolls?" I snapped.

"I can't say, ma'am."

I slapped the folder shut. "What do you want?"

"An exclusive, of course."

I flattened the folder against my chest, crossing my arms over it. "There's no exclusive, because there's nothing here."

Mariah bobbed her head from side to side. "I beg to differ. You and the Congressman are rather, shall we say, *friendly* in those pictures. Some might even say intimate."

I raked my nails over my forehead. Any moment I'd lose that little piece of pineapple I'd eaten. All I wanted was to scream at this woman to get the hell out. Instead, I did what any good campaign manager would do. I plastered a smile to my face, pointed to the folder against my chest. "I'm keeping these."

"That's fine. I have copies." Mariah gave me a wink. "Loads of copies."

"I'm sure you do. When's your article due?"

Mariah beamed with excitement. She thought she had me. "Two for the evening edition deadline."

That at least bought me some time. Immediately, my mind started whirling with everything I needed to accomplish before the story hit. Scout and I had our work cut out for us on this one, but we had time to get ahead of it.

I nodded. "Thank you for stopping by."

The cocky grin Mariah wore disappeared. "What about my exclusive?"

"I already told you, there's not going to be one."

Mariah ripped her bag up from the floor in a snit. "You're going to wish you'd given me an exclusive, lady," she chuckled mirthlessly. "I would've done right by you."

"Doubtful, but thank you for stopping by."

Ivory appeared and escorted Mariah out of the house.

As soon as I heard the front door shut, I had my phone in my hand and called Scout. "Whitaker, here."

"Scout. Grab Aaron and Liam and get over here now," I rushed.

"Whoa! Slow down. What's going on?"

"Our problems just got bigger."

"How much bigger?"

"John Edwards big."

"Oh, shit!"

"More like, Oh, fuck."

I could hear Scout slap her forehead through the phone. "Please tell me this is a joke."

"I wish I could."

"God dammit," she hissed. "Okay, we're on our way."

We hung up and I rushed to the den to start my battle plan.

My worst fears had come to life. Liam and I were exposed.

Twenty-eight

I might've thought things were bad with Anita Cole, but I was wrong.

The media was camped out everywhere. They wanted a glimpse of Liam and me together. The wolves were on the prowl and we were their prey. To make matters worse, Keating released a new promo where she bashed Liam for his affinity toward older women. I cringed every time she mentioned my age or commented on how he had turned his back on the military that had given so much to him. There wasn't a more patriotic person on the planet than William Baxter and she was shredding that part of his identity to bits all in the name of politics.

I hated her for it and I hated myself, because if the roles were reversed, I'd have done the same thing to her.

In the middle of Liam's hotel room, I stood in front of

him straightening his tie. It saddened me to see he'd chosen a plain black tie for today's interview. I'd bitched at him for so long about his ties that seeing him wear an "Elizabeth approved" one was disheartening. Hell, I didn't even realize he had a sedated colored tie.

"You're going to do great," I encouraged him. "Just remember what I told you. Don't deny being with me. Be honest. People trust you. Remind them why."

"Please come with us," Liam pleaded.

I brushed my hands down the front of his jacket over his hard chest and attempted a smile. "I don't want your interview to turn into a circus. If I go, that's what'll happen."

"All they want to know about is us. Let's give them that." He had a good point, but what I didn't want to tell him was I didn't feel strong enough to handle being in the spotlight. I was used to being in the shadows, pulling the strings. All of this made me feel out of control. I needed to regroup before facing the media with him.

I splayed my fingers across his square jaw. "When the time is right." I pushed up on the tips of my toes and placed a warm kiss to his lips. "But for now, I need you on your A-game. Go in there and wow Masters."

Liam rested his forehead against mine. A solemnness hung between us that twisted my weak stomach.

"You hate me for all of this, don't you?"

I pulled back and ran my fingers through his hair. "You listen to me, I don't hate you. This isn't your fault."

"I promised to protect you and I didn't."

I traced the line of his eyebrows with my thumbs. "But you are. By listening to me and handling things the right way, you're protecting us both."

He grabbed both of my wrists, planting kisses at my pulse points. "It doesn't feel that way to me."

I closed my eyes, relishing the feel of his mouth on my skin. We were pushing a week without any physical connection and being this close to him, touching him, immersed in his warmth and scent, had my blood sizzling with want.

Liam dropped his head to my ear and whispered, "Are you thinking what I'm thinking?" Slowly, he traced the shell of my ear with his tongue.

My body hummed with pent up energy. "You have to leave soon. We can't."

"I want you," he breathed. "I need you."

I peered up into those dark chocolate eyes, sucking my bottom lip between my teeth. He had me and he knew it.

Taking me by the hand, Liam walked me into the bedroom of the hotel suite. A large, fluffy bed covered in white cotton linens sat in the center of the room. All of the shades were drawn, granting the space ample privacy.

Liam pulled me into his arms and crushed his lips to mine. As he plunged his tongue into my mouth, a little whimper escaped my chest. He eagerly caressed my tongue, holding my face between his large hands. Step by step, I allowed him to direct me toward the bed. Every ounce of passion that had burned between us over the last several months, every moment we'd been apart over all the crap we were dealing with, was now manifested in this one glorious kiss.

"Liam," I breathed his name.

"Tell me you want me, too, baby," he murmured

against my lips.

"I do," I professed. "More than you could ever imagine."

Liam lifted me from the floor and placed me gently on the bed. In no time he had me stripped naked and spread out before him. He tilted his head and smiled.

"What?" I asked, astonished that I didn't feel exposed in front of him. He could see me. Everything about me, down to the stretch marks I had from when I gave birth to Jordyn, and still I didn't feel exposed. With him, I felt protected. Wanted. Desired.

"God, you're beautiful," he purred. "Absolutely stunning." He placed his fingertip at my throat and slipped it down between my breasts, over my stomach, stopping just short of where I wanted to feel him.

He removed his hands from my body and rushed to strip out of his clothes. I lifted to my knees and with each inch of skin he revealed, I placed soft kisses on his bare body. He moaned as I flicked my tongue over his skin. All I wanted was to know him again. Memorize him. Every inch of him. I couldn't help myself. There was a power growing between us that consumed me. This wasn't merely sex. It was more. Much, much more.

Once naked, Liam shifted, pushing me gently back down on the bed. He hovered over me, taking the opportunity to simply be in the moment. I reached up, gently caressing his face. Liam closed his eyes and leaned into my hand. Our breathing was steady but heavy. Our hearts pounded in our chests. Power escalated between us.

I hissed through my teeth as he moved his hands down my chest and squeezed my breasts. He ran his thumbs over my stiff nipples, soft and sweet, causing them to harden further. I squirmed beneath him, loving the sensation and feel of his erection against my stomach. Liam tilted his head and flicked his tongue over my aching pebble. My eyes rolled back, caught up in the pure pleasure of the moment.

He took it slow. Meticulous. Time didn't matter to him. The world would wait on us. All he cared about was being with me. He teased me, lavished me with such tenderness I thought my heart might shatter. Our bodies talked, sang, connected us to the universe, restored our souls.

"Oh God," I gasped, as he moved his face between my thighs.

Liam linked his arms around my legs, hoisting my hips up. I grabbed a pillow and shoved it over my head to scream as he dipped his tongue deep into me. He grazed his teeth across my sensitive need followed by a circle of his tongue to soothe the momentary pain. Over and over again he tasted me until I was shaking in his arms.

"You know why I love going down on you?" he mumbled against me. He reached around on the bed, fumbling for the condom he knew was there.

I removed the pillow, breathing heavily. "Why?"

Liam released my legs, rolled on the condom, and moved back up the length of my body. I could feel his throbbing erection at my center. "Because when I do this..." He shoved himself inside me. Instantly I fell over the brink. I gripped his hair in my hands, crying out as passion consumed me. He pressed his mouth to mine, pumping hard and fast. "You do that..." he finished against my lips.

Moments later he found his own release, but it was different. There was a sweetness in the way he kissed me as his climax tore through him. When he rolled over and removed the condom, I no longer felt a sense of loss like I usually did when he pulled out of me. This time I felt complete.

He drew me to him, laying my head to his bare chest. "Well that was unexpected."

I lifted my head, resting my elbow in its place. "So much for keeping things professional until you're elected."

Liam tweaked my nose. "Yeah, but we were only doing that so the media wouldn't catch us."

"True. True."

I touched my fingers to his face, tracing along the scar over his eye. "Where'd you get this?" I asked.

He probed his fingers where mine were. "I got into a fight in the eighth grade. I'll never forget the kid. He was such an ass." He chuckled. "He was interested in Kris and she didn't feel the same. He tried to kiss her and when she said no, he proceeded to force her. I found them and whooped his ass, but not before he got a good punch in on me."

I smiled and pressed my lips to his scar. "Always protecting the women you love." I stiffened as the words fell from my lips.

Dammit!

I didn't mean to say that. It just came out.

Liam pulled back a little, meeting my eyes. His smile tugged at his lips. "You could say that."

There was a loud knock at the door.

Liam looked over my head and then back at me.

"That's my ride. I was supposed to be downstairs fifteen minutes ago."

"Oh, shit!" I tried to jump up but he held me to his chest.

"I still wish you'd come with me, but I understand why you're not."

I sighed as his lips found mine in a kiss, chaste and sweet, but full of meaning. "Thank you for understanding."

"You'll at least watch me, right? I'll feel better knowing you're watching."

"I wouldn't miss it for the world. Now go knock 'em dead."

"Don't you mean, knock it out of the park?" he teased.

I smacked his chest and laughed. "Yeah. That's exactly what I mean."

Twenty-nine

I watched as Liam left then managed to sneak out of his hotel room without being noticed.

That was a feat in and of itself, but I succeeded.

Thank God for a history of backdoor exits.

Back at the Lone Star Ranch, I slipped in the front door, high on having spent some quality time with Liam.

I unfastened my blazer and untucked my camisole from my slacks. The house was quiet save the click of my heels on the hardwood floors. I sauntered down the hall toward the den to watch Liam's interview.

"Bet, is that you?" Harper's Texas twang echoed from his office. I jumped, startled to find I wasn't alone in the house.

I diverted my route to his study and popped my head inside. "Yeah. Sorry. I didn't realize you were home."

Harper leaned back in his oversized leather chair,

crossing his arms behind his head. "No worries. I just wanted to make sure you weren't some crazy stalker who snuck into the house with Ivory gone."

"Ivory's out?" I lumbered into his office. It was much like the den, all dark woods, animal heads, and earth tones. The walls were covered in bookshelves filled with volumes upon volumes of books of all genres. If it wasn't for the creepy heads and bearskin rug, his office would've been my favorite room of the house. Across from his desk sat two high-backed leather chairs. I plopped down in one, crossing my legs at the ankles.

"Yeah. He went home for a few weeks. His daughter's having a baby."

"That's wonderful!"

Harper ruffled the hair at the back of his head. "Depends on how you look at it. I think this is like her fourth kid or something."

"Wow! You'd think by now she'd figure out what's causing that issue."

"I keep telling Ivory he needs to buy her a Netflix subscription."

"Binge watching. The world's most effective birth control."

We both had a good laugh at poor Ivory's daughter's expense. When the laughter died down, I leaned forward and placed my elbows on Harper's desk, resting my chin in my hands. "We're good, right?"

Harper let out a long sigh. All of the lightheartedness was syphoned from the room. "Why him, Bet? You know better than to get involved with a politician? I mean, look what's already happened."

I shrugged, not knowing how to explain. "I didn't plan for it to happen. It just did."

Harper pushed forward, his face so close to mine that I could smell the scotch and peppermint on his breath. "Which part?"

I tilted my head, my brow crinkled. "What do you mean?"

Harper jumped up from his chair. He crossed his arms behind his back and started to pace the floor. For a moment I was reminded of Liam. "What I mean is, you didn't plan on having sex with him or you didn't plan on falling in love with him?" The bite in his inflection cut me to the core.

Cold chills formed over my skin. I dropped my head down and closed my eyes. "Both."

"Jesus Christ, Bet! You can't seriously tell me you're in love with the kid."

I sprang from my chair, my stance taut and ready to fight. "He's not a kid, Guy. Believe me when I say he's all man."

"His balls have barely dropped," he sneered.

It wasn't too long ago I'd said something quite similar to that statement. I was wrong then and Harper was wrong now.

I shook my head in disbelief. "You had no problem with his age when you introduced him to me as a potential client. What changed?"

Harper threw his hands in the air. "You changed!"

"How? How have I changed?" My voice shook with anger.

He moved closer, allowing me to see the ire outlining his pupils. "You used to tell me you'd rather be dead than get involved with a politician. They couldn't be trusted, you said. And now look at you. You're acting like a lovesick teenager over one. What is it about him, huh? Does he make you feel young? Is this some sort of *phase* for you? Like a mid-life crisis or something?"

I stepped back, barely able to keep the bile down in my stomach. "Why are you acting this way? You're supposed to be my friend."

"Am I? Am I your friend? Because the way I see it, I haven't been your friend for a long time now. He took my place. Or haven't you noticed?"

"No one's taken anybody's place."

Harper slammed his fist into the wall. "Bull shit. I saw the way you two acted around each other when you were on the trail..." A low, dejected chuckle sniffed from his nose.

"Funny you say that, because there really wasn't anything going on then."

Harper covered his eyes with his hand, applying pressure to his forehead with his index finger and thumb. "Maybe not, but it didn't take long for it to start afterward, now did it?"

He had me there. "No," I admitted. "It didn't. But in my defense, I can't help who I fall in love with."

Wow! That felt good. Saying those words out loud made them all the more real to me.

Although, by the look on Harper's face, he didn't share in my relief.

He jammed his hands into his jeans pockets and dropped his chin to his chest. There was a slight lift and fall in his shoulders as his head shook. "You're right. You can't." Harper drew in a long, deep breath and exhaled slowly. "I'm sorry I've been such an ass lately. I know with everything going on you needed me and I haven't been here for you."

I fidgeted with my sleeve cuff. Mushy stuff always left me a little unnerved. "It's okay. I haven't been the best of friend to you either."

Harper crossed the great divide between us and pulled me into his arms. I wrapped my arms up around his back and let him hold me for a moment. Unlike with Liam, I didn't feel a sliver of safety in Harper's embrace, but it was still comforting to have my friend back.

Harper curled a lock of my hair around his finger. "We're both shitty friends," he teased.

"That we are. But I think we've known each other long enough to get past our shitty ways."

He chucked my chin, and clicked his tongue. "Most definitely." Harper released me and moved back around his desk. "By the way, why are you here? I was under the impression you'd be at the studio with Baxter for his interview."

I swayed in place, hating that I wasn't there and the fact that my fight with Harper was keeping me from seeing the interview. "To put if frank, I'm a chicken shit." I wilted into the chair with a huff.

Harper propped his chin in his hand, rubbing the day old scruff along his jaw. "No you're not. You're just in uncharted waters."

"Understatement of the year, my friend."

"So, tell me, as Elizabeth McNeal the greatest political consultant of our times, not the woman who finds herself in a sticky situation, what are you going to do?"

I dragged my foot across the bearskin rug. It felt nice talking to Harper. He knew how to speak to me. "For starters, I should watch his interview. We both know Masters has a tendency for crassness."

Harper nodded. "That man made Hillary Clinton cry. And I didn't think it was possible for robots to have feelings."

"I know! He's a scary twerp." I created a circle in the poor animal's fur. If it had been alive, it would've mauled me over sheer discomfort. "Which is why I should be watching. Honestly, I should've swallowed my pride and gone." I sighed. "But I know Scout and Aaron will take good care of him."

Harper drummed his fingers against his chin. "True. But you said for starters, which means you have a plan. Lay it on me."

"I've already set it in motion."

Harper cocked his head. "That's my girl. Now, details."

I shifted in the chair. "I told Liam to tell the truth tonight. He's not to deny our interactions. His strength is his honesty and it's vital that he faces this thing head on."

Harper's eyes grew wide. "Are you kidding me?"

I shook my head. "No. I'm serious. He needs to be honest, which means I'll be forced to give an interview as well."

"And you're okay with that?"

I lifted my chin and tucked my hair behind my ears. "No, but I'll do it. Not because I love him, but because he has integrity. Liam's the right man for this job."

"You say that like he doesn't know you love him."

I dropped my eyes, hot shame burning under my skin. "He doesn't."

Harper fell back in his seat, causing it to roll. "Really? How's that? You just said..."

"I haven't told him."

"And he hasn't said anything about being in love with you?"

I laughed. "Nah. No undying professions of love from either of us."

"Hmm. I didn't see that one coming." Harper flicked his fingernails against each other. He sat up a little straighter and somehow seemed a little lighter. He smiled and reached across the desk to take my hand. "I have faith in you, Bet. You'll survive this and come out stronger for it."

"Studying up on your Nietzsche?" I made light. His head dropped in a deadpanned expression. I chuckled and patted the top of his hand. "Thanks." I moved to stand only for Harper to stop me.

"Where ya goin'?"

I thumbed behind me toward the door. "To the den. I need to, at least, catch the end of his interview."

Harper released my hand and reached for the remote on his desk. "We'll watch it in here."

"Are you sure? I don't mind going to the den."

Harper flipped through the channels. "I'm positive." He came to a stop as Corgin Masters' face appeared on the screen. "You relax. I'll grab us a couple of drinks," he stated, dropping the remote on his desk.

"Thanks." I sank back into my chair crossing my knees

as Harper maneuvered around his desk. He stopped in front of me and placed two fingers under my chin, tiling my face upward.

"You look tired."

"I haven't slept well lately."

"After this is over, go get some rest. You need it."

I smiled and nodded. "I'll try."

He kissed the top of my head and stepped out of the room. Liam's face appeared on the screen. He seemed so calm. The epitome of cool. The camera loved him. Harper had neglected to increase the volume on the television before he left, so I turned around and grabbed the remote. In my haste, I accidentally knocked over a pile of papers that had been neatly stacked on the corner of Harper's desk.

"Dammit!" I griped, kneeling down to collect the mess I'd made.

Among the papers I found a folder that looked oddly familiar.

Double dammit!

It was exactly like the one that reporter, Mariah Herbert, had given me. I grabbed the folder off the ground and moved into my seat. Inside were more pictures of Liam and me. The sex photos were there, but there were far more than I'd seen before. On top of that, there were pictures of me walking into Liam's townhouse and of us together at Bilbo Baggins talking with Gerald Samford.

My stomach knotted. We'd been under surveillance for some time. I couldn't believe the nerve of that woman. She had some balls trying to use me to get a story out of Harper.

"What a relentless..." I stopped before the curse fell from my tongue. I'd turned to the last page of the folder to discover a plastic bag tucked into a pocket. Inside the baggie was a flash drive with a large sticky note in handwriting I knew all too well.

Mr. Harper,

Here are the pics I printed. The flash drive has more, but these are the clearest.

Thank you for the bonus.

~Brandy

I stared at the sticky note, unable to move. This had to be a sick joke. There was no way Harper could do something like this to me. No, that wasn't possible.

"I hope you don't mind, but I'm out of..." Harper came to an abrupt stop at the sight of me holding the folder. "I can explain," he cringed.

I gripped the folder in my hand, popping up out of the chair. "You better, because from what I see here, you're a lying, backstabbing prick."

Harper placed the two tumblers he was carrying on the table near the door and moved in toward me. I took a step back, shaking my head. "Explain these, Guy!"

Harper raked his fingers through his hair and growled. "Fuck. You were never supposed to find those."

A heartless laugh spilled from me. "That's your explanation? That I wasn't supposed to find these? You had me followed."

"I had to!" Harper bellowed. "After I saw how close you and Baxter were, I had to do something. You weren't about to tell me the truth, and I knew you weren't thinking straight."

"You're saying you did this for my protection?" I spat.

"Baxter's a politician. I wouldn't trust him as far as I

could throw him. I knew he'd use you like he does everyone else. That's what they do."

"So, you had me followed," I reiterated in an emotionless lilt.

Harper flattened his hand over his chest. "Yes! Okay. I had you followed. There. I admit it. You happy?"

"But, why?"

"I told you why!"

I flipped through the pictures, astonished at how much he had on me. "But you leaked them to the press!"

"No! I would never do that to you."

"So how did they get them?"

Harper wrapped his arms around his chest. "Victor," he proclaimed.

I stumbled backward. "Victor Knolls?"

Harper nodded. "He came in here all high and mighty, flapping his lips about Liam and that woman. He tried to blackmail me."

"So not only did you give him real ammo, but you knew he was about to attack and you didn't warn me?"

Harper threw his arms out at me. "Just like you didn't tell me about Baxter. Even after you came into my house and fucked him under my roof, you still didn't tell me."

Ouch. He heard.

No matter. My indiscretion didn't equate to his ruination.

"Fine. We've established I'm a terrible person, Guy. I crossed the line. I messed up. But that doesn't excuse you for exposing me."

"I didn't. Victor…"

"You gave it to him."

"By accident. I never intended…"

"It doesn't matter. You did it and you didn't tell me."

His brows knitted together in a scowl. "I'm in love with you. Can't you see that?"

Whoa! That came out of left field.

My lips curled in icy contempt. I lifted the pictures in my hand and shook them. "This is what you call love?"

"No! That's twisted jealousy."

"And giving them to Victor, was that love?" I seethed.

"That was hurt. I could see in those pictures you wanted him. And then Victor showed me the pictures of Baxter having an affair with that woman…."

"He didn't have an affair with her!" I screamed, unable to maintain my control.

Harper charged forward, reaching out for me. He grabbed me by the shoulders and shook me. "He did. He did have an affair with her. You can't see it because you think you're in love with him, but you're not. If you were, you'd have told him. I get it. You just like the way he makes you feel, but I can make you feel better. I know you. I love your daughter like she's my own. I can give you everything he can't. I've waited so long for you. I couldn't let that lying, cheating bastard hurt you."

I pushed out of his grasp, sickened by his touch. "You've waited for me?"

"Since the day I met you, I've wanted you."

"Then why didn't you ask me out twenty years ago?" I shouted.

"Because you were with Russell!"

"And after that?"

"You needed time, but now, now we can be together. I

love you, Elizabeth."

I covered my mouth with the back of my hand, disgusted by the sight of Harper. "All these years...you've waited all these years to tell me that. And when I'm finally happy and in love, you spring this shit on me." I took a step toward Harper, dangling the pictures at my side. "You asked me earlier why Liam. Well, let me tell you. He's a man who knows how to treat a woman. He takes what he wants, when he wants it. He doesn't act like a pussy, slinking around in the dark, having others do his dirty work for him. He owns up to his shit, and most of all, he challenges me. He knows what I like and what I want. You could never be that for me."

Rage burned red hot inside me. My body shook with pure contempt for the man in front of me.

"You don't mean that, Bet."

"Don't call me that. Only my friend can call me that, and you are not my friend. You're nothing to me. You understand? Nothing. You will stay away from me. You will stay away from Jordyn and if I so much as see you anywhere near Liam...so help me God."

"And what about the campaign? It's your baby. You still need me for financial backing. I mean, who's going to pay that over inflated salary of yours?"

My mouth set in a grim line. "Don't you know me well enough to know I never put all my eggs in one basket? Wait. Obviously you don't when you tried to destroy my life."

Though I was angry, I'd never felt such intense heartbreak. The day Russell and I separated wasn't nearly as painful as this. Harper was right about one thing, I was different. Then again, so was he. The man I called my friend, my brother, would never have betrayed me like this.

"Elizabeth, please."

I jutted my jaw. Malice rolled off of me like a threatening storm. "Don't *please* me. As a matter of fact, forget you ever knew me."

"I'm sorry. What I did was wrong. I know that."

"Wrong? You tried to destroy me! And for what? For some trumped up idea in your head that you could swoop in and save me." I thrust the photos outward, squeezing them tight in my hand. "This is my life, Harper! Not some business deal gone bad."

"But he's a liar, too. He cheated with that woman! If you can forgive him, why can't you forgive me?"

I sailed toward him, poking a finger in his chest. "He's not a liar. He never slept with her. There was no affair. Had you actually investigated the situation instead of giving Victor real incriminating evidence, you would've learned that. But no. Instead, you wasted your money following me. And now, you've lost me."

"Elizabeth, don't do this," he entreated.

Deep down I wanted to slap him. The idea alone made me feel better, but something told me it would make him feel better, too. He'd take it as though I was getting out my frustrations and we could move on from this. That wasn't going to happen. There was no moving on from that kind of betrayal. "You did this. Not me." I pulled myself up and took in a deep breath. "Goodbye, Guy."

I rushed out of his office, flew up the stairs to my room, where I packed as fast as I could. I expected to hear him follow me, but he didn't, which proved he did have a few scruples in his head.

As I packed, I called Liam. All I got was his voicemail. More than likely he was still in the interview.

At the tone, I left my message: "Liam, it's me. I'm leaving Lone Star tonight and heading to my place in the city. There's been some...developments," I paused and stared down at my bag, a single tear trickled down my cheek. I couldn't remember the last time I cried. I swiped the traitor away and whispered, "I'll explain later."

I disconnected the call and immediately called security at HQ back in Washington.

When the officer answered, I was expedient with my instructions. "Brandy Turner is terminated effective immediately. She is not to be allowed back into the building."

"She's still here, Ms. McNeal."

Son of a....

"Okay. I want you to go to her desk and escort her from the building. Do not, I repeat, *do not* allow her to take anything with her. We'll ship it to her, understand?"

"Yes, ma'am."

I ended the call and finished my packing. My heart was shattered and my pride pulverized. The pictures sat on top of the bed next to my luggage, all crumpled and marked from my sweaty palms. I grabbed them and shoved them into my bag.

Luggage in hand, I dashed downstairs and out of the house without so much as a glance behind me, determined I'd never grace the Lone Star Ranch with my presence again.

Thirty

"I'll be on the next flight out of Dulles."

The sun faded into the backdrop of skyscrapers. The moon was translucent in the sky, waking up to take her reign over the night. As I drove down the freeway, thankful there was no traffic, I called Jordyn to let her know what'd happened. I didn't want to take any chances Harper might try to manipulate her with his lies.

"Absolutely not!" I insisted, pounding my hand on the steering wheel.

I pressed the jostled earpiece in my ear as Jordyn's high pitch appeal squawked, causing me to momentarily pull it back out. "But, Mom!" I returned the earpiece and rammed my foot on the gas pedal, taking my speed over seventy-five. I needed to get home. My head was throbbing, my stomach churning, and my eyes burned with the tears that brimmed to the edge. "No buts, Jordyn. You need to be in school. I'll be home on Sunday."

She expelled a breath in a loud whoosh. "I can't believe it. Are you sure this isn't some twisted joke? I mean, it's Uncle Harper."

I brushed another tear away from my eye, thankful she couldn't see the mess I was. "He admitted it, sweetheart, which is why I need you to stay there. I don't want him to drag you into this. You understand me?"

"You shouldn't be alone right now."

"And I won't be. Once Liam's done with his interview, I'll be in touch with them."

"Wait, you haven't seen his interview yet?"

I pulled into the drive of my Dallas home. It was strange being here so early. Staring at the pale pink colored brick brought on another wave of sorrow. Because of his betrayal, Harper wouldn't be involved in our traditional Christmas celebration. There'd be no disgusting homemade eggnog that Harper swore by or sounds of his laughter after I opened some stupid gag gift from him. He'd taken so much away and for what? His stupid pride?

"No. I feel terrible that I missed it, too. I promised Liam I'd watch."

"Oh, Mom. You need to see that interview right away."

"I'll watch the recaps on the news tonight."

I parked my car in the garage and cut the engine. "Um, Mom," she hesitated, "it's gone viral."

"Oh God no!" I climbed out of the vehicle and popped the trunk, extracting my bags. "What the hell did he say? Why haven't I heard from Scout?"

"Trust me, Scout's busy. But you've got to fucking see this. Like now."

"Language, young lady. Geez." I waddled my bags into the house and dropped them in the laundry room. "I just got into the house."

"Hurry, Mom. I want to hear your reaction."

"Fine." I grabbed my laptop bag and marched into the kitchen. "What website should I go to?" I extracted my laptop and plugged it in.

"It doesn't matter. It's everywhere."

My stomach curdled. This didn't bode well. For a politician's interview to go viral was usually an indication of a major screw up.

I fired up my laptop and picked the first news site I had saved under my bookmarks. Instantly Liam's face appeared with the caption: *Hollywood romance meets Washington DC politics.*

Dammit! They were making a mockery of him. I'd directed him wrong. I should've had him be more discreet. What had I done?

My already watery eyes were now blinded by tears. My heart filled my throat making it hard for me to breathe.

"Mom? You still there?"

"Yes," I managed. "I seriously fucked up, didn't I?"

"Language, Mom," Jordyn jibbed. "And watch the video for God's sake."

I clicked the video box and turned up the volume.

Corgin Masters sat across from Liam, his long legs crossed and a stack of cards sagged in his hand. "You've had a bit of a rough go of it recently," Masters chuckled, rubbing his lips together. "First the pictures of you and

Anita Cole, the wife of General Michael Cole, surface and now these photos of you and your campaign manager have emerged. Would you say you enjoy the company of older women?"

Ouch! I cringed at that question, but Liam remained calm and smiled. "Corgin, I believe age is nothing but a number. In regards to Mrs. Cole, she was and still remains a friend, and as for Ms. McNeal," he waited a moment, "she's an amazing person who could run circles around me on her worst day."

"You would know," Masters pumped.

Liam, so professional, didn't respond.

Realizing Liam wouldn't take the bait, Master continued, "So you claim you and Mrs. Cole were never intimate."

Liam didn't even flinch. His smile unwavering. "As far as I know, Mrs. Cole has never strayed from her marriage. I have nothing but the utmost respect for General and Mrs. Cole. This country owes them both a great debt for their service."

"Well said," Masters noted. "And what about Ms. McNeal? Those pictures of you two...yowza!" Masters fanned himself with the cards in his hand.

"As I said before, Ms. McNeal is an amazing woman. She is an impeccable campaign manager and..."

Corgin smirked, biting onto Liam's hesitation. "Yes?"

"I deny nothing in regards to my relationship with Ms. McNeal. We have shared certain intimacies as two consenting adults do."

I fist pumped. He nailed it just as we practiced.

"Then how about your relationship with Kristin Page?

She recently made a statement that you two were nothing more than friends. How do you respond?"

Liam smoothed his tie and graced Corgin with a full smile. A smile I knew all too well. He was about to do something possibly dangerous to the campaign. I slapped my hand over my eyes and groaned.

"Here comes the good part," Jordyn rasped into the phone. I ignored her. It might've been good for her, but Liam was about to go off script and I was freaking the hell out.

"Most men can tell you exactly how many women they've loved in their lives. We might've had our fair share of romances, but there are those few women who stick with us. In a way, they mold who we become."

Corgin leaned in, intrigued by where Liam was going.

"In my life there have been three such women. The first was Kristin Page. She was my best friend throughout elementary school and as a teenager, she became my first real kiss. It's safe to say I loved her then and I love her now, though my love for Kristin is much different now."

"So, you're more than friends, unlike what she suggested?" Corgin probed.

"Let me finish, please," Liam politely replied.

Corgin bowed his head. "Of course. I apologize, Congressman."

I hugged my arms around my stomach, glued to Liam's expression. He was happy. Content.

"After that first kiss, Kristin and I knew something was different. In later years we understood what it was." Liam dropped his eyes to his hands. "To answer your question, Corgin, Kristin and I are only friends and will only ever be friends, because Kristin's gay."

My mouth hit the ground. "Holy shit!" I gasped.

"I know, right!" Jordyn cheered.

"I never got the gay vibe off her. I knew they were hiding something; I just thought she was shy. It all makes sense now."

That explained why when I vetted Kristin I never found any former relationships. She kept them concealed, which also made her the perfect candidate to stand at Liam's side for events. "Shit! He just outed her on television."

"Listen," Jordyn shushed me.

I settled myself by leaning against the counter. "As of yesterday, Kristin informed her family of her secret, and as her best friend, I was proud to be by her side." Liam looked into the camera, and grinned. "I'm so very proud of the first woman I loved in my life, and I stand proudly by her decision to tell her family."

"That's fantastic, Representative Baxter. I shared a very similar experience about six years ago with my partner. We've never been happier."

I clapped my hands over my mouth. Liam had won Corgin over by being honest. I'd been right. All he had to do was tell the truth. This was him. Out in the open. No secrets to hide.

"Congratulations, Corgin. Love is a beautiful thing and should be cherished. Which leads me to the last woman I've loved in my life."

"Wait! We're skipping the second? That doesn't seem fair?"

I barked in laughter. Liam owned him now. I'd never

seen an interview with Corgin Masters where he was on the edge of his seat waiting for the candidate to speak. He was usually derailing them hard and fast.

"The second was my college sweetheart. I was ready to marry her, but sadly she decided I wasn't the one."

Corgin awed. "So, then the third one?"

Liam templed his fingers under his chin and grinned. "The third one..." he let out a romantic sigh. I was on pins and needles waiting to hear what he'd say. "Has no idea I'm in love with her."

"How's that possible?" Corgin gasped. "Who is she?"

The corner of Liam's mouth twitched. "Why, it's the woman in the photos, Corgin. Elizabeth McNeal."

Jordyn clapped and squealed. My eyes grew wide. I covered my mouth as tears streamed down my cheeks. He loved me. He really loved me!

For all of two seconds his announcement thrilled me. Then it struck me. He just announced that he was in love with me on television and it'd gone viral. The Republicans had to be foaming at the mouth over his confession.

"Mom!" Jordyn squealed. "He loves you!"

"I heard him," I whispered.

The two sides of me were pulling me in every which direction. The woman in me was floating on air, happy and in love. The strategist in me was trying to figure out how to handle the situation.

"You okay?"

"I...ah..." As my mind whirled with scenarios, the doorbell rang. "Someone's at the door. Let me call you back."

"Be careful. It could be Uncle Harper."

I hadn't considered he might follow me to my house. "I won't open the door if it's him. I promise."

"Okay, call me back. Love ya."

"Love you, too."

As I closed my laptop, we disconnected our call. I walked down the hall to the front door. Taking a peek in the peephole, I started to cry. Liam, sans his tie and jacket, with his hands jammed in his pockets, stood outside my door. I unlocked the deadbolt and threw it open.

"I can explain," the words flew out of his mouth, but I didn't care to listen. I flung myself into his arms, and pressed my lips firmly against his. His hands cupped the back of my head, tangling in my hair as our kiss deepened.

The dam of my heart broke. The river of love flowed through my veins. My pulse raced. My body trembled. For the umpteenth time today I cried. I couldn't believe any of this was happening. My heart hammered with the knowledge that I got to love him. Really love him.

The rasps of our heavy breathing hummed inside my ears. A stifled moan escaped my lips as he broke away. "I love you," he breathed.

"I love you, too."

"You do?"

"Yes! God, yes!"

Liam showered my face with kisses, trailing his mouth down my neck. I clung to the fabric of his shirt, refusing to let go.

"So you're not mad at me?"

"Of course I am. Are you crazy? Announcing something like that on live television."

Liam pulled back, his chocolate orbs peering deep into

mine. "I am. I'm crazy for you. And I couldn't take them tainting my feelings for you anymore. This isn't some sleazy affair as they've tried to make it out to be. I had to set the record straight."

"You could've warned me!" I kissed him hard and unabashed.

Against my lips, he mumbled, "You would've tried to stop me."

"Because this could lose you the race," I argued.

"Who cares? If I lose, I lose, but I refuse to lose you. I can't live without you. This last week has been hell for me."

I leaned back in his arms, laughing. "I can't believe you!"

Liam smoothed away the tears that clung to my cheeks with his thumbs. "Believe that I love you."

I combed my fingers through his hair, unable to control my need to touch him. "I believe you. And I love you. With all my heart."

One look at him and my world was realigned better than it ever had been. Everything would be okay, because even if we lost the election, we'd won each other. Together, we were stronger, and no matter the obstacles we had to endure in the future, we would face them together.

Thirty-one: Election Night

I stared at the television chewing the inside of my cheek. At any moment, Associated Press would announce the final numbers in the election.

"God, this is so close," I crooned.

Scout nudged me in the ribs. "Stop worrying. He's got this."

I waved my hand out toward the screen. "There's no guarantee he does."

While Liam announcing to the world that he was in love with me actually helped his ratings, it didn't stop the flood of media from ripping him to shreds. Our massive lead was now a neck and neck battle of votes. It was officially anyone's race.

Liam stepped in behind me, wrapping his arms around my waist. He placed a soft kiss on my shoulder. The only saving grace to having outed our relationship to the world was that we no longer had to hide our feelings in the shadows. Liam enjoyed that part a little too much.

"Nervous, are we?" he tittered, taking my earlobe between his teeth.

"How can you be so calm?"

His arms tightened around me and he rocked me slightly. "Why shouldn't I be? I have you. And if I lose, I still have my seat in the House."

"But it's not the Senate," I whined.

"And who's to say I'll never get there?" He pressed a kiss to my jaw. "There's power in the House. I can still make a difference."

"I know. You're right. I just want this so bad for you."

Liam turned me around in his arms. "For us. Always for us."

I grinned. "Yes, for us."

He rubbed his nose against mine. "I love you so much."

My heart ran wild every time he uttered those words. "I love you, too."

I spun back around in his arms, looking out over the room. All the faces I loved the most in the world, along with a few new ones, stood around the conference table with small plates of goodies in their hands. Aaron stood by his and Liam's parents, who were deep in conversation with my daughter. They seemed intrigued by my overly animated woman-child, discussing her latest adventure to the Rockies. Nestled in the back was Kristin with her new girlfriend, Jennifer. A woman that Liam and I both approved of. Even good ol' Gerald Samford was sitting amongst us, carrying on with a pretty blonde volunteer.

There was only one face missing in the crowd — Guy Harper. While I knew I shouldn't miss him, I did. It was because of him that I was standing in the arms of the man I loved, but it was also because of him that I carried the ache of betrayal in my chest. Maybe one day I could forgive him. I hoped so. There was too much in our past that I didn't want to lose, but for now, I couldn't see a future friendship between us.

"You're thinking about Harper, aren't you?" Liam whispered so only I could hear him.

I nodded. "I'm sorry."

"Don't be. You have every reason to think of him right now." Liam nuzzled his nose along my jaw. "I'd be disappointed in you if he didn't cross your mind. You see, the woman I love isn't cold or heartless and it would take a cold, heartless bitch to forget her friend in this moment."

"Liam," I squeaked, looking around the room. "Language."

"What? It's not like I said fuck."

I shook my head, laughing.

"Only a few more minutes," Scout announced.

A few minutes longer that our lives hung in the balance and while I was happy, happier than I had ever been in my life, there was a secret burning inside me.

I closed my eyes and let the magnitude of it all wash over me. Everything we'd dealt with and all that we were about to face. I hated keeping things from Liam, but for the sake of the day, the secret that burned in my heart would remain there.

"Lizzy?"

My eyes popped open and I lifted my face to the voice that soothed me. "Hmm?"

"Where are you?"

"I'm here," I whispered. "Just nervous is all."

Liam pulled me away from his chest and turned me to face him. His dark eyes reached into my soul. "No. There's more."

Damn his ability to read me.

"No. No. There's not."

Liam took me by the hand, and dragged me toward the door. "Come with me."

"Isn't it a little early for victory sex?" I teased, allowing him to pull me along. He ignored my comment, trailing us into the empty office space next to the conference room.

Inside the room, he closed the door behind us and pulled me into his arms. I accepted his embrace and sought his lips for a tender kiss.

Liam stepped back, holding my shoulders at arm's length. "Talk to me, Lizzy. Tell me what's going on inside that beautiful mind of yours."

I stepped back. Normally I'd force a smile, but Liam would see right through it. Instead, I turned away from him so he couldn't see my countenance. "Nothing's wrong, sweetheart. I'm worried about the race is all."

"I call bull shit, Liz. You've been off since yesterday, but tonight it's worse. So we're staying in this room until you talk to me."

I whipped around astounded he'd suggest such a thing. "We can't! We have to see the election."

He crossed his arms over his chest, standing stone cold. "Then you better get to talking."

I sniffled, annoyed. Things used to be simple for me. I gave the orders, people followed. Liam broke my chain of command and I knew he was serious. We were stuck in this room until I spilled the beans. "Fine. I do have something to tell you." I crossed my arms behind my back. "You might want to sit down for this."

Liam cocked his head, curious, but obeyed.

I paced for a moment, trying to get my bearings. "I don't know how to tell you this."

He rocked forward in his seat, a hint of amusement and maybe a little concern painted his face. His smile, tender and happy, wreaked havoc on my heart. "Just say it."

I stopped and faced him, swallowing down the fear knotted in my throat. I clenched and unclenched my fists as I blurted out, "I'm pregnant."

Liam slumped back in the chair, his eyes wide, and his mouth flopped open. "You're joking, right?"

Well, that wasn't the response I'd expected. We'd talked about this many times, about my need to not have any more children. Liam was adamant that he didn't care if he ever had children. He understood my not wanting to go down that road again. All he cared about was us being together.

"No," I whimpered.

"How do you know?"

I dropped down in the chair next to him, hanging my

head. "You know my doctor's appointment yesterday?"

Liam nodded.

"Yeah, well, he told me."

"And you're just now telling me?"

"I didn't know how. I wasn't sure how I felt about it. And then there was this." I threw my hand out toward the conference room. "The election. I didn't want to take that away from you."

Liam stood up, turning his back to me. "And how do you feel about it?"

I wrung my hands together, staring at the back of his head. His shoulders slightly slumped and his stance seemed almost defeated. "Honestly, I was scared to death at first, but the more I thought about it... Liam, women my age have babies all the time. It's not that big of a deal. Besides, this is me and you. I can't imagine anything more perfect. Well, except maybe Jordyn."

"So, you're happy? You want the baby?"

"Yes."

Liam spun around, a smile as wide as Texas plastered across his face. "I'm really going to be a father?"

I nodded frantically, tears spilling down my cheeks, but laughing. "Yes... yes."

"I'm going to be a Dad!" he whooped.

Well, that was unexpected.

Liam dropped to his knees, taking my hands in his. "How far along are you?"

"A few months."

"But how?"

"Well, you see, when a man and a woman engage in intercourse..."

"You know what I mean," he deadpanned.

"The best I can recall, we failed to use a condom that night in my office. I guess it's true what they say — all it takes is one time."

Liam laughed in rapt amusement. "We really were reckless that night."

"You're telling me."

He placed his hand over my stomach. "We're having a baby."

I rested mine over his. "We're having a baby."

Together, we stared down at our hands splayed over my belly.

"Marry me," Liam whispered.

"What?"

"I know it's sudden and I don't have a ring, but I'll get one. A quaint, classic cut diamond that suits your beautiful fingers. But there's no one in this world I want to spend the rest of my life with more than you."

"Just because I'm pregnant doesn't mean we have to get married."

"I'm not asking because of that. Though, I do love the idea of us being a family." He tilted my chin, brushing his thumb along my bottom lip. "I want you as my wife. So, I'll say it again. Elizabeth McNeal, will you marry me?"

I sucked my bottom lip between my teeth, a smile pulling at my cheeks. "Yes. I'll marry you."

Liam jumped off the floor, pulling me up out of my seat with him. He lifted me off the ground, kissing me hard.

"Hey, you two," Aaron's voice interrupted our moment. "AP's making the announcement now. You might want to get in here."

Liam rested me back on my feet and swung around to Aaron, beaming. "I'm going to be a Dad."

"Yeah," Aaron stated nonchalantly. "We all heard you."

I burst into laughter.

"Congratulations. Now let's get going."

"And I'm getting married," Liam added with an almost childlike enthusiasm.

"And you could be a Senator of the United States, but we're not going to know until we get our asses back in that room."

Liam took me by the hand and we followed Aaron back into the conference room. We were greeted by happy faces, handshakes, hugs, and a multitude of congratulations.

"Shh! Quiet down. They're making the announcement," Jordyn hissed.

Liam and I moved to the center of the room. He tugged me to his chest, resting his hands on my stomach and his chin on my shoulder. We watched as the announcer spoke.

"Representative William Reid Baxter will take the Senate seat for the state of Texas."

What came over me was a mystery to even myself, but by my reaction one might've thought I was at a football game and my team just scored the winning touchdown. I bounced up and down in his arms, crying out in victory.

Liam turned me to face him, his lips pressing to mine. "We did it!"

"I love you."

"I love you, too."

Before he could kiss me again, Liam was ripped from

my arms. People crowded around him, shaking his hand, patting his back, and congratulating the newest and youngest member of the US Senate.

I moved out of the way, allowing Liam to have his moment, which he deserved. In the corner, a frail hand touched mine. I looked down to find the hunched over Gerald Samford smiling up at me.

"I knew that boy had gumption," he bragged. "And if you ask me, madam, he's going all the way."

I grinned, and watched as Liam moved out toward the front of the crowd to make his speech. "One election at a time."

"Mark my words, that man right there will be our president one day." He patted my forearm. "And he's going to have one hell of a wife by his side."

"You don't think I'm too much of a Marilyn?" I jibbed.

Samford barked a hoarse laugh. "My dear, you're the whole package. Jackie and Marilyn rolled into one. He can't lose with you."

Liam's voice resonated out over the crowd. I watched as he basked in his moment, thanking those who supported him. The media swarmed into the room, carrying video and digital cameras to get the first few glimpses of the newest Senator. The crowd went wild as he spoke. I'd witnessed many victory speeches in my day, but this was the first time I'd ever been truly proud of my client.

"But most of all, I'd like to thank my lovely fiancée and the soon-to-be mother of my child, Elizabeth McNeal. Without her, I wouldn't be standing here today." He extended his hand toward me. "Come up here, Lizzy."

I blinked several times, thinking back over all we'd been through. Had I known then what I knew now, the heartache we'd endure and the love we'd share, I could honestly say, I'd do it all over again.

Samford pushed me forward. "Get up there, honey."

My eyes focused only on my future, I straightened to my full height and adjusted my jacket. Pride filled my veins and love surged my soul. No longer was I the woman behind the curtain. I stepped out in front of the crowd and took my place by Liam's side, forever to be in the spotlight.

The End.

Acknowledgements

I was recently reminded that it takes a village to rear a child, and the same premise applies to publishing a book. For me that village is a conglomerate of individuals who have seen me through every step in the process of making this novel come to life. I wish to express my undying gratitude to all of the people who provided me the support I've needed through their many talents, time, and most of all, love. Sadly, page space and time only allow me to mention a few names, but know I love each and every one of you for taking a moment to read this story of mine. You, my readers, are what keeps me plugging away. Thank you!

To my husband and son, I love you both more than there are words created. Your undying love and support are what pull me out of bed each morning. Thank you both for being my rock.

A good writer isn't worth their salt without the backing of a good editor. Amy Gamache, thank you for kicking me in the hind end when you know I can do better. I couldn't do this without you, girl. Love ya!

This book would've remained nothing more than a creative writing piece had it not been for Sarah Canady. She read the three page version of what is now part of chapter sixteen and immediately saw potential. Because of her, this book is a reality. Thank you so much, my friend. I love you dearly!

Every so often, someone enters your life unexpectedly and takes it by storm. Melanie Moreland has been that storm for me. I cherish her wisdom, experience, but most of all her friendship. She has been the friend I needed when I didn't realize I needed one. Her name is a constant in my household now, and I am so proud of her and her recent success. I'm lucky to call her my friend. I love you, Mel!

If there were ever two people who I would claim are the world's greatest beta readers, they would be Katy Patrick and Mary Shilling. These two women are brilliant, funny, and true friends. I'm blessed to have them both in my life. Love you, ladies!

I'm sure if Jo Richardson had to endure any more instant messages from me that proclaimed: "Oh my God! I seriously suck!" and "I can't write *bleeeeeep*!" she'd be ripping her hair out. But I love her for her ability to endure my incessant babbling without going bald. She helps me keep my sanity when I think I might lose my marbles. I love you loads, Jo!

To Jada D'Lee and Lindsey Gray, thank you for making my book look beautiful. You both have an eye for details that are unmatched. Love you both!

Thank you to all the ladies at Enchanted Publications. Your support and guidance is immeasurable. I'm blessed to be surrounded by such talent and great friends.

To my publicist, Kristi Falteisek with Sassy Savvy Fabulous PR, thank you! Thank you for everything!

Jeanne's Sexy Divas, my beloved reading group — y'all are awesome! That is all!

Thank you to Dr. Tiffany Cartwright, my former government professor at Collin College, who restored my love for politics and all things government. It was her enthusiasm that rekindled my love for political science, which brought William and Elizabeth to life. I'll forever be grateful to her and the time I spent in her class.

And last but not least, the winner of the Ugly Tie Contest — Jenn McElroy. Several months back, I held a contest through my newsletter and Facebook page that I called the Ugly Tie Contest. The prize included the winner's ugly tie to be featured in this book. The salmon face tie submitted by Jenn won, and appeared in chapter sixteen. Congratulations, Jenn. Your ugly tie will live on in infamy around Liam's neck. Thank you so much for participating.

About the Author

Jeanne McDonald is an author, a mother, a wife, a student of knowledge and of life, a coffee addict, a philosophy novice, a pop culture connoisseur, inspired by music, encouraged by words, and a believer in true love. When she's not spending time with her family, she can be found reading, writing, enjoying a great film, chatting with friends or diligently working toward her bachelor's degree in literature. A proud Texan, Jeanne currently resides in the Dallas/Fort Worth area with her family.

Other Works

A Ray of Hope
The Truth in Lies (The Truth in Lies Saga I)
The Certainty of Deception (The Truth in Lies Saga II)
The Truth Be Told (The Truth in Lies Saga III)
Indulgence (Taking Chances #1)
Compass

Coming Soon
Satisfaction (Taking Chances #2)

Other Titles Offered by Enchanted Publications

59669771R00215

Made in the USA
Charleston, SC
09 August 2016